Dave Zeltserman lives in the B͏[...] novel. Serpent's Tail also publishe͏[...]

Praise for *Pariah*

'*Pariah* is all I know of bliss and lament...bliss at reading a superb novel and lament at knowing that Dave Zeltserman has now raised the bar so high, we're screwed. This is the perfect pitch of reality, history crime, celebrity, plagiarism, and sheer astounding writing. It needs a whole new genre name... It's beyond mystery, literature, a socio/economic tract, a scathing insight into the nature of celebrity and in Kyle Nevin, we have the darkest, most alluring noir character ever to come down the South Boston Pike or anywhere else in literature either. I want more of Kyle and more of this superb shotgun blast of a narrative... If every writer has one great book in them, then Dave can rest easy, he has his and it's to our delight and deepest envy' Ken Bruen

'Mean like bad whiskey and sophisticated like good scotch, *Pariah* is a rare find and a scorching read. This accomplished novel features a great blend of strong narrative voice and a realistic, multi-layered plot that lays bare the dark soul of South Boston's underworld. In Kyle Nevin, his main character, Zeltserman has a dark Celine creation that is as literary as he is noir. To my mind this novel provides the final word on the Southie's demise and does so more artfully than its predecessors. Brimming with historical anecdote, rife with keen sociological insight, Zeltserman invests his novel with a veracity found mostly in non-fiction. However, this is a novel and a damn entertaining one, one that reminds us that reading the book truly is more informing and riveting than seeing the movie' Cortright McMeel

Small Crimes

'Zeltserman delves deeply into his specialty, an unorthodox look at the criminal mind – the 'unlucky' guy who can fool himself way too long. It kept me turning pages and glancing over my shoulder' Vicki Hendricks

'*Small Crimes* is a superbly crafted tale that takes the best from mid-century noir fiction and drops it expertly into the twenty-first century. Like the very best of modern noir, this is a story told in shades of grey. Immensely subtle, and written with a rare maturity and confidence, the story of troubled ex-con/ex-cop Joe Denton always keeps you guessing. This deserves to be massive. At the very least, it must surely be Dave Zeltserman's breakthrough novel' Allan Guthrie

'So noir…all the way to a surprisingly bold ending… Fairly zips along' *Guardian*

'Zeltserman creates an intense atmospheric maze for readers to observe Denton's twisting and turning between his rocks and hard places. Denton is one of the best-realised characters I have read in this genre, and the powerfully noirish, uncompromising plot, which truly keeps one guessing from page to page, culminates with a genuinely astonishing finale' *Sunday Express*

'Zeltserman's breakthrough crime novel deserves comparison with the best of James Ellroy' *Publishers Weekly*

Turn to page 275 to read the opening chapter of *Small Crimes*.

Pariah

——Dave Zeltserman——

A complete catalogue record for this book can
be obtained from the British Library on request

The right of Dave Zeltserman to be identified as the author of this work
has been asserted by him in accordance with the Copyright, Designs and
Patents Act 1988

First published in 2009 by Serpent's Tail,
an imprint of Profile Books Ltd
3A Exmouth House
Pine Street
London EC1R OJH
website: www.serpentstail.com

ISBN 978 1 84668 643 6

Designed and typeset at Neuadd Bwll, Llanwrtyd Wells

Printed in Great Britain by CPI Bookmarque,
Croydon, CR0 4TD

10 9 8 7 6 5 4 3 2 1

For Ellen Zeltserman, my mom

Acknowledgments

There are a lot of people I'd like to thank.

My beautiful wife, Judy, of course, for all of her support, not just for this book but throughout my career, and really from the very first moment I met her.

To my editor, John Williams, and my publisher, Pete Ayrton, for both their help and the enthusiasm that they showed this book.

To all my early readers for all their great feedback: Laurie Pzena, Duke Roth, Mike Lombardi, Jeff Michaels, Ken Bruen, Cortright McMeel, and especially Alan Luedeking, whose careful read and line edits were invaluable, as they've been with all my books.

To my agent for this book, Sara Crowe. The subject matter for *Pariah* made this one a challenge, to say the least, but we got it done.

To my crack team at Profile Books/Serpent's Tail: Ruth Petrie, Emily Berry, and Niamh Murray for their superb efforts in copy editing, proofing, and getting the book out there. Also to Jamie Keenan for his brilliant cover art. And in advance to Rebecca Gray and Meryl Zegarek, who did an excellent job promoting *Small Crimes* in the UK and US, and I'm sure will be doing an equally great job with *Pariah*.

Chapter 1

Jesus, it felt weird stepping out of Cedar Junction a free man. June 8th. End of an eight year stretch. All that time lost because of a rat bastard. Thinking about Red Mahoney and what he cost me brought the bile up again. Setting my jaw, I decided enough of that. Not now, anyways, not during my first few moments of freedom. I'd have more than enough time later to think about Red. I took a deep breath and walked slowly over to the visitors' lot, enjoying the smell of the air outside of the prison walls and the heat of the sun on my face. Danny was supposed to pick me up. I stood squinting at the parked cars looking for him when a horn blasted to my left. About thirty yards away sitting in the driver's seat of a rusted out Honda Civic was Danny with a big dopey grin breaking over his face. He gunned the engine and shot forward, damn near clipping me before stopping the car inches from where I was standing. I got into the passenger seat.

After eight years he had changed more than I would've thought. His hair had thinned and had receded high enough to where I could see deep lines carved across his forehead, and even though he had that big grin plastered across his face, a tiredness seemed to weigh down his features, making it look almost as if he was the one who had just gotten out of prison. I ignored all that, though, and we hugged the way two brothers who haven't seen each other in ages would.

'Fuck, it's been a long time,' Danny said.

'No shit.'

That took an edge off of his grin. 'About not visiting you, I'm sorry, Kyle, but you know, first they stuck you in Texas, then Kansas, and then when they put you in here, with work and all this other shit that kept coming up...'

'Forget it,' I said, stopping him. 'I wouldn't have wanted you to see me in any of those places anyway. Let's just get the fuck away from this shithole.'

'Still, with you being right here in Walpole I should've come. Fuck, I don't know, things just got kind of crazy—'

'I said forget it.'

He nodded slowly, some hurt showing around his eyes, and drove to the security gate. The prison guard had us open the trunk before he waved us through.

'What did he think?' Danny asked. He was trying hard to grin, but this time it wasn't quite sticking. 'That we were smuggling out one of your buddies?'

I ignored him and told him I'd like to see Ma first. 'Let's find a place to buy her flowers,' I added.

He gave me that same slow nod again, his grin completely gone and replaced by something far more solemn. We drove in silence. I took a pack of Marlboro 100s out of my prison-issue shirt and tapped the last cigarette out of it. After lighting up, I tossed the crumpled box out the window, then sat back and inhaled deeply, filling my lungs with smoke and taking some comfort from it. I caught Danny eyeing me. When we were kids we both smoked to prove ourselves tough guys, and we both gave it up later when Red complained about it being a dirty habit. Back in prison I started up again. Now that I was out I was planning to quit, but I would have to ease out of it. I asked Danny if he could stop off someplace so I could pick up some more cigs. He gave me a dull nod and stopped off at the first convenience store we came across so I could run in and pick up a carton. Coming out, I stuck a fresh pack in my shirt and asked if he wanted a cig, but he declined. After he pulled back into traffic he started talking casually about the Patriots and the Sox as if the last eight years never happened.

'It took you getting sent off to prison for the Sox to finally win a World Series. Could you imagine if we were running books in New York when the Sox were down three nothing to the Yankees? We would've cleaned up. Nothing I like better than taking money off asshole Yankee fans. And the Patriots. Holy fucking shit. Three Super Bowls? Can you believe that shit?'

I cut him off and asked him what happened to his Beemer.

'I had to sell it,' he said, smiling weakly. As brothers, Danny and I look a lot alike, but one big difference is he's got a weak mouth. It makes him look kind of feminine at times. I guess he took after our dad with that, because Ma had nothing but strength in her face.

'I needed to pay my lawyer,' he continued. 'And shit, I don't make nearly enough in construction to afford stuff like Beemers. It was time to live within my means. But the Honda's fine. It runs. That's all that matters, right?'

I gave him a cold look in response. 'What year is this piece of crap?'

'There's nothing wrong with this car. And it's an '88, so big fucking deal.'

I squinted over, saw the odometer was at 300,000 and counting. 'You don't know how embarrassing it was seeing you drive up in this tin can. Chrissakes, Danny, what the fuck's happened to you? Don't you have any self respect anymore? I still can't believe you agreed to move out of Southie.'

'Kyle, you're making a big deal over a car. It's transportation. That's all it is. Something to get you from point A to point B. It doesn't define who you are. It's not like I just served eight years in prison for armed robbery.'

I saw a little 'fuck you' smile flash across his face. There was a lot more truth to what he said than he could've imagined. When I got arrested, I took it like a man. I kept my mouth shut. I didn't make any deals – not even after I found out the truth about Red. I served out my full eight years; the first five in the federal penitentiary system, splitting time between Beaumont and Leavenworth, the last three in the worst shithole Massachusetts has to offer. I refused the early paroles that were put in front of me. When I left I made sure I was free and clear. Danny, on the other hand, when he got busted shaking down a nightclub, he took a plea that made him give up his old life. As part of the deal he had to move out of Southie and keep away from past associates. And for what? One to two years in Billerica or one of the other medium security joints? The place would've been Club Med compared to where I served my time. But that was his choice. I just thank God he didn't rat on anyone.

Danny stopped off and bought flowers for Ma, but we didn't talk the rest of the way. When we got to the cemetery in West Roxbury where Ma was buried, I caught Danny giving me a sideways glance.

'You okay?' he asked.

I nodded, not trusting myself to say anything.

Ma's plot was under a Japanese Maple tree. It was nice. Her gravesite looked clean and well cared for. There was a small wreath by the headstone and other flowers placed along it. I took the flowers Danny had bought and added them to the ones already there. I stood and read the headstone and thought about Ma. She died two years after I was sent to prison. I still remember her sobbing in court when the judge sentenced me to five to eight years. I don't think I'll ever forget the way her soft round face folded into creases as she sobbed. Every time I'd close my eyes and see her sobbing like that, I'd promise myself all over again that someday I'd pay Red off nicely.

'It looks peaceful here,' I said. 'It looks good. You've been doing right for Ma.'

'I come here every week to keep things up,' Danny said. He put his hand on my shoulder, added, 'Ma died quickly. She didn't suffer.'

I knew he was lying. I had my lawyer look into it since all Danny would tell me was she fell ill, and I knew she had stomach cancer. I read enough about that on the Internet to know that Ma didn't die easy. From what I read, stress can play a role in cancer, and I couldn't help feeling that her worrying about me in prison had something to do with her getting sick. If she were still around when parole was first offered to me, I would've taken it but she was already gone by then.

'That's why I took the deal I did,' Danny continued in a soft voice, almost as if he were reading my mind. 'Ma had just gotten sick. I couldn't go to prison and leave her alone.'

I nodded and turned from him so he couldn't see me wipe the tears from my eyes. Any minute now I was going to start sobbing worse than Ma that day I was sentenced, and I didn't want Danny seeing that.

'Let's get out of here,' I said, my voice choked.

I moved quickly away from Ma's grave, the world blurring around me. By the time I got back to Danny's rusted out junker, I was feeling worse than I'd felt that day I'd heard about Ma's death.

Even worse than when my lawyer couldn't get me a day's pass to attend her funeral. I forced my thoughts back to Red and how I was going to pay him back, and I felt the tension ease enough to where my head stopped throbbing.

As we drove away from the cemetery, Danny started to mention how he might be able to get me a job at his construction site. It took me a few moments to clear my head of thoughts of Ma and Red before I made sense of what he was saying.

'I knew there was a reason you took a job like that,' I said, feeling a renewed sense of pride in my little brother. 'I've got something else in the works for the two of us, but maybe we can squeeze this in. What do they got there?'

'What do you mean?'

'For us to rip off. Steel, copper, come on, what do they have for us to score on?'

'I don't want to rip them off, Kyle. I'm just asking if you want help getting a job there.'

'You're fucking kidding me.'

'There's nothing wrong with an honest day's work.'

'Says who?'

He didn't bother answering me, and I could feel my jaw muscles tightening as I stared at him. What the fuck happened to him? How the hell did he turn into such a moke? I swallowed back what I wanted to say. It wouldn't do any good, and besides, I needed the old Danny back, the Danny Nevin who had no problem busting up a joint and kicking out teeth if a payment was late.

'Danny,' I said as calmly I could, 'what I've got in the works is big. Massive big. I'm going to need you in on it with me.'

'I don't know…'

'We'll talk later,' I said, shutting him up before I lost it and told him what a disgrace he had become. The rest of the drive he looked like he was tormented. It made me both want to laugh and slap him silly. I guess I could understand it. With me out of the picture he had fallen into a loser mentality. He got used to a shit way of life and had convinced himself that's all there was going to be. He just needed to be shaken up a bit and reminded what the old days were like. A week, two weeks tops, and I'd have the old Danny back. Christ, the thought of doing construction work every day was worse than prison, worse even than waking up in a shithole like Cedar Junction each morning. At least in prison when you did your time you were let go. With the life Danny was now trying to lead the only release would be a cold grave. Thank God I was out now so I could look out for him.

West Roxbury and Brighton were both neighborhoods of Boston, but you had to leave the city and cross through the upper crust town of Brookline to get from one to the other. Danny was driving through the student ghetto part of Brighton when he pulled off of Commonwealth Ave. and onto a narrow roadway barely wide enough to navigate along without scraping against the cars parked on both sides of the street. The street signs marked one of the sides as a no parking tow zone. That's the thing with students, no respect for the law. Danny pointed out an old brownstone as his apartment building.

He pulled behind the building to park. Opposite the small six-car parking lot about twenty yards away were dumpsters belonging to a Chinese restaurant. At four o'clock in the afternoon I could already see rats climbing along one of them. It smelled like the back of a fish market.

'You got to be shitting me,' I said.

He noticed what I was looking at and shrugged, telling me it was no big deal.

'What do you mean no big deal? You've got rats crawling all over your back lot.' I peered harder at the dumpsters. 'Aren't they supposed to keep covers on them?'

'Forget it, Kyle. The rats usually stay over there, anyway.'

'Usually? You're not telling me you get rats in your apartment?'

He gave me a weak smile, his eyes tilting away from mine. 'Once, but Eve nailed it with a frying pan.'

'Jesus fucking Christ.'

I got out of the car and the stench from rotting food nearly bowled me over. My time in prison, and specifically Cedar Junction, left me hypersensitive to stenches like this. I picked up a brick lying a few yards away and threw it at the dumpsters. I missed the rat I was aiming for, but the brick made a loud clang when it hit the metal dumpster and the rats scattered. I counted at least eight of them as they ran off. As I was watching where they went, an Asian man in his thirties wearing a stained T-shirt, baggy khakis and an apron tied around his middle came out of the restaurant's back door. He spotted the small dent in the dumpster and then the brick lying next to it. He stared back at me fuming, anger twisting his face.

'What the hell are you doing?' he yelled.

'Put covers on those damn dumpsters like the law requires!' I yelled back.

'I'm calling the police on you!'

'Yeah, well, fuck you! I'm calling the sanitation board on you!'

He flipped me the bird. I took a couple of steps towards him, but Danny moved quickly and grabbed me by the arm.

'Kyle, come on, man, it's not worth it.'

I calmed down enough to nod and tell him that I agreed. The Asian man brought his other hand up so he could give me a two-handed salute. Then, after spitting on the ground, he disappeared back into the restaurant.

'You okay?' Danny asked.

'Yeah, I'm okay. How about helping me out with something.'

'What?'

I led the way to the dumpsters. When I looked at Danny, I

could see a dim glimmer of his old self in his eyes. Without having to say a word, we worked together putting some muscle into tipping the dumpster over so the garbage and rotting food inside of it spilled out towards the back doorway. It took some work, but we got the dumpster pushed up against the door. We tried to do it quietly but we still made enough of a racket I was surprised no one tried the back door to see what we were doing. With some more sweat we got the other dumpster tipped over also and on top of the first one. Both of us grunting, we pushed it up against the door. When we were done, we both stank, both of us with dumpster sludge dripping from our clothes, and both of us just about laughing our asses off. I was laughing so hard I could barely breathe. Nearly blind with tears, I found the brick I had tossed earlier. Danny was doubled over, his face a bright red. He tried pulling me away.

'Let's get the fuck out of here,' he said as he gasped for air.

I let him drag me to the back door of his building, then I chucked the brick at the dumpsters we had knocked over. The clanging noise this time seemed louder than before. I heard the restaurant's back door banging against the dumpsters we had put in its way, then the guy inside swearing as he realized what happened. He started yelling how he was going to call the police and I damn near ruptured something inside. Danny pulled me into his apartment building.

'Fuck, that was fun,' he said, wheezing hard now, his eyes nearly on fire they were sparkling so brightly. 'I've missed that. I haven't laughed this hard in years.'

'Me either.' I was holding onto my knees for support. This was the best I'd felt since being arrested. I sniffed and remarked how we both smelled like something that would make a skunk puke.

Danny grimaced as he got a whiff of his shirt. 'Yeah, we do. Let's get upstairs and clean ourselves off before Eve comes home.'

'Who's this Eve you keep mentioning?'

'My girlfriend. You'll meet her later.'

'You two serious?'

He gave me a wry little smile. 'Yeah, I think so. Let's go get cleaned up.'

Danny led the way up the backstairs to his apartment, and as I saw the cracked plaster along the walls and the garbage piled up in the small alcoves, whatever good humor I was feeling faded. I couldn't believe the shithole my brother was living in, but I held my tongue. His apartment turned out to be a small cramped one-bedroom, with one room serving as a combination living room and dining room. A yellowish-brownish water stain bled across the ceiling and the wall-to-wall carpeting was some cheap industrialized shit that needed to be replaced – it was far too stained and dirty to ever be cleaned properly. Given what he had to work with, he had the place fixed up about as nice as it could be. My guess that was Eve's doing. As Danny moved through the apartment opening windows, I looked behind some of the prints of Southie that were hung up on the walls and saw they were there to cover cracks. It pissed me off thinking of Danny living in a dump like this, but I held my tongue.

'Brought a little bit of home with me,' Danny said.

I looked up and saw him smiling, and realized he thought I was admiring one of his Southie prints of Carson Beach. I didn't bother answering him. He stood awkwardly for a moment trying to pretend we weren't standing in the middle of a shithole and suggested I take the first shower, that he'd toss our clothes in a washing machine the building kept for their tenants in the basement. The bathroom was about as cramped as the rest of the apartment with barely enough space to fit a toilet, sink and shower. Still, it felt nice taking a shower where the water wasn't either ice cold or scalding. And I have to admit it was nicer than I would've thought taking a shower in private for the first time in over eight years.

I dried off and put on a heavy dose of Brut before leaving the bathroom to make sure any traces of dumpster smell that might've lingered were covered up. Danny had a pair of boxers on as he sat smoking a joint in the combo living/dining room. He handed it to me while he went off to get me a change of clothing. Drugs weren't my thing, but I took a few hits, and put on the faded jeans and black T-shirt that Danny brought back for me. Before heading off to prison we were the same shirt and pant size, but his jeans were now loose on me and the T-shirt was tight across the chest. Danny remarked as much. He finished sucking on the joint that I had handed back and stubbed out the embers.

'I had a lot of hours to kill in the weight room.' I pulled on the jeans to reveal the several inches of extra space. 'And this is my one benefit from not drinking any beer over the last eight years.'

'Well, let me fix that.' Danny got a couple of cold Michelobs from his fridge and tossed me one, then took his into the bathroom. When I heard the shower running I sat down and drank it slowly, trying hard to relax. I was a free man and I should feel free. But that was easier said than done. I needed to re-establish myself, and more important, I needed to square things with Red. There was no way I could breathe easy knowing that sonofabitch was out there enjoying life, not after what he did to me. And not just to me, but to Danny and my ma and hundreds of others who had trusted him. When I got up for another beer I heard the unmistakable whine of a police siren and then saw a red light flashing from Danny's open bedroom door. I made my way over there, and through the window I could see a police cruiser parked by the overturned dumpsters. A couple of officers were talking to some of the restaurant workers. The prick who had given me the finger earlier was with them and he kept pointing animatedly towards Danny's apartment building. The cops looked bored. Even from where I was standing, I could see one of them trying hard to suppress a smile. I watched for a while, then went and got another beer. After ten minutes the red light stopped strobing in through open bedroom door.

Danny stepped out of the bathroom. He raised an eyebrow at me and asked if he had heard a siren.

'You sure as fuck did. The cops were out back.'

'They didn't knock on any doors or anything?'

'No, but that Chinese prick tried getting them over here. He was hopping up and down pointing at your building. I hope they cited the motherfucker for not keeping his garbage covered.'

'That little fucker.' A wide smile spread across Danny's face. 'What do you say tomorrow we tip over those dumpsters again?'

'No, I don't think so. As long as they keep their garbage covered from now on I'll let it slide. If they don't I'll take care of it a different way.' I wasn't going to say anything, at least not then, but seeing Danny sitting there looking all happy and content I couldn't help myself from asking him how he could stomach living in a place like this.

He shrugged, still smiling his dopey smile. 'Come on, Kyle, it's got to be more spacious than your cell at Cedar Junction. More accommodations too, right, bro?'

'I had no choice where they stuck me. But you choose to live here, for Chrissakes.'

He ignored me while he took a baggie filled with pot from under the sofa cushion and rolled himself another joint. A hard grimness had tightened his face. He lit the joint, inhaled deeply on it, and held the smoke for a good ten-count before exhaling. A couple more hits softened his features. He looked back at me and flashed a careless smile.

'I didn't have any choice either, Kyle, not if I was going to stay out of prison so I could take care of Ma when she was sick. You think it was my choice to move away from the old neighborhood? But shit, this place isn't so bad. Eve's had it under rent control since she was a student, making it cheap as hell. Neighborhood's kind of fun and it's only two miles from where she works. Fuck, I haven't even shown you a picture of Eve yet.'

He took another long hit on the joint, then tried offering me it but this time I passed. As I said before drugs aren't my thing. When I was Red's right hand man, we made a lot of money dealing but there'd be hell to pay if he ever caught you using. As he used to like to say: 'Boyos, I demand clear minds and actions from me lieutenants.' Pretentious little prick, always acting as if he were born and raised in Belfast instead of K Street in South Boston. Anyway, even without his fucking rules, at the level I was at I needed my wits and aggression to survive, and I couldn't afford to soften either with pot, and it was too hard to hide the effects of coke. I got used to keeping away from drugs. Even in prison I avoided them. I didn't want to give the cocksuckers running the place any excuses to stretch out my maximum eight-year sentence.

Danny's dopey grin was mostly back, any traces of the grimness from a few minutes earlier were gone. He pushed himself off the sofa and left the room. When he came back he handed me a photo. The girl in it was thin with long stringy red hair, and from what I could tell given the angle the photo was taken, not much in the tits department. As thin as she looked she had a pale moon-shaped face with a nose that made me think of a pig. Like with every other aspect of his current life, he had settled badly.

'Nice, huh?' he asked.

I nodded. I had criticized him enough for one day. Earlier I'd seen flashes of the old Danny. I knew his true self was buried somewhere in this joke of a life he was leading, and given a little prodding, I'd bring him out like a fucking butterfly from its cocoon. The image of that brought a smile to my lips.

'I knew you'd think so too.' Danny was beaming at the photo of his plain-Jane girlfriend. 'Meeting Eve's the best thing that ever happened to me.'

I handed the photo back to him so he could admire it closer up. 'What plans do you got for tonight?' I asked.

Danny took another long hit from his joint, then stared bleary-eyed at his watch. 'Eve should be back in a half hour. I thought we'd go out for dinner, have a few drinks.'

'What? Just you, me and her?'

'That's what I was thinking.'

'Chrissakes, Danny, I'm just out of prison after eight fucking long years. I thought you'd get a party together for me. Bring in a few of my buddies from the neighborhood.'

His eyes dulled to the point where they matched his smile. 'I couldn't do that, Kyle,' he said. 'I can't contact any of them 'cause of my plea arrangement. You wouldn't believe the hoops my lawyer had to jump through so I could maintain contact with you.'

'They were trying to keep you away from your own brother? The only family you got left?'

'Yeah.'

When I first found out about Red's treachery, it was like a rage had been ignited inside me, and it has been burning steadily ever since. For the last eight years that rage had been my one true companion. Now with this bit of news it flared up, choking me off. For a few seconds all I could see was red – the color, not the traitorous rat. I took a few deep breaths and was able to bring the rage back to a low simmer. When I could, I told Danny the joke was on them.

'What do you mean?'

'Not now. I'll tell you in a few days when I got things worked out. Anyway, fuck them. It's been what, seven years since you made your deal? No one's going to notice if you cheat on it now.'

'They will. I got a few enemies from the old days waiting to drop a dime on me.'

'Bullshit.'

'It's true, Kyle. They already made a few bogus calls, one even last year. The cops investigated each of them. Thank God I had witnesses who could corroborate where I was.'

'You got names for who made these calls?'

'Just suspicions.'

'Give me the names.'

He hesitated, then, shrugging, said, 'Tom Dolan and Mike Halloran. I can't prove it, though.'

I nodded as I remembered those two. Dolan owned a liquor store on Dorchester Street that was on Danny's collection list. If I remembered right, at one time he got stubborn about paying his monthly dues, and stayed stubborn until a crowbar was taken to both his kneecap and his whiskey section. Halloran was just some dumb low-level punk who thought he could run his own book in the neighborhood. Red heard about it and next thing you knew Dolan was being fitted for a new set of dentures. In the old days, Danny did good work.

'I'll make sure word gets out on what happens if anyone rats you,' I said. 'So what do you say, we head back home tonight for a little celebrating?'

Danny shook his head. 'I can't risk it, Kyle. The DA's office is serious about that plea. And there's no time expiration on it. The arrangement's for life. If they catch me breaking it I'll go away for a minimum of three years.'

'Danny, with me out, no one's going to risk ratting you.'

'I just can't do it. I'm sorry.'

I was going to try arguing but looking at the dumb stoned expression on his face I knew there was no point.

'Fuck it,' I said. 'We'll go out to dinner with you and your girlfriend, then I'll take myself off to Scolley's for some celebrating.'

Danny nodded, his eyes glazing over as he stared off at a print of a crowd watching the St Patrick's Day Parade winding down

4th Street. I went and got myself another Michelob. I was going to have to get Danny off the grass if I was going to bring back his old self, but I had some time for that. The job I was planning out wasn't going to go down for a few weeks. The third beer was starting to give me a buzz. I guess after the stretch I just finished without a drop of alcohol, I'd become a bit of a lightweight. Danny finished the joint he was working on then got himself another beer also. We sat, chilling, mostly making small talk about how life was in the federal system and then later at Cedar Junction. It was nice just the two of us sitting there bullshitting like that. It brought back old memories from when we were kids. When I tapped out a fresh cig, he did a slow double take as if he couldn't quite comprehend what it was at first.

'Not a good idea, bro,' he said.

'What?'

'Eve doesn't want anyone smoking in here.'

'You're shitting me, right?'

'No, bro.'

I didn't need this shit. I was finally starting to feel better and I had to have a fucked-up discussion over whether I could smoke a cig? I lit up, using an empty Michelob bottle for the ashes. Danny looked on, too stoned to really care much one way or the other. For the first time he noticed the carton of Marlboro 100s I had put by the sofa, and he made a comment how it would be better if I hid the carton in his closet.

'Why's that?'

'Eve might throw it out.'

I gave him a look to see if he was serious, and as best I could tell he was. Reaching over, I pushed the carton under the sofa, then did a slow burn as I finished the cigarette and dropped the butt into the beer bottle. I was just starting to calm back down when his girlfriend unlocked the front door and walked in. In person, her tits were as small as they looked in the photo. She had nice legs, though, I'll give Danny that. When she saw me sitting on the sofa next to Danny, she didn't bother putting on an act. There was nothing but ice in the look she gave me. Still, she was my brother's girlfriend, so I started to push myself up to give her a kiss, but she short-circuited me by moving in quickly and offering a small frigid hand instead. It was like shaking hands with an ice cube.

Danny, grinning a stoner's grin, said, 'This is my big brother, Kyle, I've been telling you about.'

'Yes, I know. I recognize him from the newspapers.'

Something about her superior-than-thou tone really pissed the shit out of me. 'Where the fuck's my head,' I said. 'You're my brother's girl, for Chrissakes.' Before she could move I stood up and gave her a tight embrace and a big wet kiss on her cheek. I felt some satisfaction feeling her squirm in my arms, but shit, it was like hugging a stick of wood. When I let go, I felt like I needed to check myself over to make sure I didn't pick up any splinters.

'From now on handshakes between us are sufficient,' she said, her pale gray eyes seething.

'That's not how things are done in my family,' I said.

'What's going on?' Danny asked, looking with some alarm at his girlfriend and then me.

'I don't have a fucking clue. Ask her.'

Eve's pale skin flushed a light pink as she met Danny's bewildered eyes. 'I'm just having a lousy day. Let's start over. Kyle, it's wonderful to meet you.'

She reached over and gave me a brittle hug and a quick peck on the cheek. I could've had some fun with her right then, but I behaved myself. After all, she was my brother's girl, at least for the moment.

Danny was still giving Eve a puzzled look, some concern cutting through his pot-induced haze. He said, 'I was thinking the three of us could go out and celebrate Kyle's release. Maybe you could call up Linda and see if she wants to join us, see if we can make it a foursome.'

'Linda met someone.'

'Who?'

'Some guy at a club,' she said quickly, her eyes shifting from Danny's.

'Call one of your other friends then. Shit, they're always moaning how there aren't enough single guys in Boston.'

'Danny, my head's killing me. You two go out and have fun. I think I'm just going to stay in.'

'Hope your head feels better,' I said.

She nodded in my direction, not bothering to make eye contact, then disappeared into the bedroom and closed the door behind her.

Danny just sat there looking confused. 'What the fuck?' he said.

'I don't think your girl likes me very much.'

'Why wouldn't she?'

I didn't bother saying the obvious. That she thought I was a bad influence. Or maybe simply that she just didn't want anything to do with a convicted armed felon. I wondered briefly if Danny ever told her what he used to do and decided he didn't. Danny's eyes had fixed on someplace off in the distance. I could see the transformation in them as the obvious cut though his drug-fogged brain.

'If it's going to cause you problems with me staying here, I'll look for someplace else to go.'

'No, bro, my place is your place.'

'That's good. Stand up.'

He stood up. I gave him a real embrace, not the quick little hug we gave in the car. 'I got plans for us, Danny,' I said softly, making sure to keep my voice low. 'When we're done, we're going to own this fucking town again.'

I took a step back, feeling strong emotion for my brother. For the first time since stepping out of prison, I felt connected to Danny, at least the way I used to feel about him.

'Look, I'm heading out to Southie.'

'What about us going out for dinner?'

'We'll do it another time. Stay here and work things out with your girlfriend.'

'Yeah, I guess I should. You need anything?'

'I could use some cash. A cell phone. Your car keys.'

He tossed me a set of keys, then emptied out his wallet and handed me forty-eight dollars. Checking his pockets he pulled out something that looked like a gizmo that could've come from Star Trek.

'They shrunk these things to almost nothing,' I said as I held the phone in my palm.

'You want me to show you how to use it?'

'I'll figure it out.'

I gave him a little tap on the shoulder and told him I'd let the old neighborhood know he was still kicking and breathing. He nodded, watching somewhat wistfully as I left the apartment. I stood outside the door listening. The walls were thin and I could hear everything as plainly as if I were in the same room with them. I heard her leave the bedroom and tell Danny that she was not going to pimp out any of her friends to me, that that was where she was drawing the line. She'd let me stay there for a few days but she was not pimping out any of her friends.

'What are you talking about?' Danny tried arguing, his speech having the same soft, slow cadence of any stoner. He didn't have a chance in hell against her. 'All I was saying was getting one of your friends for a foursome.'

'Right. Your brother's just out of prison. All he wants is a dinner date. Right.'

'And what would be the harm if they connected?'

'Are you kidding me? He's a convicted felon. I'm not introducing any of my friends to someone like him. And God knows what diseases he picked up in prison. I've watched *Oz*. I know what they do in prison. And I don't want him smoking in our apartment. I'm not an idiot, Danny. I saw the cigarette stub in the beer bottle. I could smell the cigarette smoke.'

'He had one cigarette.'

'I don't care. I don't want him smoking in here!'

'Come on, Eve. He had the window open. What else is he supposed to do?'

'Why should I have to be subjected to his cigarette smoke? Or worry about him burning the place down? If he needs to smoke that badly, let him go outside.'

'Ah, shit. Come on. We're on the third floor. You're saying he has to run down three flights of stairs every time he wants to smoke?'

She was going on, telling Danny that was exactly what I had to do while he tried half-heartedly to argue with her. He couldn't get a word in. I left then. The rage simmering inside had started to heat up and I needed to get away before I went back in there and kicked her teeth down her throat. The last person who talked about me like that was my old man, and that was when I was thirteen. I still went after him with a steak knife and if he hadn't been able to wrestle it away from me, I would've sliced him open. He beat the shit out of me – broke a few bones, but he realized he'd better watch his mouth around me. He was cautious after that with what he said, even to Danny. Up until the day he took off after stealing eighty grand from a local loan shark, he watched what he said to the two of us.

I stepped out of the building's back doorway. It was past six and the sun was a bright orange and dropping fast, but it would still be light for another hour or so. The Chinese guy from before was alone by the two dumpsters shoveling garbage back into them. He seemed to be struggling with it, his arms rubbery as he lifted the shovel up almost over his head to dump off each load. When he spotted me he did a kind of double-take and then started shouting. I ignored him. The mood I was in I thought it would be best. Still, as I got in Danny's car, I started worrying about him memorizing the license plate. I was deciding whether I'd better warn him about calling the police when he started pounding on my front window. Spittle flew from his mouth as he called me a few choice names and threatened to have me arrested. I lowered the window. He stuck his index finger towards my face, still spitting as he yelled, and I snapped the finger like a twig.

I twisted his broken finger until he dropped to his knees, then I smacked him in the face with the car door as I got out. A gash had opened up on his forehead and the blood from it dripped over his eye and down his cheek and then onto his white T-shirt. He started crying, his mouth forming a big gaping round 'o'.

'You have any idea who I am?' I asked him.

When he didn't answer, I put pressure on his finger until he shook his head.

'You should read your newspapers and not be such an ignorant fuck,' I said. 'If you were to call the police on me you and your family would disappear. It wouldn't matter where I was, I'd still have enough juice to make it happen. Maybe your bodies get dumped in the ocean, or chopped up and spread over landfills. It wouldn't matter. No one would ever have a clue what happened to any of you. You think I'm making this up?'

He shook his head frantically without waiting for me to twist his finger again. I let go of his finger and watched as he made little moaning sounds, all the while rocking back and forth as if he were engaged in some sort of silent prayer.

'What happened today was your fault,' I told him. 'If you showed this neighborhood the proper respect it wouldn't have happened. You keeping your garbage uncovered attracted rats to the area. And I'm not even mentioning the smell. People live around here, and what you did wasn't fair to them. You understand that?'

He nodded, his head moving up and down as if someone had grabbed it and shook it. He had his eyes squeezed shut, but he was paying attention to what I was saying.

'As long as you cover your garbage from now on, you and me are fine. If you don't we're going to have big problems. I mean really big fucking problems. So are you and me going to have any more problems?'

He shook his head.

'I want to hear you say it.'

In a low stilted voice, he forced out that the two of us were not going to have any more problems.

'Go get your finger taken care of,' I said. I helped him to his feet. He ran off holding his injured finger. I sat back in the car, paralyzed, wondering what the hell was wrong with me. If he talked, him and his family would disappear like I told him. I wasn't kidding about that. If the police arraigned me they'd have to drop their charges once they lost contact with their only witness. Even though I didn't have to worry about going back to a place like Cedar Junction, if he talked it would bring me police attention that I couldn't afford. With them watching me and snooping into my business, I would have to delay my plans by months, maybe even longer. Which would be all that more time before I'd be able to look for Red. In the old days – well, fuck, in the old days no one would've dared get in my face like that, but if someone had ever been stupid enough to try, I would've taken care of them.

Ah, fuck it. I decided he got the message. He wasn't going to talk. You'd think being out of prison and getting a chance for the first time in years to let off a little steam by working over a fucking ignorant moke would've relieved some of the pressure inside, but all the incident did was put me in a darker mood. I took out Danny's cell phone and figured out how to use it. I swore I wasn't going to call Janet, at least not until things were better for me, but in the mood I'd slipped into I couldn't help myself from calling her mom. I had that number burned in my skull. When her mom answered the phone, I heard the hesitancy in her voice as she recognized me, but she didn't hang up. Mary always liked me, and I knew she wouldn't hang up on me.

'Kyle, you know I can't give you Janet's number,' she said with a soft sigh.

'Ah, Mary, what do I need to bribe you with? A bottle of Bushmills?'

'She's married now with children.'

'Mary, how do I need to sweeten this? Make it a sixteen-year-old malt?'

'Kyle,' she said. 'You've got to let this go. It's not right for you to be calling her now. Besides, what would be the point?'

'Mary, I am going to be calling her. If you don't help me, I'll find someone in the old neighborhood who will. But I need to talk to Janet. After all, we were engaged before my arrest.' I thought back on all the Oprah and Dr Phil shows I killed time with, and added, 'I need this closure.'

Another deep heavy sigh, then, 'All you're going to do is talk to her?'

'Jesus, Mary, no matter what you've been reading in the papers I'm not an animal.'

'Promise me, Kyle.'

'I give you my word.'

There was a long ten-count where I wasn't sure whether she'd hung up on me, then, 'And the gift that you mentioned?'

'On your doorstep first thing tomorrow.'

'Make it a case of Bushmills.'

'A bit steep,' I said. 'At Scolley's the same information would probably only cost me a pint.'

'If anyone there knows it, that is,' she offered, a sly note edging into her voice.

'Someone there will know it. Or at least know someone who does. But Mary, 'cause I like you I'll make it four bottles of the good stuff. That's a combined seventy-two years. Almost double your own age.'

That got a laugh out of her. At this point she had to be topping sixty, and her liver, from all the abuse she's given it over the years, had to be more like a ninety-year-old's. How she was still alive was anyone's guess.

'Four bottles it is,' she agreed. 'Anyway, you'd find Janet easy enough without my help. But Kyle, as you promised, you'll just be calling her for, uh, closure, and nothing more.'

'Scout's honor.'

She laughed again. 'And when were you ever a scout?'

'In my heart I've always been one.'

She sighed and gave me Janet's phone number. 'Now, I'm not telling you her address,' she said. 'You just call her this one time so you can move on. Who knows, maybe it will help Janet too. I know there's some torment there concerning you.' She hesitated, then added, 'You're just out of prison today, is that right, Kyle?'

'That's right, Mary. They opened those pearly gates for me only a few hours ago.'

'Maybe this time you can try to make a better go of things,' she said. 'Try living the straight and narrow for a change and not get yourself in any more trouble.'

'I can't do that, Mary. Jesus, you of all people should know what I'm going to have to do to get those four bottles of Bushmills for you.'

I hung up on her then ignoring her half-hearted protestations. After sitting quietly for a few minutes, I called the number she gave me. After the fourth ring a woman answered, her tone guarded as she asked if I was Danny. It had been over eight years but I had no trouble recognizing Janet's voice. Hearing her brought a tightness to my throat.

'Nope, not Danny,' I said. 'Why would you think Danny would be calling you?'

'Kyle,' she said, her voice turning sour.

'That's right. Now answer my question. Has my little brother been in the habit of calling you?'

'You're an idiot. According to the Caller ID, the call was being made from Danny's cell phone.'

I was confused and told her as much. 'What the fuck's Caller ID?'

'It tells you who's calling. Hang up, and I'll call you right back and you'll see for yourself.'

'I don't know the number for this cell phone.'

'I already have it. It showed up as part of the Caller ID.'

I hung up and after a minute or so realized Janet wasn't calling back. I redialed her number. This time her answering machine clicked on.

'I don't know what fucking game you're playing but unless you want me showing up in the flesh or calling your husband and letting him know what you used to do at the Squire Inn to make us money, you'd better fucking pick up—'

She picked up. 'What are you calling for, Kyle?' she demanded, trying to sound angry but I could hear the fear in her voice. 'I'm married now. It's been over a long time between us.'

'What's with this bullshit, telling me you're going to be calling me back and then leaving me waiting?'

'I'm sorry—'

'Don't give me that shit. And don't think I'm overlooking you calling me an idiot before. You should know me well enough to know what that could end up buying you.'

'I said I'm sorry. It threw me hearing your voice. I needed a few minutes to think. And I apologize for what I called you. It slipped out. How'd you get my number?'

'Mary sold you out for four bottles of whiskey.'

'I should've guessed as much. What a wonderful mother I ended up with, huh? Maybe those four bottles will finally finish the job on her liver. God, I hope so. What do you want, Kyle?'

'Ten thousand dollars,' I said.

She laughed, but it was tired and with not much life to it. 'And how do you figure that?'

'It's what you owe me.'

'I do, huh?'

'That's right.'

'What would happen if I called the parole board and told them you were trying to extort ten thousand dollars from me?'

'Not much, I would think. I didn't get paroled. If you read the stories in the papers, you'd know that. I served out the full sentence so I wouldn't have to worry about anyone trying to hold that over me like you're trying right now.'

There was a long silence, then, 'How do I owe you ten thousand dollars?'

'It's what I invested in you. Implants for example. Thanks to me your husband gets to enjoy nice firm cantaloupes instead of the shriveled oranges I used to have to deal with. And let's not forget all the other things I did to make you presentable. A partial list would include braces, nose job, jewelry and health club memberships. I spent far more than ten grand on you, but I decided to give you a break and charge you only thirty cents on the dollar seeing how you're a bit used up at this point.'

'This is how you spent your days in prison, thinking something like this up? Anything I might've owed you I paid back a long time ago with what I had to do to get money for your lawyer. I'm not paying you another cent.'

'It's not negotiable.'

'Fuck you!'

'Is that any way to talk with children around?'

She lowered her voice. 'If that's some kind of threat—'

'You should know me better than that. I'm just concerned that one of your little ones might be listening and picking up your bad habits.'

'Look, Kyle, I'm sorry how things ended with us, but I needed a chance to make a real life for myself, and I've done that. Maybe now that you're out of prison you can do the same for yourself.'

'Maybe I might, but it doesn't change the fact that you owe me ten grand. If you're short on cash, I can let you work off your debt in trade.' I waited while I heard her breathing on the other end. She didn't say anything but I could hear her breathing. Maybe I could even hear her heart beating. 'I'll give you a higher hourly rate than you deserve. A thousand bucks an hour. One long night on your knees, and you'll be paid off.'

'That's what this is about,' she said, her voice cold enough to freeze.

'Nope, not at all. Just giving you options.'

There was a long silence before she told me never to call back there again.

'I know what you're capable of, Kyle,' she said. 'But you have to know what I'm capable of too.'

She hung up then.

For a long time she'd been under my skin, especially with the way she broke things off between us; going through my lawyer the day after the eight-year maximum sentence was handed down, and then her stone silence to my letters. It felt good knowing I'd gotten under her skin also.

I was surprised she was still in the area, even more surprised that she'd let her mom know how to contact her. More than anyone, except maybe Red, she knew what I was capable of, and knowing that I would've thought she'd have the common sense to have moved thousands of miles from Boston with a new name and identity. Maybe she'd convinced herself that I'd end up being killed in prison, or even more far-fetched, come out a changed man. Or maybe it was simply that her husband knew nothing about me, and she never had the heart to tell him. More likely he had no idea about her either, or at least who she used to be. Anyway, she knew me well enough to know my one phone call wasn't by any means the end of it.

Fuck her. Let her stew in worry and agitation for a while, the same as she left me stewing those years in prison.

I found myself breathing a little easier than before. Not much, but some. It would take finishing things with Janet and squaring my debt with Red before I'd ever really be able to feel like my old self again. This was a start, anyway.

My call to Janet put me in a good enough mood to make a couple of other calls I needed to make. Then, whistling a happy tune, I turned on the ignition and headed towards Southie.

Chapter 2

I made two stops on my way to Scolley's. The first was to Flynn's
Liquors, where with some relief I saw John Flynn's beefy self
behind the counter. I was glad to see him. It would've made
things harder for all concerned if he had hired help working that
night instead of himself. Not that it would've mattered much as
far as the eventual outcome.

John Flynn looked up from his newspaper as I entered the
store. His eyes remained dull for a moment, then as he recognized
me his face deflated as quickly as if it had been a punctured
balloon. He tried covering up his disappointment by a forcing a
big toothy smile. Lumbering slowly to his feet, he held out a sickly
white fleshy hand for me to shake.

'Jesus, Kyle, I read you were being let out. Just today,
wasn't it?'

I took his hand. It felt soft, almost like I was squeezing a hunk
of lard. He had gotten larger and fleshier since I had seen him
last, his skin more of a sickly pale dead fish color. One would've
thought looking at the two of us that he was the one just out
of stir.

'That's right, John. A free man as of today.' I patted his bulging
stomach. 'You look like you've been eating well. Business been
good?'

His smile weakened. I could tell he was trying to figure out the safest thing to tell me, and settled on that he had no real complaints. All at once he winced and slapped his forehead.

'Where the fuck's my head. Let me get you a welcome home gift,' he said.

He walked around the counter and made his way to the refrigerated area in back. He returned a minute later and tried handing me a six-pack of Guinness. When I didn't take it from him, he placed it awkwardly on the counter.

'This is what you're calling a welcome home gift? After eight fucking years?'

'It's a gesture, Kyle.'

'You want me smack your fucking head against this counter? That would be a gesture also.'

He blinked as he stared at me, his smile cracking badly under the strain.

'I don't know what you want, Kyle,' he said.

'I want you to show me some fucking respect. Red's been on the run, what, six years now. You've had six years to get nice and fat, which I can see you've done, and this is what you're going to offer me, a six-pack of beer?'

He aged as he stood staring at me, his smile now completely gone. 'What can I get you?' he asked.

'A case of Bushmills.'

An internal debate flickered in his eyes as he tried to decide whether without Red in my corner it was safe to tell me to go screw or if he still needed to fear me. The debate ended. He looked away, his heavy jowls sagging. He decided smartly that he still needed to fear me.

'I'll get you the case,' he said.

'The sixteen-year-old malt.'

That stopped him, a pained look spreading over his large fleshy face.

'You trying to kill me here—' he started. One look at me, though, and he turned away, mumbling that he'd see what he had in back. I watched as he walked away, then took a can of Guinness and drained it slowly. In the old days he'd be hit for two bills a week. Over six years that would add up to more than sixty grand and now he was going to start bitching and moaning over a few bottles of whiskey? The thought of that made me almost start knocking over shelves, but I decided to just be mellow. I guess I needed to give him time to adjust to how things now were.

He came back red-faced and breathing hard as he carried a case in his arms. When he put it down in front of me I saw the case was half-filled.

'That's all I have in inventory,' he said.

I thought he might be lying to me but decided to give him the benefit of the doubt, and told him to have the rest waiting for me when I came back the next week.

He nodded, a dull film falling over his eyes.

'And for Chrissakes, get some fresh air occasionally. And some exercise. I've seen guys taken out of isolation with more color than you.'

'I'll do that. Are we finished?'

'Almost. You got a screwdriver you can loan me?'

Alarm showed in his eyes. 'What do you need a screwdriver for?' he asked, his voice coming out almost as a squeak at the end.

I couldn't help laughing seeing him trembling. 'Take it easy, John. Don't have a heart attack or nothing. I'm not going to stick a screwdriver in your eye if that's what you're thinking. It will just save me a trip to the hardware store.'

He looked sick as he searched through a drawer under the cash register and came up with a flathead screwdriver, just the type I needed. Relief spread over his face as I put it in my pocket.

'I'll be by next week for the rest of my welcome home present,' I said. 'Be good, John. Lose some weight.'

I stacked the rest of the six-pack on the case and carried it all out of the store. I wondered briefly if he had ever done anything to me to make him seriously think I'd want to stick a screwdriver through his eye. Maybe he had tried tipping off the cops on me at some point. Maybe even wrote an anonymous letter to the courts for my sentencing. I was going to have to ask around, but more likely than not, it was just his nerves. When I got to the car I put the whiskey in the trunk and brought the Guinness into the front seat with me. I drained two more cans, and then set off for my second stop, an alleyway off of East Broadway.

One of the tricks I learned from my years with Red was to hide cash around so if you're ever on the run you can get your hands on it without having to go to the bank or your home, and just as importantly, so the government and your lawyers don't have a clue about it. Red did it on a much larger scale than me, hiding cash in banks all over Europe, using aliases for each account. What I did was hide bundles of cash around Boston. It might sound risky, but it wasn't. Unless you knew where the cash was, you weren't going to find it. I didn't have to worry about some dumb moke stumbling on any of it.

I counted the bricks on the far end of the alley, and found the one that was loose enough where I could pull it out with a screwdriver. Sure enough, taped on the inside of the hole was a packet of hundred dollar bills wrapped tightly in cellophane. The packet had been there for a decade. When I unwrapped the cellophane, I was relieved to see the bills were still in good shape, no worse for wear after all this time. I flipped through the packet and counted the three grand that I was expecting. With spending money in my pocket, I headed to Scolley's, which was less than a mile away.

When I stepped into Scolley's it was as if the place had been frozen in time. Nothing had changed. Same cracked Budweiser mirror on the side wall to my left, same cheap Kelly Green upholstered barstools scattered around the bar, same worn parquet floor and, of course, the same dim fluorescent lights that barely lit the place. Joe Whalley had always been a fixture at Scolley's, and he was there as usual working the bar. Joe's hair had gone completely white making his face appear even redder than I remembered, but other than that he hadn't changed a bit. I looked around and recognized most of the regulars propped up on the same barstools they always sat on, the same ones they'll probably someday will to their heirs. Some of the regulars might've looked a little thicker in the middle, maybe their hair a little thinner and their faces more lined, but not much else had changed with them either. I think I even recognized a few of them wearing the same clothes they had on the last time I was in Scolley's. And each one of them was staring at me with the same hostile alcohol-glazed looks they always gave intruders.

Joe recognized me first. 'Holy Mary, mother of God,' he exclaimed, his eyes crinkling with genuine affection and a big grin breaking out over his ruddy face. 'Look who's back from the dead. Kyle Nevin. Get your ass seated so I can set you up!'

I looked around and saw smiles stretching on most of the other patrons' faces. A few, though, turned away, their expressions becoming grim as they stared down at their drinks. I noted who they were, and their reactions didn't surprise me. Especially Fred Connor's.

Charlie Maguire had been sitting on my old barstool. He hopped off and showed a toothless grin on his round eighty-year-old face, welcoming me to take his place. I put my arm around the old rummy and told him next time to try remembering his false teeth before leaving home, and that made his grin wider and even more like a jack o'lantern's. After taking my place at the bar, Joe grabbed my hand first and held it in his two large meaty paws.

He's had a warm spot in his heart for me ever since twenty years earlier I stood up to Red and declared that from this point on Scolley's was sacred ground and that they were to be taken off his collection list. Red didn't like it but he wasn't going to fight me over something like that. Not with everything I was doing for him.

After I freed my hand from Joe, I shook hands with the other patrons who had gathered around while others good-naturedly patted me on the back. Joe yelled out that drinks were on the house to welcome me back home, and he was right about that; Scolley's had always been like a second home to me.

Joe got busy, first placing a shot glass of Bushmills in front of me, along with a pint of Guinness, then pouring drinks for the rest of the crowd. I shook loose a cigarette. Before I could take out my Zippo lighter, Joe had my cigarette lit. 'You're looking good, Kyle,' he said with a wink. 'Maybe a bit pasty, but a few days in the sun will take care of that. Lost some weight, have you?'

'About thirty pounds,' I said. I took the smoke deep into my lungs and let it out through my nose. 'Back to my old fighting weight of two-ten.'

Drinks all around were lifted for a toast given by Joe. Fred Connor muttered something under his breath during the toast, while Bill Mullan sitting next to him showed a smirk over their private joke. Neither of them bothered to touch their glasses. Joe gave the two of them a cold eye, but I chose to ignore the insult. Hell, I was back home after eight long years, fuck the two of them. I sipped the Bushmills, noting that Joe hadn't skimped and had poured me the sixteen-year-old malt. I then took a long drink of the Guinness and appreciated the richness of it. Draft Guinness was like nectar of the Gods, the canned version I'd been drinking earlier just didn't cut it.

'Nothing better than Guinness out of the keg,' I said.

'Mother's milk,' Joe agreed. 'It's been far too long, Kyle. I've missed having you here. And what about your little brother, Danny? Is he still alive, or what?'

'Barely,' I said. 'He's living in Brighton, if you can believe it. A shithole of an apartment if I've ever seen one, maybe one step above the cell I just got out of. And you should see the girl he's shacked up. Tits the size of ping-pong balls. She's got nice legs and a nice ass, I'll give her that, but the fucking mouth on her. I almost put my foot down her throat.'

'She mouth off to you, did she?'

'Not in front of me. She waited until I left the apartment. But I could hear her from the hallway.'

'Hard to believe Danny would put up with that.' Joe shook his head, a scowl creasing his face. 'And hard to believe he'd end up this way. A sad thing to hear. But still, why hasn't he graced us with his presence all these years?'

I finished the Guinness, and Joe took away the glass to pour me a fresh one.

'Because of his plea arrangement,' I said.

Joe looked away from the beer he was pouring so he could stare off into the distance and try to remember what I was referring to. Slowly he nodded as it came to him.

'That was years ago,' he said. 'I'm sure he could come back now without any problems.'

'He's afraid the DA's office would nail him if he tried.'

'That sounds a tad paranoid to me.'

'Maybe.' I took a sip of the fresh pint Joe had just poured me, enjoying the creaminess of the foam topping off the pint. 'He's convinced there are some rats out around looking to drop a dime on him first chance they get.'

'Well, you tell Danny I've got an axe handle back here for anyone who tries a stunt like that,' Joe said.

Of course, Joe knew now that I was out I would do far worse

to any rat than what he could do with an axe handle, but I told him I'd relay the message. I emptied the shot glass and watched blissfully as Joe poured me another. 'You know what I've been dreaming about at night the last few months? Those roast beef sandwiches of yours.'

Joe gave me what could only be described as a look of utter pride, then took three roast beef sandwiches from a mini-refrigerator he keeps under the bar and popped them into a toaster oven. His wife cooks up fresh roast beef everyday, and Joe, using plain Wonder Bread with a perfect combination of mayo, mustard and Swiss cheese, whips up a stack of sandwiches as close to heaven as I've found. I wasn't kidding him. Over the last month I'd find myself waking up at night drooling like a baby as I thought of them.

While Joe was busy waiting for the toaster oven to ding, several of the regulars moved their barstools closer so they could ask me about prison. I told them how the federal prisons were a cakewalk compared to Cedar Junction, how that place was a different beast entirely. Martin Foley clapped me on the back and asked if anyone in there tried giving me a hard time.

'Nope. The guards baited me at times, but I ignored them and it never got physical. Not that they never gave a prisoner a beating for the hell of it, but with me they had to be more cautious, not knowing how much payback I could arrange for them. As far as the other prisoners went, they're like wild dogs. They have a sixth sense of who's weak and can be victimized and who should be avoided. Me, they avoided. But to be honest, not a lot of shit went down in there.'

I took a long drink of my beer, then went on, telling them about the special wing they had at Cedar Junction called the DDU. 'Departmental Disciplinary Unit,' I said, taking my time pronouncing each word. 'You get sent there and you'll do twenty-three hours a day in isolation. A year or two of that will drive almost anyone nuts. The threat of that mostly kept the animals in check.'

Fred Connor made another comment half under his breath, and his buddy, Bill Mullan, got another snide laugh out of it. I was about to turn to the two of them when Joe put a plate with three roast beef sandwiches in front of me, along with a couple of bags of potato chips.

'I made some calls around,' Joe said, the wrinkles along his eyes crinkling good-naturedly. 'Spreading the word that you're here tonight. See if we can give you a proper party.'

As he was saying this the door to Scolley's opened and two women in their mid-twenties walked in, a blonde and a brunette, both sharply dressed in short miniskirts, silk blouses, and stilettos that accentuated their athletic and well-shaped legs and showed off their calves beautifully. The brunette was wearing sheer black stockings, and as she and her friend made their way to one of the small tables in back, her eye caught mine and she gave me a bare trace of a smile that got my heart pumping a bit harder.

'Who's the brunette?' I asked Joe.

Joe craned his neck to get a look at them at their table. Somehow he had missed their grand entrance, or maybe I was giving him an excuse to get another look.

'Her and her blonde friend? A couple of the gentrified folks who've moved into Southie recently. The likes of them are driving the price of apartments sky high here. She's not one of us, Kyle. But she and her friend are certainly nice to look at.'

'They certainly are at that.' I stopped to take a bite of one of the sandwiches stacked up on my plate, the roast beef just about melting in my mouth. I savored the taste for a few moments, then added with a wink, 'Even more so when you've been locked away for eight years.'

Fred Connor chose at that moment to make another snide comment to his buddy, Mullan. I couldn't hear what he said, but the way they both laughed got me turning around and nearly off my barstool. Joe stopped me by putting one of his large paws on my hand.

'Enjoy your sandwiches, Kyle. I bet you haven't had anything quite like that in a while.'

I nodded slowly, turned back to my food and took another healthy bite of the sandwich, but couldn't quite enjoy it as much thinking of those two smirking at me.

'Nothing at all like this,' I conceded. 'Food you got in the joint you had to hold your nose while you ate.'

I heard some hushed whispering behind me and once again caught the brunette giving me both the eye and a faint smile before looking away. Joe noticed it too. He leaned in close to me, speaking low so none of the other patrons next to me could hear.

'A few weeks back she left here with Tom Dunleavy, and a month or so before that, Mike Callaghan. Her friend has done similar. Now you didn't hear any of this from me.'

Joe and his propriety. As long as I had known him he had always put women on a pedestal. Saying what he did to me would be hard enough. Coming right out and admitting the obvious, that the brunette and her friend came to Scolley's trolling for bad boys, would be near impossible for him.

I nodded and pushed the remaining piece of the sandwich in my mouth and chewed it slowly, all the while giving the brunette a long look. She had a nice shape to her and soft lips that got my blood racing and my imagination running. I was about to pick up the plate and bring it over to her table so I could join the two of them when Martin Foley asked me another question about what the prisoners were like in Cedar Junction. I decided to sit back down and spend more time with my friends. I'd have plenty of time for the brunette and her friend later.

'You've got three basic types,' I told both Martin and the crowd listening in. 'Hardcore lifers, losers who are in way over their heads and psychos. The worst of the worst. But because of the long shadow of the DDU, they mostly watch themselves. But I did see some bizarre shit over the last three years.'

I took a long drink of my beer and told them about Darren Lusker. 'This sonofabitch was pure psycho. He had strangled his seventy-year-old mother and sodomized her body for weeks before the cops found him. The guy was just this thin, bony piece of shit. Looked like you could break him in two with your bare hands if you wanted. A lot of cons wanted to, but you had the DDU to worry about, so he was mostly left alone.'

'Fuck,' said Martin. 'I remember reading about him. He killed someone in prison, didn't he? Then committed suicide?' A couple of the others sitting nearby nodded. I took another drink of my beer, then finished half a sandwich before continuing.

'Yeah, well, that's not exactly the way it happened. One of the losers tried making a name for himself by sticking a shiv into good ole Darren. Cedar Junction is responsible for making every license plate in Massachusetts, and this guy had gotten a sliver of sheet metal and made a shiv out of it and snuck it into the showers. So there's Darren minding his own business, totally oblivious to what's about to happen, and the fucking loser comes charging across the showers when he slips and falls and ends up with his own shiv buried under his ribs. He flapped around like a fish for a minute or so before dying only a few feet from where Darren was standing. The next thing you knew the guards come storming in, whaling away at Darren with their nightsticks, then dragging him off to DDU. And you know how I know all this?'

Martin shook his head slowly, his eyes dull and glazed with the shots of Chivas he'd been pouring down religiously.

'I was right there in the showers when it all went down. I'll tell you, I enjoyed watching that little motherfucker finally get what was coming to him.'

I was polishing off the rest of my pint when I heard Fred Connor make another comment under his breath to his buddy, and then the two of them laughing. I'd had enough of their bullshit, and turned to Connor and asked him if he'd mind sharing with the rest of us what was so goddamned funny. Connor met my stare head on, his own black eyes shining with violence.

'Nothing that funny,' he said. 'Me and Bill were just speculating whether you took it up the ass or gave blow jobs. Because that's what they do to child killers in prison, isn't it?'

'What the fuck are you talking about? I got sent away for armed robbery.'

'Fuck you, Nevin, we both know what you did.' Connor had pushed himself off his stool, his eyes now small holes as he stared at me. He was a big barrel-chested man with broad shoulders and thick arms. I got off my barstool also. Others sitting around started to scatter. Out of the corner of my eye I could see Joe reaching for his axe handle. I signaled for him not to bother.

'And why don't you tell me what I was supposed to have done?' I asked softly.

'You fucking piece of shit,' he swore at me. Then he turned to the rest of the crowd. 'How can all of you idolize this piece of garbage?' he yelled out to them. 'This isn't someone human! This isn't someone you should be sitting around buying drinks for! This is nothing but a cold-blooded parasite. You all know what he's done. You all know what happened to my little girl. And to those other innocent girls. What the hell's wrong with all of you!'

Six years ago, after Red went on the lam, the Feds dug up the basement of Kevin Flannery's mom's house on a tip and found the bodies of four dead young girls, Sue Connor being one of them. She was only seventeen when she was reported missing, and the rumor was she was one of Red's girlfriends. Red was in his early fifties back then and fucking anything with a skirt that looked nice and was at least old enough to be out of elementary school. But the thing was Flannery's mom was close to ninety when those bodies must've been buried down there, and at that time she was as deaf as a doornail and nearly blind. She was also close to being a cripple and wasn't about to navigate the steps down into the basement. Anyone wanting to set Red up could've snuck down there and buried those dead girls.

Fred Connor turned back to me after imploring the crowd, his eyes wet and his face tear-stained. He was holding a beer bottle menacingly in his right hand. I told him he should leave now while he still could.

'I'm not leaving here until I have some justice for Sue,' he said, his jaw muscles rigid, his face hardening with a combination of hate and determination.

'You're acting crazy,' I said. 'If Red killed your girl, I doubt her body ever would've been found. But even if he did, how am I responsible?'

'Everyone knows you did Mahoney's killing back then. Sue and those three other girls were all strangled to death. What was it, Nevin? Mahoney get off watching you kill them for him? Did he get off more knowing they were buried right here in the neighborhood?'

'You're fucked up right now, Connor. I suggest you leave now before you get fucked up worse.'

Fred Connor's eyes glazed for a moment, then he smacked the beer bottle he was holding against the bar. It was a stupid thing to do. He could've shattered a glass easy enough against the oak surface of the bar, but he would've had to hit the beer bottle against something harder, like stone or cement, to shatter it. All he accomplished was having the bottle bounce back in his hand and nearly hit him in the head. Out of the corner of my eye I had been noticing Bill Mullan trying to creep up on me. The same moment Connor tried to shatter the beer bottle, Mullan flew at me to grab me from behind. I stepped to the side and stuck out my hip and he nearly went over it. As it was, he was off his feet, caught straddling my hip and as helpless as a baby. I grabbed him by his big ears and slammed him face first into the bar. I let go so I could deal with Connor. There was a loud *whack* from where I had left Mullan, and I knew without looking that Joe had finished the job on him with his axe handle.

A lot of the steam had gone out of Connor's face. Things weren't working out as he and Mullan had planned. Still, he was a big burly hulk of a man, so instead of running like he should've, he somehow figured he still had a chance, and he jumped forward swinging his beer bottle. The problem was he had no clue how to fight, and I did. All I did was step aside. As his arm swung past me I grabbed him by his wrist with my right hand and hit him hard in the elbow with my left palm, putting all my weight behind the blow. His arm bent in an unnatural way. By that and the way he screamed I knew I had shattered it. Before he could do much else, I grabbed him by the ears, just like I had done to Mullan, and swung his head down as I lifted my knee. The collision was brutal. He nearly bit his tongue in half. I let go of him and he collapsed to the floor, either dead or out cold. A small pool of blood and loose teeth gathered by his face. I looked up and saw more people had come into Scolley's while the fight was going on, and from the looks on their faces, none of them were rooting for Connor. The brunette was still in the crowd, and her dark face was smoldering. Her eyes locked on mine for a moment before I turned back to the bar. From the looks of it, Mullan hadn't fared much better than Connor. His body was slumped over the bar and Joe stood over it swinging his axe handle into his open palm.

'I swear, Joe,' I told him. 'I don't know what the fuck Connor was talking about. I had nothing to do with his girl's death, or any of the other girls they dug up. And as much as I hate that rat bastard, Red Mahoney, I sincerely doubt he had anything to do with them either.'

'You don't have to explain yourself to me, Kyle,' Joe said, his face flushed from the violence that had just occurred. He grimaced as he gave a sideways glance at the dent the beer bottle had made to his beloved bar. 'I knew these two were trouble as soon as I heard their mutterings. I should've thrown them out then. I apologize for that, Kyle.'

Martin Foley must've checked on Connor because he came rushing to the bar all breathless.

'He's still breathing,' Martin said.

'So's this one,' Joe said, pointing a thumb towards Mullan.

'You want to call for an ambulance?' Martin asked.

'Nah, not necessary.'

Martin nodded, and he and Steve Sullivan grabbed Mullan by his arms and dragged him towards the back doorway and to the alley beyond that. Two of the other regulars grabbed Connor and did the same. Joe yelled out that drinks were on the house and that brought a cheer to the room.

Joe set me up first with a double shot of Bushmills and a fresh Guinness, also sticking a couple more roast beef sandwiches in the toaster oven for me due to my plate having been tossed to the floor during the melee. The old duffer, Charlie Maguire, made himself useful with a mop cleaning up the pool of blood and broken teeth while Joe got busy pouring drinks for the rest of the crowd. Quite a few more people had come into Scolley's by then. I recognized most of them. Not all, but most. I took the double shot in one gulp, feeling both the alcohol burn and the high from the violence. As I sipped on the Guinness, more of the crowd came over to pay their respects and to shake my hand. Before too long Connor and Mullan were forgotten.

As Joe was putting another double shot in front of me, he leaned in close and asked over the din roaring through the place whether I knew for a fact that Red Mahoney was a rat bastard, or if it was just speculation on my part.

'I know it for a fact,' I told him, moving close to his ear so he could hear me. 'His crooked FBI buddy testified as much on the stand when he went on trial three years ago. But I suspected it almost from the start. The FBI was waiting for me at the bank. They knew what was going down. The kicker is that rat bastard planned out the job, then sold me out so his FBI buddy could score a few brownie points and take some of the pressure off Red.'

Thinking about all that made me too mad to speak for a moment. I sipped slowly on the whiskey while Joe shook his head, also too angry to do anything else.

'Unbelievable,' he said at last. 'And you kept quiet to the Feds about him.'

'Yeah, I did. Just as he knew I would.'

'May he rot in hell,' Joe said.

'Someday he will, and I'm going to help him get there.'

Joe raised an eyebrow towards me. His voice even lower so I had to strain to hear him, he asked, 'You don't by any chance know where he is, do you?'

'If I did I'd be heading there now. But I've got ideas. And I know things the FBI doesn't.' I took another long sip of whiskey and met Joe's gaze. 'And remember, he may well be number three on the FBI's most wanted list, but there are plenty of dirty FBI agents who don't want him found. Me, on the other hand, I want him found. More than anything. I just don't want him turned over to the Feds, at least not alive.'

Now it was my turn to wave Joe close, bringing him leaning forward on his elbows with his ear turned to me so no one else could hear me. 'Timmy Dunn,' I asked him. 'Can he still be trusted?'

'Yeah, a good heart in that one. He'd pull his own tongue out before saying a word on anyone.'

The new plate of sandwiches was ready. I nodded to Joe as I grabbed them and a fresh round of drinks and headed to the table in the back where the brunette was sitting. Her blonde friend was gone, but she was still there, her dark face still smoldering. I put my food and drinks on the table and sat down next to her. It had gotten loud and raucous enough in Scolley's that we had to lean close to each other and talk with our mouths inches from each other's ears to keep from shouting.

'That was quite a show you put on earlier,' she said, her breath hot against my ear, her voice with a nice throaty purr to it. 'You've got me all excited. Here, feel.'

She took hold of my hand and held it up to the side of her face. Her skin felt like it was on fire.

'Nice meeting you, too,' I said after I got my hand freed. 'By the way, my name's Kyle.'

'I know who you are.'

'You do, huh?'

'That's right. I've been reading about you. My name's Nola.'

She held out a small hand to me. Her large brown eyes held steady on mine as I took it. Like her face, her hand was as hot as an iron.

'How do you know I haven't been reading about you also?' I asked.

She laughed, showing a nice soft curvature to her throat. 'I don't think that's possible,' she said. 'I don't rob banks or anything.'

'You don't do anything exciting, huh?'

'Oh, I do plenty of exciting things. Just nothing to get my name in the papers.'

She had taken my hand and had it resting on her thigh. Showing me again that bare trace of a smile from earlier, she started to inch my hand up towards her open skirt. I stopped her.

'Not now,' I said, and I took my hand away from her.

Her eyes lustful, she asked, 'Why? I thought you were a tough guy?'

'That may well be, but Scolley's is like my home. I'm not disrespecting it, and I'm not disrespecting Joe either.'

She gave me a quizzical look. I pointed out Joe working behind the bar. 'Joe Whalley,' I said. 'He owns Scolley's, and has been like a dad to me ever since he bought me my first drink at thirteen.'

A large group had come over to the table to welcome me back to the neighborhood, Tom Dunleavy being one of them. Dunleavy, his long face red with alcohol and his pale eyes like glass, pumped my hand affectionately. Shouting so half the room could hear, he said, 'Now that you're out, Kyle, you and me, we're going to run Southie again. Fuck Red Mahoney. You and me Kyle. Anything you got in the works, you give me a call.'

I caught the wink he gave Nola – not that she reciprocated; she reacted by tensing up and looking away. Still, I told him I would call him, but there was a fat chance of that ever happening. Not that I cared he had fucked Nola. That was weeks before I met her. I couldn't care less about that, and as long as I was fucking her later that night, he could give it to her tomorrow and every day afterwards for all I cared. Back in the day, though, Dunleavy had been nothing but an errand boy. The lowest rung on the ladder so to speak. He always thought he was one of the boys, but that was only in his own mind. And he demonstrated perfectly why we never looked at him as anything but a joke; getting drunk and shooting off his mouth in front of a crowd that included strangers from outside the neighborhood. He was close to the last person I'd hook up with on a job unless I needed a fall guy. For that he'd be about perfect.

The crowd dispersed, and Joe made his way over with a tray full of fresh drinks. After he left, and Nola and I were more alone – at least as alone as you can be in a bar jammed to the rafters with twice as many people as it's legally allowed to hold – Nola moved her chair closer to mine so she was just about sitting in my lap. With her eyes full of mischief, she leaned close and whispered in my ear, asking if I was going to own Southie again.

'It just well may happen,' I told her.

'How about prison? Did you own prison?'

I saw some tenseness in her face, and knew what she was really asking.

'If you're worried that I might've caught AIDS—'

'That's not it at all—'

I stopped her. 'That's okay,' I said. 'You've got a legitimate right to be concerned but there's a lot less of that homosexual shit going on in prison then you'd think from watching TV, at least at a place like Cedar Junction where they've got the threat of hell on earth hanging over your head. During my stretch, nobody touched me and I didn't touch anyone. I was purely a solitary man, if you catch my drift. And hell, since I don't use drugs I could be one of the lowest risk dates right now in Boston as far as AIDS goes, or any other STDs for that matter.'

That seemed to satisfy her. And it was the truth. At both the federal prisons and at Cedar Junction the hardcore lifers and psychos knew well enough to leave me alone, and I had no interest in taking advantage of the poor bastards who'd been turned out. Call it my Catholic upbringing, but I felt guilty enough taking matters into my own hands. Anyway, I wasn't going to risk having my term extended – and as a result of that, my payback to Red pushed back – for something like that, so as much as I could I minded my own business while in prison.

Nola moved in closer to me, and the two of us even got chummier, if you can believe it possible, with my arm around her thin shoulders, and her scooting herself over so her leg was pressed hard against mine, then her casually placing her hand so it rested inches from my crotch. I let her hand stay where it was. The rest of the time we were just into each other as we whispered stuff back and forth. At times friends of mine would interrupt us and I'd pull away from her so I could shake hands and take their good wishes, and of course Joe would somehow show up at our table with fresh drinks whenever ours were empty, but when it was just Nola and me alone at the table it was as if the rest of Scolley's didn't exist. At one point I asked her about what happened to her blonde friend, and that just got her laughing.

'Why, don't you think I'm enough for you?'

'I was just wondering, that's all.'

'I sent her home. After seeing you in action I didn't want to share you with her.'

She flashed me a wicked grin, and again started pulling my hand under her miniskirt. This time, though, I didn't stop her. I found out quickly enough that she wasn't wearing any underwear. She was so wet down there it surprised me, making me think for a few seconds that she'd had a bladder accident, and I found myself checking to see if there was a puddle under her chair. But that wasn't the reason for her wetness. Before too long she was working my finger back and forth, and then after a minute or so of that she let loose with a low orgasmic moan. Her whole body seemed to shudder with it. I was ashamed. I quickly removed my hand and looked around to see if anyone had noticed us, particularly Joe. It didn't seem as if anyone had. Through the crowd I could see Joe was busy at the other end of the bar pouring drinks and gabbing with a couple of the old-timers. I looked around and a few people seemed to sense I was looking at them and they smiled back at me, but there was nothing in their faces to indicate they had noticed what had gone on. Still I couldn't help feeling ashamed.

Nola leaned in close to me so she could whisper in my ear how turned on she was.

'You have me tingling all over,' she said.

I wondered then whether I was dealing with a full-fledged nut job. There was no question she was an exhibitionist. And she definitely got off on danger – the way she set her sights on me, and walking into a place like Scolley's wearing a miniskirt with no underwear. And how hot she got witnessing me beat two men unconscious – or to death for all she knew. Or for all I knew for that matter. From what she had whispered to me earlier, I knew she had read every newspaper article she could about me, and I couldn't help thinking that she had come to Scolley's hoping I'd be there. That she had targeted me. Still, though, I decided for one night it didn't matter. She could be as crazy as she wanted to be. I stared bleary-eyed at my watch until I could make out that it was almost three in the morning. The crowd at Scolley's had dwindled to maybe a third of what it was during its peak, and it seemed as if things were winding down. I suggested to her that we find someplace to be alone so I could make her tingle even more.

'I have a condo by the waterfront,' she said.

I nodded. I got to my feet and nearly staggered due to the night's drinking. I did a quick accounting, and figured I'd had more than a dozen whiskeys, and at least the same amount of pints. In the old days a long night of that type of drinking would just be getting me going, but after eight dry years I was feeling the effects enough that it left me stumbling. I righted myself, holding onto the table until I felt steady on my feet, and then told Nola I'd be right back, that I had a trip to the boy's room I needed to make. Normally I have a bladder like an elephant's, but after pouring down all that booze I needed to give a good bit of it back. Nola showed a sly little smile and suggested she'd join me in there. I shook my head. 'No, God no,' I told her, and I left her standing there, the disappointment showing on those big brown eyes and soft lips of hers.

It took a while to return all the booze I'd drunk, and when I came back Nola was waiting eagerly for me. Myself, I could barely walk straight, and I cursed myself for drinking as much as I did. I also counted my blessings that Fred Connor was as dumb as he was. If he had bided his time and waited he'd have no trouble clobbering me to death in the state I was now in.

Nola wrapped one of her tanned thin arms around me and held on tight. I was glad she did. I needed the support. On the way out, I stopped off to talk to Joe. I tried handing him five hundred dollars for the way he had taken care of me and any damage that might've been caused by the fight, but he wouldn't take my money.

'Jesus, Kyle, I should be paying you. 'Cause of your visit I did a week's worth of business in one night. The cash register's flush right now, my boy.' He paused, showed a tight grin that didn't make it anywhere near his eyes. 'You might like to know that the back alley has been checked and your two friends must have crawled off into the night.'

'You think they're laying in wait for me?'

He shook his head. 'Not the shape they were left in. My guess they're both getting their jaws wired up and whatever emergency dental work they can. And don't worry. This is your home, Kyle. Those two ever show up here and I'll be busting their heads myself.'

When we shook hands, Joe pulled me close so he could whisper to me without Nola listening in. 'Be careful with that one, Kyle,' he said.

I waved farewell to Joe and the remaining crowd at Scolley's. Charlie Maguire was still serving sentry duty, tottering slightly on his feet. He gave me a drunken salute as I walked past. When Nola and I were at the door I heard Joe yell out to the remaining stragglers to finish their drinks and be on their way, and that brought out a chorus of moans and complaints. Once we were outside, Nola wanted to know what Joe had whispered to me. 'He gave me ten to one odds that I end up expiring tonight from a heart attack. I put a C-note on the bet. If I end up dead because of a stroke or asphyxiation or some other reason, make sure to collect.' She gave me a skeptical look, but chose not to push it.

She had taken a taxi to Scolley's, so we walked the half a block to where I had parked Danny's Honda Civic. When she saw the car I could see the disappointment spreading across her face.

'My brother's,' I told her. 'By the end of the year I'll be driving a BMW seven series. Anyway, it's not the car that defines a man, but his actions.'

That brought a smile to her lips. When we got in, she gave me an Atlantic Avenue address, then bent over as she reached for my fly.

'What the fuck are you doing,' I demanded as I pushed her head away. 'Fuck. I just got out from an eight-year stretch. You trying to put me back in for exposing myself in public?'

She leaned back, insulted, her arms crossed. 'I don't get you,' she said. 'I thought you're supposed to be a wild man.'

'No,' I corrected her. 'I'm cautious. That's why I'm still alive.'

I turned the car and headed towards Beckler Ave., one of Southie's true blue collar neighborhoods, the opposite direction from the Atlantic Avenue address that she had given me. She noticed it and asked me about it.

'I've got an errand to run first,' I said. 'Then I'll be giving you what you've been begging for all goddamned night. Until then, just keep it in your skirt.'

She got moody then. I had to bite my tongue to keep from breaking out laughing as I caught glimpses of her with her brow all furrowed and her mouth scrunched into a tight little oval. As nuts as she might be, she was quite a piece of ass, and I felt my mouth watering as I caught the outline of her tits pushing hard against her silk blouse. I forced myself to stare straight ahead before I got myself in trouble. Both of us sat quietly until I double-parked in front of Mary's. Nola looked around, her eyes curious as she asked me what was going on.

'Nothing too interesting,' I said. 'Just stay in the car.'

I popped the trunk, took two bottles of Bushmills sixteen-year-old malt out of the box John Flynn had given me, and carried the remaining four bottles up to Mary's front door. It was sad seeing the dilapidated shape her two-bedroom ranch-style home had fallen into. Even in the dim light given off by the streetlamps I could see her front yard was nothing but a mass of weeds with garbage strewn around. Several shutters were hanging loose, and the house badly needed a paint job with the old paint peeling off in large pieces. Holding the box in one hand, I rang her doorbell several times. After waiting a couple of minutes I rang it again and heard her yell out hoarsely, asking who the hell was bothering her at a quarter past three in the morning.

'It's me, Mary,' I yelled back. 'Just here to pay off a debt.'

She kept me waiting a good five minutes more before she opened the door wearing a threadbare bathrobe that she must've had since the fifties. As dilapidated as her house might've been, she looked in even worse shape. Ninety if she looked a day. Her face was as wrinkled as a raisin and large sections of her scalp showed through her sparse gray hair. Her color didn't even come close to matching that of a dead fish. Bundled up as she was in her bathrobe, she looked like she might've been all of eighty pounds underneath it. She peered in the box I was holding and then gave me a harsh look.

'Janet called me last night,' she said. 'Read me the riot act. Doesn't want anything to do with me anymore.'

'Yeah, well, she'll get over it. Give her a few days.'

'No she won't. She told me what you said to her. I trusted you, Kyle.'

'I called her for closure,' I said. 'Just like I told you I would.'

'You called demanding ten thousand dollars from her! And threatening her!'

'We all get closure in different ways. Why don't I bring this box into your kitchen? You can make me some coffee and we can talk about it.'

She stood stone-faced, glaring at me, and ageing even more in front of my eyes. It was like some weird magic trick. I had to blink to make sure I was seeing what I thought I was seeing. Then moving quicker than I would've thought possible, she slapped me in the face. It was like being hit with a wet sponge, I could barely feel it, but I still took a step back.

'I don't want you ever calling me again,' she said.

'Mary, don't you think you're overreacting? Why don't we act sensible, have some coffee and talk it over.'

'Get out of here!'

I shrugged and took a step away.

'And leave that whiskey like you promised!'

I started laughing then. I couldn't help myself. But I did make a promise. 'Lost a daughter but gained four bottles of fine whiskey in the process,' I said. 'All in all a good deal for you, Mary.' I left the box where it stood, then walked to the car without bothering to look back.

'What was that all about?' Nola asked, her eyes growing wide.

I started the car up and told her it was a long story not worth getting into. She kept pestering me, though, wanting to know why that old woman slapped me, and even more, why I let her. To shut her up I slid my right hand under her skirt while handling the steering wheel and a cigarette with my left. The streets were in bad shape and we hit quite a few potholes on the way to Atlantic Ave., and with each one Nola dug her nails hard into my hand. By the time we reached her address my own hand was bleeding while her skin had flushed a bright feverish pink. Her building was one of those new luxury ones that were popping up along Boston's waterfront to take advantage of all the white-bread suburbanites loaded with money wanting to move back to the city. I pulled up next to a fire hydrant, shook loose the last cigarette from the pack and sat thinking.

'Let's leave the car here,' she said, her voice a breathless whisper.

'You got any coke?'

'I don't need any. You've got my head pounding as it is. Come on, let's go inside.'

'You didn't answer me. You got any either on you or inside?'

'No, I don't do coke. Come on, let's get you inside… me.' She giggled over her pun, then pulled on my arm but I didn't budge. After thinking some more I told her to get out. That I was going to be heading back home alone. She looked at me as if I were speaking in some foreign language that she didn't understand.

'Let me make this plainer for you,' I said. 'Get the fuck out of my car.'

'What's going on?'

'I decided I don't want to fuck any hole that willingly accepted Tom Dunleavy's two inches. Now get the fuck out while you still have some teeth in your mouth.'

Her jaw dropped as if she'd been slapped. Then with her eyes narrowing and her dark face mottling with anger, she commented how I must've turned queer while in prison. That I was sucking on cigarettes all night because of some oral fixation. Being generous, I pretended not to hear her and asked her to repeat what she said. She realized that she better not and fortunately left the car without saying another word. I watched her storm away, her small hands clenched tightly into fists. As I stared almost hypnotically at the shape her ass made bouncing under her tight miniskirt, I cursed myself for drinking as much as I had that night. In the old days before prison it wouldn't have mattered, but back then I was in my early thirties, not forty-two like I was now. I also had some tolerance for alcohol. Now I felt nothing below the waist. Not even a stirring. The alcohol had left me dead down there. That was why I had pushed her away earlier when she tried reaching for my zipper. The same reason I had taken the side trip to Mary's, hoping to talk her into putting a pot of coffee on. I badly wanted to sober up so I could give Nola what she was wanting. A few lines of coke might've done the trick, but without that there was no hope, and I couldn't risk her spending the night flogging on a dead piece of flesh only so she could spread the word about it later at Scolley's.

I closed my eyes for a moment picturing what could've been, then cursed myself one last time before performing an illegal U-turn and heading back to Danny's.

Chapter 3

I almost didn't make it back to Danny's apartment that night. I couldn't remember which side street off Commonwealth Avenue to take and came close to just pulling over and sleeping in the car, but I kept circling a stretch of Commonwealth Ave. and taking different streets until I stumbled upon the right one. At one point I came across a couple of punks trying to boost a late model Mustang. They were both in their twenties. Both with shaved heads and wearing sleeveless T-shirts to show off their tattoos. I knew what they were doing, and they both knew that I knew also. The larger of the two put his finger to his lips in a hushing type gesture, the other gave me this dead stare and ran his thumb across his throat as a threat. Like a couple of punks like them would stand a chance with me. In the mood I was in that was almost enough to get me out of the car and busting their heads. Instead I leaned on the horn and kept leaning on it. At first they stood their ground, glaring at me, pissed, then they got nervous and started hopping around like chickens with their heads cut off, both cursing me as they ran off. Watching them scamper away like that brightened my mood. A few people opened their windows and yelled at me to shut the fuck up, and I yelled back that I was stopping a couple of punks from stealing a car. One guy suggested that I should've let them steal it, that at least I wouldn't have woken up the neighborhood at four in the morning. Even with that lack of gratitude I was feeling more like my old self. When I eventually found the side street Danny lived on, my mood brightened even more.

It was well past four in the morning before I finally got back into Danny's apartment. He had left a pillow and a folded up sheet for me, and I flung the sheet over the sofa and tried to lay out over it. The problem was the sofa was only five feet long and I'm over six feet, so I had to carry over one of the chairs to keep my feet from hanging in midair. I felt wiped out. My routine in prison had been lights out at nine, then a bullhorn blasting at five-thirty each morning to get us moving to the showers. I closed my eyes hoping I'd be tired enough to fall quickly asleep but like every other night over the last eight years my mind started racing as it played back that last bank job.

I never liked the location of the bank. When I planned any armed robbery, I looked for easy access to two or more major highways. With this bank I'd have to drive in local traffic for a good eleven miles before I'd be able to reach a highway, and anything could happen during those miles. The road could get shut down for any number of reasons and I'd be a sitting duck. I told Red I didn't like the access to the bank, but he was insistent that I do the job. He confided in me then, telling me how he'd been tipped off about the Lombardo family stuffing two million dollars' worth of Federal Reserve Notes into a couple of safety deposit boxes, and how I had to hit the bank before the notes were moved by the end of the month. I should've realized something was up. First, it was too good to be true, and second, he was too easygoing about it, too relaxed. Usually before a big job he'd be fidgeting. Not this time, though. I should've seen through that nice big palsy smile of his – the same one I'd seen him give dozens of people over the years before he'd screw them. But it just never occurred to me. I'd been working for Red since I was seventeen and during those fifteen years had grown to be just about his right-hand man. Me or Kevin Flannery, take your pick. During those fifteen years I'd done so much for him and had so much dirt on him. Why would he fuck me? Especially since if I returned the favor I'd be able to put him away for a few dozen life sentences, maybe even a couple of Federal death penalty raps. And then there was his constant talk about rats. How they were the lowest form of scumbag. Not that anyone would ever argue the point, not in our neighborhood, anyway. We were all brought up the same – being taught that nothing in the world was lower. When Red once got his hands on a rat who was trying to tip off the police about one of our jobs, he demonstrated to us personally what needs be done when a rat is caught, and it wasn't pretty – not that any of us minded watching. Mentally I took notes, and someday I'll give Red the same demonstration up close and personal.

The job was just me and Jimmie Clark, and it should've been a piece of cake, with Jimmy holding shotgun while I drilled open the two safety deposit boxes that Red had given me the numbers for. Ten minutes in and out. Easy. Too easy. As soon as we entered the bank I knew something was wrong. I could feel it. When I heard the shouts barked out from behind and caught a glimmer of all those rifles lined up inside the bank in front of us, I dove to hug the floor, and even so took a bullet in the shoulder and another in the thigh. Jimmie was a little slower to react and he was cut in half. The story given in the papers later was that Jimmie had turned and pointed his shotgun at several of the FBI agents, but that was a load of crap. Even as I was lying on the floor bleeding from my two bullet wounds I knew that the plan was to execute me. That I wasn't supposed to leave the bank alive. Jimmie and me were about the same size, we were both wearing ski masks when we entered the bank, and originally he was going to drill the boxes while I held the shotgun but we switched up in the car—

To Ed.: The only reason Jimmie and I switched up was because he had a wicked hangover from the night before mixing tequila with whiskey, and the poor sonofabitch didn't think he could take listening to a drill. A little life lesson there for all Irish boys – don't mix your hard alcohols unless you want to end up gut shot in a bank lobby. —K. N.

—So the plan, at least for one of those murderous fucking FBI agents, was to leave me dead in the bank, but the sonofabitch had to change it once I was lying prone on the floor. At that point it would've been impossible to stand over me and put a bullet in my head unless all the FBI agents at the banks were in on it, and fortunately they weren't.

When the ski masks were pulled off me and Jimmie, I could see the disappointment in that bastard's face once he realized Jimmie wasn't me, and then later heard him insisting to his fellow officers that he saw Jimmie moving the shotgun towards him. The other FBI agents just stood grim-faced over the results of the operation. I could tell from their reactions that none of the other agents were in on the execution plan, but they all went along with that scumbag's story. I'd long since found out his name, and also with a little digging discovered that he was connected with Red's childhood buddy, John William Carr. The FBI agent Red had in his pocket for years. But more on that later.

During my first two years in the joint I racked my brains trying to figure out who had ratted me and Jimmie. I couldn't come up with anything that made sense, or think of anyone other than Red who would've known what was going down. All I could think was that Red's private booth at the Corrib Pub where we talked must've been bugged. Or that maybe Jimmie had told someone, but that made no sense. He was a true professional and as closed-mouthed as they come. The kicker was while I lay in the hospital in blissful ignorance over what Red had done to me, the

Federal Prosecutor on the case was offering to put me in witness protection if I'd testify against Red. I kept my mouth shut. Fuck if I'd ever be a rat. Even two years later when they arrested John Carr and he unloaded his full story about him and Red, how Red would routinely rat for him so he could score points in the FBI, and how in return he would protect Red by warning him about ongoing investigations and busting his competition, I refused to believe that Red had set me up. But then word filtered down how Carr mentioned my last bank job as one of the ones Red had given him – that the pressure had been building within the FBI to take down more of Red Mahoney's operations, and Carr needed to give his bosses one of Red's top dogs to take the pressure off. It all clicked then, including the reason for the execution orders. There was no way Red could risk ratting on me unless he knew I'd be killed inside that bank. He knew me well enough to know what would happen if he left me alive.

I have to think that that scumbag FBI agent screwing up and leaving me alive had more to do with Red going on the run than him being tipped off to the case the FBI was building against him. He knew he'd only have a few short years to build distance between the two of us. And he knew he'd need every second of it.

Red Mahoney. The king of the rats.

Thinking about him and all that had happened got the juices stirring just like they did every night. For hours afterwards all I could do was stare at the ceiling, my jaw muscles hardened to the point where they ached.

Just like every other night.

I think I had drifted off for maybe an hour when Danny woke me by reaching for the pair of jeans that I had folded next to me. At first he was just a blur, but after a long moment my eyes were able to focus and I could see that he was going through my pockets.

'What the fuck?' I asked, my voice not much more than a

croak. I could barely hold my head up. I knew I was squinting badly, the light from the windows hurting my eyes.

He gave me a dumb lopsided grin and jangled the set of car keys that he had taken from my pockets.

'Sorry to wake you, bro, but I need the car.'

I pushed myself up. I had to hold my head in my hands – the damn thing felt like it was encased in lead. My mouth was so damn dry, like I had swallowed a handful of sawdust. The light from the windows shot little daggers into the back of my brain, and I had to squeeze my eyes shut against it to stop the assault.

'Where the fuck are you going?' I asked, my voice still raspy and still not much more than a croak.

'To work, bro. It's how I help pay for this apartment you're taking advantage of.'

As painful as the light was, I had to look up at him, not quite believing he really said that to me. 'What did you just say?' I demanded.

He tried staring me down, but he couldn't quite manage it.

'I was just kidding,' he said. 'It's too fucking early to think straight, you know, the words just slipped out. But I didn't mean anything by it, bro. You know I'm glad to have you here.'

From the look on Danny's face I knew that comment had gotten stuck in his head thanks to his girlfriend relentlessly harping on it.

'She doesn't want me here, does she?' I said.

Danny made a face. 'She'll be fine with it. She just needs a day or two to adjust.'

I tried looking around. It hurt my head moving it too fast. 'Is she around?'

'Nope. Eve left half an hour ago. She told me you were dead to the world in here. I didn't think I'd wake you getting my keys back.' He flashed me a shit-eating grin. 'You look kind of green around the gills, Kyle. A hard night drinking at Scolley's?'

'Yeah, I must've left the joint a fucking lightweight. Shit, I didn't drink half enough to be feeling this bad. Right now I've got the mother of all hangovers. And she's a beauty.'

'You got to ease into it, bro. Been away a long time, you know.'

I nodded, my head throbbing too much to want to say anything.

'Anything eventful happen last night?' Danny asked.

I started to shake my head and regretted the action immediately as more little silver daggers flew through my brain.

'Just the guys from the old neighborhood getting together to welcome me home,' I said.

'So who's Nola Nilssen?'

He handed me the business card that he had taken out of my pocket along with the car keys. I had forgotten Nola had given it to me. I squinted hard at the card until I could focus on it. Up to that point I don't think I knew her last name. It sounded Swedish, but she didn't look it given her dark hair and olive-tanned complexion. According to the card she was a salesperson working at a men's clothing store on Newbury Street. Smart career choice; it would be hard for almost any guy to turn her down, especially after she measured their inseams.

'Just someone trying to sell me a suit,' I said. I opened my mouth wide, gagged a bit. 'Fuck, I feel like I've been chewing on a wool sock.'

'I'll make you some coffee,' Danny offered, then left the room for the kitchen. I sat for a while trying to keep my head from spinning off. When it felt like my head might actually stay attached to my body, I pushed myself to my feet. I swayed back and forth like I was on a boat before I could steady myself. My head was fucking swimming, but I made my way to the small galley kitchen and joined Danny, the two of us barely able to fit in it. I poured myself a glass of water, drank it, then poured another.

I was starting to feel a little better. Danny took a bottle of aspirin from one of the cabinets, opened it and handed it to me. I chewed on a handful of tablets and nodded thanks to him.

'You still take your coffee black?' he asked.

'You better load it up with sugar.'

While the coffee was brewing, I made my way back to the sofa and collapsed on it. I fished around for the carton of cigarettes under it and took out a fresh pack. I was in the middle of lighting up when Danny came into the room. He was going to say something, but the look on my face stopped him. Instead he handed me a mug large enough to hold half a pot of coffee. I was grateful for it, and as such took only a few long puffs on the cig before stubbing it out.

'I've got to get going, bro,' he said. 'I'm late as it is.'

'You're really going to abandon me my first full day out of prison?' I asked. 'You're sure we're related?'

'Kyle, I'm sorry, but I need the paycheck.'

I took a long sip of the coffee. It felt good going down and even better hitting my stomach.

'It's bad enough you didn't join me at Scolley's last night,' I said.

'I already told you my reasons for that.'

'You're just going to fucking leave me like this?'

His smile weakened as he looked past me impatiently. 'Bro, I have to go to work. I need the money.'

'They give you sick time, right? All working-class mokes get sick time, don't they?'

He gave me a hard smile in return for calling him a working-class moke. 'Yeah, I could call in sick,' he said, his voice flat, 'but I wouldn't get paid for it.'

'How much do you make a day?'

He calculated it out in his head. 'After taxes and FICA, about a hundred and twenty. If I work overtime, more.'

'You got to be shitting me. You break your balls each day for that?' I found my wallet under the pillow where I had left it, and took two hundred dollars from it. 'This should take care of you for today, right, Danny?'

He took the money from me and studied it. 'Where'd you get this?' he asked.

'What are you talking about? You ever know me not to be flush with cash?'

'You were broke yesterday coming out of prison,' he insisted.

'Yeah, well, that was just a temporary cash flow problem easily solved. So what do you say? You going to take the day off?'

Danny nodded and stuck the two hundred dollars in his pocket. While he called in sick, I made my way to the bathroom. After ten minutes or so of standing under the shower, I started to feel more human again. I dried off, splashed on some of Danny's cologne and left the bathroom with the towel wrapped around my waist. Danny had found the two bottles of Bushmills that I had brought up from the other night, and was sitting on the sofa studying the labels.

'This is good stuff,' he told me.

'Fucking right it is. Think of those two bottles as an apartment warming gift from your old buddy, John Flynn.'

That brought a genuine smile to Danny's lips. 'Just a bit of arm-twisting required, huh?'

'None at all. John was more than happy to oblige.' I took one of the bottles from Danny, opened the seal, and took a long drink. The whiskey helped clear my head better than the aspirin, water and coffee combined. I handed the bottle to Danny and he took a swig himself before passing it back. I took one more shot, then plugged the bottle back up. I could feel the warm flush of the alcohol spreading across my face, my hangover now mostly a memory.

'I'm going shopping later so I can quit having to wear your

clothes,' I told him. 'In the meantime, though, I could use a clean shirt and a change of underwear and socks. The jeans will be okay for another day.'

'No problem, bro.'

Danny left the room and came back less than a minute later with what I was asking for. I got dressed quickly, told Danny I'd take him out for some breakfast. 'Later I'll tell you about the job I'm planning out for the two of us. But I think it would be better if we get some food in our bellies first.'

Danny shifted his weight from one foot to the other, an uncomfortable look twisting his mouth. He looked away from me.

'I don't know, bro,' he started. 'I'm kind of happy with the life I've got now. I don't really want to go back to what I used to do. You might be better off figuring out your plans so they don't include me.'

'Don't shit me, Danny.'

'I'm not.'

'You're happy living like this?'

'Yeah.'

'Busting your hump making a hundred and twenty dollars a day?'

'Nothing wrong with that.'

'Bullshit. That's a loser mentality, Danny. You and me, we used to have only the best. Remember what those days were like? Before going away, I was wearing Brooks Brothers everything, except underwear, which was Armani's. You also. Now you've got me wearing some no name brand. You can't be serious that you're happy living like this.'

'Nothing wrong with the underwear I gave you.' He stuck his chin out challenging me to argue otherwise. 'I bet it's a hell of a lot better than what they gave you in prison.'

'Yeah, a little anyway. But that's not the point. I didn't bring you up to live like a fucking loser. Like a blue-collar moke. The job I've got worked out is going to put two mil in our pockets. With that type of cash you can do whatever the fuck you want afterwards. You want to do construction then, fine, but at least you'll be doing it wearing a pair of silk Armani's covering your ass.'

Danny shook his head, laughing. 'Two million, huh? That's a fucking pipe dream, Kyle.'

'No, it isn't. And let me make this part clear. It's two million each. One job and we're out. It's not some ongoing concern that we're going to have to sweat out over the years.'

I saw the subtle change in his eyes as he started to take me more seriously. He wetted his lips, asked, 'That's it, huh? One job and we're done?'

'That's it. The heavy lifting will take less than a couple of hours.'

'Fuck.' His stare shifted off into the distance as he thought about it. I could see in his hardened face glimpses of the old Danny. 'Any bank job and the feds will be all over you.'

'It's not a bank job.'

'What is it then?'

'Later, after we eat something. But Danny, you should know me well enough to know that I'm not talking out my ass here.'

He nodded, because he knew that if I was saying it was going to be two mil, then it was going to be two mil. I didn't know the neighborhood so I asked him where he wanted to go and he suggested a place a few blocks from his apartment that we could walk to. As we stepped outside, I told him where I should be taking him was the K-Street Diner.

'We'd get a real breakfast there,' I said. 'Homemade corned beef hash, pancakes with some weight to them and the best fresh brewed coffee I can remember ever tasting.'

Danny nodded. 'Yeah, K-Street was always good. Especially after a hard night's drinking. Been thinking of it much?'

'Only every morning for the past eight years.'

He laughed at that. 'I have to admit there are days I miss it too.' He hesitated, as if he were trying to decide whether to turn around so we could get his car and drive back to Southie and the K-Street Diner, but the moment passed. 'The place we're going to is almost as good,' he told me without too much enthusiasm.

I didn't push him on the matter. There probably was a chance some scumbag would drop a dime on him if we went to the K-Street, even with the full knowledge that I was back on the streets. If a couple of shmoes like Connor and Mullan could try what they did, then who the fuck knew what anyone was capable of anymore? In the old days, back when Red, Kevin Flannery and I ran roughshod over Southie, a stunt like theirs would've cost them a lot more than a few teeth and some blood. But there wasn't any respect anymore. Or fear. And I put that entirely on Red. With him turning out to be nothing more than a rat bastard, why should there be any respect? For Chrissakes, for years the guy was looked on as the unofficial mayor of Southie. Half the kids growing up in the projects probably thought he was the real mayor! People throughout the neighborhood worshipped him. Yeah, he was a crook, but he was our crook. He was the guy who took care of Southie, who watched all our backs. Of course it was all a fucking lie. Everything he did was for his own benefit, but so what? It worked. It kept people in line, at least until he had to fuck it all up and make us all into nothing but jokes. Now thanks to him the rats were running wild. He set the example and they followed. Who could blame them?

Danny and I had both fallen into our separate dark thoughts, and neither of us talked or even paid attention to each other until we placed our orders. The waitress was something else. A fat college girl with purple hair and matching shade of lipstick. Enough thick black mascara had been slathered around her eyes to make her the envy of any raccoon, and she had more nose studs and lip piercings than should've been physically possible. She must've been going for a look somewhere between goth and headbanger, but Christ, the sight of her gave me the willies. I guess it was an act of rebellion and a way for her to get noticed. Still, as she walked away, I pointed a thumb at her and asked Danny how he'd like to wake up with something like that some morning.

He peered over at her before giving me a deadpanned stare. 'I'm sure you've woken up with worse over the last eight years. And before that too, bro.'

'What the fuck did you say?'

'You heard me, bro.'

He was giving me a hard stare, challenging me, but at the same time strumming his fingers nervously against the table. For whatever reason he was trying to get a rise out of me. I suppressed the smile fighting to come loose. I also swallowed back a crack I was going to make about those living in glass houses with titless girlfriends should be careful about throwing stones, or something like that. Instead I warned him that he'd better start showing more respect to his older brother. 'You're too young to be fitted for dentures,' I added.

'Fucking Christ, I was just making a joke.' He shook his head, scowling, still strumming hard on the table. 'You've got no sense of humor, bro. And you're so fucking judgmental. That girl's just trying to find herself, and you have to make fun of her? For Chrissakes!'

'What's your problem?'

'What's my problem? How about that I'm adjusting to my new life here trying to put Southie far behind—'

'Yeah? Fuck you are. That's why you've got pictures of Southie all over your apartment?'

'That doesn't mean shit.' He looked away from me and absentmindedly tugged on his lower lip, showing me that his gums were receding badly. 'These days I can look myself in the mirror. I'm doing an honest day's work for the first time in my life. Fuck, I got a girl I care about.' He seemed stuck for a moment, his voice drifting off and the muscles along his jaw and mouth tightening. Slowly he rotated his eyes towards me. 'You're sure about the number you gave me?'

'Yeah, I'm sure about it.'

The waitress came back carrying a pot of coffee. As she poured me a cup, she kept peering at me through her painted-on lone ranger mask. 'How do I know you?' she finally asked.

Danny had been fidgeting while she poured the coffee. I knew he was anxious to get more details about the job I had in mind. Pushing a hand through his hair and at the same time showing a smart-alecky grin, he told her, ''Cause he's a celebrity. Don'cha read the papers? That's my brother. Big bad Kyle Nevin.'

A glint of life broke the sullen dullness masking her eyes as she placed the name. 'You're that gangster?' she asked.

'Fuck that,' I said. 'I'm just a poor Southie kid from the projects who made good.' That brought out a short laugh from Danny. I took a sip of the coffee and nearly spat it out. Mud would've tasted better. 'I can't drink this shit,' I told the waitress. Disgusted, I asked her to bring me a Coke instead. Her complexion had been a milk white when I first saw her. It might've even dropped a shade as she carried the coffee away.

'Nothing's wrong with the coffee here,' Danny said as he sipped his.

'You lose your sense of taste since moving here?'

'Nope. The coffee's just brewed stronger than you're used to, that's all. If you gave it a try you'd like it. Come on, bro, open yourself up to new experiences. You're not in Southie anymore.'

'Fucking right I'm not.' I didn't know whether Danny was screwing with me or not. All I knew was the coffee tasted like shit. To get the taste out of my mouth, I lit up a cig. That brought our freak show of a waitress trotting back to the table, moving as tentatively as if she were making her way across broken glass. 'You can't smoke in here,' she told me. 'Boston's got a smoking ban.'

'You're fucking with me, right?'

'No, sir.'

'Since when has Boston decided you can't smoke when enjoying greasy food at a shit diner?'

'I don't know.'

'If you don't know then my suggestion is don't worry about it.'

'Sir, you have to put that cigarette out.'

I flashed Danny a hard grin. 'Can you believe the balls on this one?' I asked him.

'Nope.'

'Why don't you tell her what happened to the last person who gave me lip like this.'

'You tell her.'

I turned to the waitress, my grin completely gone. 'We cut her up for fish bait.'

Out of the corner of my eye, I could see Danny struggling to keep from bursting out laughing, probably more from the way the waitress's jaw dropped than anything else. 'I hear the bluefish are biting now in Quincy Bay,' he added, still struggling to keep a straight face. 'Shit, bro, we'd get a weekend's worth of bait off her.'

'Not only that, look how much we'd save on fishing hooks.'

She looked from me to Danny trying to decide if we were kidding. Still unable to make up her mind, she went back up front to the grill area, moving a lot quicker than at any other time. As soon as she was gone, Danny burst out laughing. 'Thanks, bro,' he said, 'I needed a good laugh.'

'What the fuck did I say that was so funny?' I asked as deadpanned as I could.

He sat back in the booth, more at ease than before. There was still some anxiety tugging at his mouth, but not like before. I knew he wanted to ask about the job, but although he'd been away from the game for years, he knew the rules. No talking about a job in public. It was just stupid, even if you could guarantee no one sitting nearby was listening in. Anyway, for the most part Danny was able to sit back and relax while we waited for our food, and that made it easier for me to relax. When I shook out a second cig, Danny told me that as much as he was disgusted by Red Mahoney, he had to agree with him about cigarettes being a dirty habit.

'You keep smoking them, Kyle, they'll kill you,' he said, nothing but genuine concern in his tone. It touched me, and I nodded in agreement.

'Yeah, I know,' I said. 'But when you're in the joint you've got so little to look forward to each day other than the next cig. Now that I'm out I'm going to try to cut down, see if I can quit them again.' I hesitated for a moment, then added, 'I'm not trying to give you a hard time either, Danny, but you should lay off the grass also. All that stuff does is make you stupid. And I can't afford that.'

He nodded, accepting that without taking any offense. It was peaceful the two of us sitting there, like we were two brothers again who'd take a bullet for each other if needed. When our food was ready, it was brought out by the short order cook. He pretended not to notice the cig I was smoking. He also shook a little as he put the plates down in front of us. After he walked away, Danny looked up and down the aisle and noticed also that our freak-show waitress was no longer anywhere to be seen.

'I think we scared the shit out of that girl,' he said, a large grin breaking out over his face. 'Fuck, and I come here all the time.'

'All the better,' I said. 'Fear's always a good thing. Means they'll take better care of you in the future.'

The food wasn't bad. It was no K-Street Diner, but it wasn't bad. The corned beef tasted like good quality and was cut in thick chunks. The pancakes were lighter than I liked, but still not bad. I was surprised to see Danny had ordered a vegetarian omelet. For as long as I could remember he was a steak and eggs guy for breakfast. I told him about the roast beef sandwiches at Scolley's.

'Same as I remembered, maybe even better. Fuck, I'd been dreaming of them for years. Next time I'll remember to bring you home a few.'

Danny nodded as he pushed some of his omelet onto his fork, but didn't say anything. I waited until he finished more of the omelet, then asked him, 'You know what else I've been dreaming of? A thick juicy sirloin steak from Morton's. One that's rare enough so the cow's still kicking. Tonight I'll take you and Eve there, and we'll have my welcome home celebration dinner then.'

He made a face and told me he wasn't sure that would be such a good idea. 'Eve's a vegetarian,' he added.

'So, she doesn't have to order steak. They've got fish, and probably vegetables too.'

'Yeah, well, I think it would upset her seeing you go to town on a hunk of bloody meat. And you know, I've been cutting down on red meat also. There's an Indian restaurant we go to a lot around here that's good. Also, a Japanese restaurant that's got pretty good sushi. How about we go to one of them instead?'

I took a long drag on the cig, letting the smoke fill my lungs. I let it out slowly, taking my time, still not quite believing what Danny said. 'You should try growing yourself a new set, little brother,' I told him.

'Fuck you.'

'I don't know. Sounds to me like your skirt's wearing your old ones on her belt. Telling you what you can and can't eat. Jesus, I can barely even recognize you right now.'

'First off, don't call Eve my skirt. I could be marrying her. Second, I've been cutting out red meat for my health, not 'cause of anything Eve's been saying.'

'Yeah, well, I'm not eating raw fish, or anything that smells like soiled laundry at Cedar Junction. Tonight you and me are going to Morton's. You can leave your skirt, excuse me, your girlfriend at home. A steak every once in a while isn't going to kill you.'

'Whatever you say, bro.'

I was glad to see some anger flushing Danny's face. At least more of his old self was slowly being dragged out. Still, though, I couldn't enjoy the rest of my breakfast, not with thinking how pussywhipped he had become. For the first time I was reconsidering whether I really wanted him in on the job with me. The problem was I needed someone with me whom I could trust, and these days Southie was teeming with rats. I had heard so many stories through the grapevine of all the rats who came rushing out of the woodwork once Red went into hiding. You no longer had a clue who you could trust, who was still a stand-up guy. Danny, his old self anyway, I could trust. Back in the days he was as fearsome as any. And no one was more loyal. The old Danny was now buried under the veneer of a blue-collar pussywhipped sushi-eating moke that his titless wonder of a girlfriend had painted on. But there were cracks in the veneer, and I could still catch glimpses of his old self – like when we tipped over the dumpsters, and when I busted on that freak show of a waitress. It was more, though, than just needing someone I could trust. Danny was my little brother. I couldn't just leave him the way he was. With some real money behind him and his confidence back, he'd be his own man again, maybe even find a girl with a figure a little curvier than a stick, and maybe someone who knew better than to mouth off about a family member smoking a cigarette in the apartment.

We ate mostly in silence, the only noise coming from one or the other of us grunting occasionally. When the short-order cook came over with the check, I handed him an extra hundred to give freak show.

'Make sure she gets it,' I warned him, ''cause I'll be checking that she does. And I'm holding you responsible.'

He gave me a short worried nod and promised she'd get it, and I didn't have any doubts that she would. When we were out on the sidewalk, Danny gave me an elbow in the ribs. 'A soft spot for that heavy metal chick, huh? Hey, bro, understandable after all that time in prison. Why the fuck not. Have something a little freaky for a change.'

'I don't think I could ever screw something that freaky,' I said. 'Not unless I was unconscious first. Besides, I'd end up getting stuck like a pincushion if I tried taking a roll with something like that.' I squinted up at the sun for a moment, then told Danny that I called Janet the other night.

'No shit? How'd you get her number?'

'From her mom. You know Janet got married?'

Danny shook his head. 'All I know is she disappeared right after your sentencing. There were even rumors floating around the neighborhood that you had her taken care of.'

'Christ, who was spreading *that* shit?'

Danny shrugged. 'They were just rumors that were going around. Whenever I heard them I'd shut the joker up. So how'd it go?'

'We'll see. I got some satisfaction but it's not over yet, not by a long shot.'

'You know where she lives?'

'She's local,' I said. 'I'll find her.'

He thought about it as we walked, then told me that maybe I should just let it go. 'It was a long time ago, bro. Maybe it would be better to just move on, you know?'

'Yeah, well, that's not going to happen.'

'Maybe it should. It can't be too healthy holding all these grudges inside. Red Mahoney, Janet, how many others, Kyle?'

'How many others? Anyone who's fucked me, that's how many others. Jesus, Danny, I shouldn't have to be telling you this. They're the rules of Southie, little brother. This is what we were brought up on. Anyone fucks you, you fuck them even harder. Fuck them 'til your dick's raw and bloody if you have to. Are you telling me that if you saw Red Mahoney walking down the street, you wouldn't pick up that brick over there and beat his head in with it?'

Danny turned grim-faced as he considered the question. 'Yeah, I probably would. But that doesn't mean that's all I think about.'

'Yeah, well, he didn't fuck you as bad as he did me.'

'No, he didn't,' Danny conceded. 'But it doesn't sound to me like Janet fucked you. It just sounds like she wanted a new life—'

I cut him off. 'Aw, Danny, please, don't even try saying anything more. Let me have a little respect for you.'

He turned red-faced. 'You're so fucking closed-minded. I can't suggest anything to you. There's not even a chance for personal growth with you.'

'Will you shut the fuck up about personal growth? That's all I've been hearing from you.' I looked around quickly to make sure no one was within earshot. 'The two million is real. Can I count on you or not? 'Cause if you're going to keep acting this way, tell me now so I can make other plans.'

His face flushed with anger as he stared back at me. 'What the fuck you think?' he asked.

I gave him a hard look, hoping that I could somehow pull the old Danny out. The one who'd act like a man and quit whining about this personal growth shit – and show some balls around his girlfriend. I had an idea then how I could do it. How to bring back the old Danny for good, not just little flashes of him. Clapping him hard on the shoulder, I lied and told him that I knew I could count on him. 'Sorry for giving you a hard time, little brother. Let's get your car, we've got some shopping to do. Afterwards I'll tell you how we're going to make two mil each.'

I picked up the loose brick that I had pointed out, and the two of us headed back to his building. He asked me what the brick was for, and I told him we needed it for one of the items we were going to be shopping for. He didn't bother questioning that.

Chapter 4

Our first stop was to get me a cell phone, and I ended up getting an extra one for Danny that we could use as walkie-talkies. After that we went to a department store so I could buy some new clothes. It was a far cry from Brooks Brothers, and I thought briefly about going to one of my other stashes and getting enough money so I could buy a decent wardrobe, but decided to keep enough cash out there for an emergency. This stuff was just going to be temporary, and then I'd do things right. We loaded the packages into the car, and when I heard Creedence's 'Who'll Stop the Rain' playing on the classic hits station that I'd tuned in, I stopped Danny from pulling into traffic until the song ended.

'Where next?' Danny asked after some Stevie Nicks shit came on and I turned off the radio.

'South End.'

The South End and South Boston are different worlds. South Boston, or 'Southie' as we called it, is a mix of poor and middle-class neighborhoods with low-income projects and dock work setting the tone for the neighborhood. Growing up it was almost entirely Irish Catholic. Even before I got arrested that had started to change. The South End, while bordering Southie, was a different beast entirely. While Southie was corned beef and cabbage, the South End was quiche. That probably describes it better than anything else I could come up with. The place was filled with overpriced trendy restaurants and rich soft yuppies who'd never been in a fist fight in their lives – and wouldn't have a clue what to do if they got in one. It was also the gay part of town, not that I cared one way or the other about that, but it was as good a place as any to go hunting if for no other reason than the cops really didn't give a shit – no matter what lip service they gave otherwise.

When we got to the heart of the South End – Tremont Street – I told Danny to slow down until I spotted what I was looking for, then had Danny pull over and let me out.

'Find a place to pull over a few blocks from here. I'll call you.'

Danny nodded, his eyelids dropping, his face a blank slate, just the way he used to always be before a job. It did my heart good to see him like that. I handed him the brick that I had picked up earlier and shut the door behind me. Half a block away was the coffee shop advertising Wi-Fi Internet access. I walked in and spotted a couple of people tapping away on their laptop computers while they drank their strawberry lattes or caramel mochachinos with whipped cream, or whatever the fuck they were drinking. I bought a paper and ordered a plain coffee from a thin girl with long stringy hair who seemed surprised I didn't want one of their more 'chic' and exotic flavors. She even asked me if I was sure I wanted only plain coffee, and not one of their flavored latte drinks. I dumped a few packets of sugar in the coffee, then found an empty table, walking past a man in his twenties with a goatee and wire-rimmed glasses sitting alone and staring intensely at the laptop's screen. I wanted to make sure he was on the Internet, and he didn't disappoint me – from the glance I took it looked like he was reading the *NY Times* online. I sat for a few minutes sipping my coffee, then left the shop and walked to the end of the block to a bench where I buried myself in the newspaper, all the while keeping one eye on the coffee shop.

I sat waiting for a good twenty before the mark left the shop and headed in the opposite direction from where I was sitting. I called Danny using the walkie-talkie feature, and told him the mark was heading up Tremont, then I started moving fast. It was one-twenty in the afternoon on a Thursday, so traffic was light and no other pedestrians were within sight. I spotted Danny crawling up Tremont, and I pointed out the mark to him. When he got alongside the guy, I yelled out to the mark that he left his wallet on the table. That stopped him. His free hand went to his back pocket, which was all the time we needed. I grabbed for the laptop, and as the mark realized what was going on and tried to pull back, Danny was out of the car and clocking him on the side of the head with the brick. He never turned fully around to see me, and he never got a look at Danny. The reality of the situation, the guy was no more than a hundred and sixty pounds soaking wet, and a slap on the side of the head with an open palm would've done the trick, but I was glad to see Danny use the brick. Not that I cared whether or not some effeminate mochachino-swilling yuppie had his head bashed in, but that type of violence was what I needed to bring the old Danny back. The brick made a nice dull thud against his skull, and kind of crumpled it in a bit. The last I saw of him, his eyes were rolling back into his head as he dropped to the pavement, either unconscious or dead for all I cared. I didn't wait around to see which. Before he hit the ground, Danny and I were back in the car driving away with the guy's computer under my arm.

There was nothing like planning out a job and seeing it go exactly as you thought it would. It didn't matter how big or small the job was, just knowing you could go out into the world and take whatever the fuck you wanted, there was no other feeling like it. Both Danny and I were riding sky high from it. He turned to me, a hard smile locked on his face and the heat from the violence burning on his skin, and told me he hadn't felt this alive in years.

'Fuck, that was something,' he said. 'All I gave him was a little love tap. You'd think the way he hit the ground that I slaughtered him. Any idea what this is worth?'

I had turned it on to check out the processor and what software it had installed. It had everything I needed, including a Wi-Fi interface.

'Between three and four thousand,' I said.

'Yeah? We going to sell it?'

'Nope. We need it for the job I'm planning.'

He raised an eyebrow at me dubiously. 'What the fuck?' he asked. 'You even know how to use one?'

'Yeah, I know how to use it. I didn't tell you this, but I got halfway through an Associates Degree in Computer Technology while at Cedar Junction.'

'No shit?'

'No shit.'

Laughing, he asked, 'So what are we going to do? Hack into a bank, or something like that?'

'Nothing like that. I'll go over it all later. Right now let's find a bar on Newbury Street, get some lunch and have a few beers to celebrate.'

'Fuck Newbury Street and all those rip-off joints. Let's take a trip out to Lynn and one of the strip clubs out there, see if we can get you taken care of, like what I should have done for you last night.'

'I appreciate the thought, Danny, but we're only a mile or two from Newbury Street. Let's go there. Maybe I'll buy a new suit first.'

He smiled as he remembered the card he had found in my pocket from Nola Nilssen. I gave him the address and he let me out in front, with us arranging to meet later at a restaurant a couple of blocks away.

'You're not going to fuck her right in that store, are you?' Danny asked, his grin stretching wide.

'What type of animal do you think I am?'

He didn't bother answering, just waved as he drove off. I stood frozen for a moment. The high from the mugging left the blood pounding hard through my body, and it left me more alive below the waist than I'd felt in years. To be honest, the reason I drank as much as I did the other night was I was afraid drunk or sober what I had down there was nothing but dead flesh. Now I felt I could give Nola everything she'd been begging for.

The clothing store was an upscale one, maybe even a place I would've shopped at before my arrest. As I wandered in, I checked the material of the suits and some of the price tags, and it looked like they started at two grand. I saw Nola inside the store. She was dressed more conservatively than the night before in a silk blouse, suit jacket and a skirt that went down past her knees. My guess, she was wearing underwear beneath it. When she spotted me, the cheerful smile she was flashing dropped clean off and her eyes narrowed to small angry holes. Hell hath no fury, right? I walked close to her, and could feel the freeze coming off her. She whispered low so only I could hear, asking me what the fuck I was doing there.

'Just here to give you what you were asking for last night,' I said. I grabbed her hard between the legs. She gasped, her body squirming, trying to resist. I squeezed harder until she gave in. A soft moan escaped from her, and then remembering where she was, her eyes darted left and right trying to see if anyone was noticing her.

'You're going to get me fired,' she whispered.

'What I'm going to do is get you fucked.'

'No, I can't. Not here, not now—'

I squeezed harder between her legs. I could feel her body

giving in to me. 'Do I have to drag you to the dressing room?' I breathed hard into her ear.

She shook her head. She didn't need any more convincing. The exhibitionist in her won out, her skin already burning hot from the idea of what we were going to be doing.

'You go to the dressing room first. I'll bring a suit in, pretend I'm waiting on you.'

I squeezed one last time, getting one last soft moan out of her before letting go. She didn't keep me waiting long. Less than a minute later she walked into the dressing room, her face flushed as she held up several suits. She let them drop and moved quickly to embrace me. I turned her around before she had a chance to and bent her over. As I grabbed her skirt, she whispered in a hushed voice not to rip it. I pulled it off, but I left it in one piece. She had silk panties underneath, and I ripped those to shreds getting them off her. Jesus, she was beautiful, her waist thin enough to get both my hands around it, and the rest of her just the perfect amount of curves. Looking down at her, I realized what I had between my own legs was more than just alive, it had become a raging beast, and before long I was sharing it with her. She tried to be quiet, and I couldn't help smiling every time a soft moan escaped from her. It seemed a long time before we were done. Then she surprised me, getting on her knees and getting another rise out of me. A long time after that we were both getting dressed. Her skin was flushed from what we did, but her eyes had started to turn queasy as she imagined what was waiting for her beyond the dressing room door.

'I'm going to get fired for this,' she said softly, resolutely, as she fastened her skirt over her now bare bottom. 'I can't believe I did this.'

Since there was no other place to put them, I balled up her ruined panties and shoved them in my pocket.

*To Ed.: I'm trying to keep this as clean as I can, which is
hard given what a crazed fucking nympho Nola was, but if
you want to add something about how I first handed Nola
her panties back to her so she could wipe her mouth off with
them, feel free. —K. N.*

'Don't worry about it,' I said.

'Oh well,' she said. 'Easy come, easy go. There are other jobs
out there.'

'You're not going to get fired.'

She gave me a weak smile letting me know she didn't believe
that, then reached for my hand and squeezed it. 'If I get fired, I
get fired. It was worth it. That was the most exciting sex I ever
had. You had my head pounding like it was going to explode.'

Yeah, no shit it was exciting for her. Fucking a badass mobster
at work with everyone there knowing exactly what you're doing.
There wasn't another girl alive I would've tried something like
this with, but with the way she acted the other night I knew she'd
go along with it. The only thing that would probably turn her on
even more would be to fuck in a church confessional while the
priest was listening in on the other side. Jesus, she was a freak,
but she was a gorgeous one.

'What are you?' I asked.

She gave me a confused smile. 'What do you mean?'

'Your last name. Nilssen. It sounds Swedish, but you don't
look it.'

She gave a half-hearted laugh, the worry over being fired
showing clearly in her eyes. 'It's Norwegian, actually. My dad's
side of the family. My mom's Portuguese. I guess I don't look like
the typical blond, fair-skinned Scandinavian, huh? Were you
worried I was married or something, and that was my husband's
name?'

The thought hadn't even occurred to me that a sex freak like her could be married. 'Yeah, a little,' I told her.

'You've got nothing to worry about. I'm completely unattached.'

I had finished dressing, and she gave me a troubled smile as she glanced at the dressing-room door. 'Maybe I should leave first?'

I waved it away. 'We'll leave together.' I saw the dread in her eyes as I reached past her and opened the door. Waiting outside of it must've been the store manager. He wasn't a bad looking guy, maybe a little light in the shoulders, but he had the athletic look of a yuppie who hits the treadmill at least an hour every day. His face stood aghast as he stared first at me and then Nola.

'I should have called the police on you two,' he said, staring mostly at Nola, his voice a hushed whisper as he tried to keep this from the rest of the customers and salespersons in the store. 'Nola, what in the world were you thinking? Don't bother answering that, you're fired, just get out of here. And you, sir—'

Before he could say anything, I grabbed him by the jaw and squeezed tight, digging my fingers in until I was pressing hard on bone. He tried to grab for my hand, and I bent his wrist over and sent him to his knees. Through tears, he tried telling me he was going to call the police on me.

'You could,' I said, 'but it wouldn't be very smart. If you've been reading the papers or watching TV you'd recognize me, and you'd know how dumb that would be.'

I could see the faint glimmer in his eyes as he made the connection of who I was. He looked like he was going to be sick. I sped it up since I didn't want to be splashed on.

'You know who I am then,' I said. 'Most of what they've been writing about me are just rumors, none of which can be proved. But you want to know something? Half those rumors are true. You don't want to become one of those rumors, do you?'

He shook his head, trying hard not to look at me.

'Nola's keeping her job,' I told him. 'And she's got special privileges from now on, including coming back here with me whenever I damn well want. Do we understand each other?'

He muttered that he did, and I helped him to his feet and brushed him off. Out of the corner of my eye, I could see Nola was on fire. I knew she wanted nothing more than for me to take her back into the dressing room, and if I had it in me I would've. Instead I gave her a hard kiss and told her to call me if there were any problems.

I know it's going to sound clichéd to say this but as I left the store I felt like I was a fucking god. Like I could punch through walls, that if I wasn't careful I'd shoot up into the sky like a rocket ship. A raw energy buzzed through me. It was as if the last eight years never happened. As if I was invincible again, and all the people walking past me were nothing but raw meat for me to tear apart with my bare hands. Remember Jimmy Cagney from *White Heat*? *I'm on top of the world, Ma!* Yeah, I know, all that sounds clichéd, but it's the way I was feeling.

When I joined Danny later he could see the change in me, but he didn't say anything about it, just showed an amused grin and asked how my shopping went. I told him it went well, that I got measured for a new suit. He got a chuckle out of that. 'Yeah, she measured you for over an hour, huh, bro? Right there where she works, Jesus, you've got a set of watermelons on you, Kyle, but no one's ever said otherwise.'

He had been nursing some beers while waiting, and he signaled the waiter for another round of what he was drinking. When the waiter brought them over we both ordered our steaks rare. The old Danny was back sitting across from me, but I knew he'd been back the moment he bashed that guy's head in with a brick. Christ it felt good sitting there with him, doing nothing more than enjoying our beers and mellowing out and knowing that I had him back. Like a pit-bull, all he needed was the smell of blood to bring out his true nature. When the steaks came, I don't think anything ever tasted better. Both our spirits were soaring as we left. On the way back to his apartment we stopped off to pick up a couple of cases of beer, then I had him circle his neighborhood while I had the laptop out. I had him stop and back up to a copy store we'd passed.

'A lot of businesses now are set up to have wireless networks,' I explained. 'It makes sense. This way if you have a business like this copy store, anyone can come in with a laptop, and as along as they have something called a Wi-Fi interface, they can connect to the Internet. The beauty of this is sometimes the signal is strong enough so an asshole like me can connect from outside the store without anyone knowing about it.'

Danny was nodding, but by the empty look in his eyes I could tell it was just white noise to him. 'I'm majorly impressed, bro,' he said. 'You really did take courses in this shit.'

'Yeah I did.' As I was talking to him I got onto a site that lets you do a reverse phone number lookup. The site had Janet's phone number in its database, and I now had her home address. Another site gave me directions to her home. After memorizing them, I told Danny I needed to learn this computer shit for what we were going to be doing. 'I also needed access to the Internet, and taking the courses gave me an hour a week in the prison library. You wouldn't believe the information they make available out there.'

I shut down the computer and had Danny drive back to his apartment. On the way we tossed the brick into a trash can. As he pulled into his parking spot, I noticed the dumpsters to the Chinese restaurant both had covers on them. Danny noticed it also and smiled, commenting how tipping them over must've taught them a lesson. I didn't bother explaining that the real lesson was taught by snapping the guy's finger and smacking him in the face with a car door. In this world that's how you get someone's attention. Anyway, it worked. It no longer smelled like rotting fish back there and I didn't see any rats crawling around. We walked up the three flights to Danny's apartment with him carrying one case of beer while I loaded myself up with the other case, along with the laptop and the packages making up the small wardrobe that I bought. Once we were inside I turned on the stereo to give us some ambient noise so no one could listen in through the walls, then we loaded a cooler with ice and sat drinking beers while I told Danny about a guy I met at Cedar Junction doing time for a string of B & Es.

'Manuel Lorentz,' I told Danny. 'We overlapped at Cedar, with him finishing up his last year while I was starting there. Lorentz was working out in the boondocks past 495, hitting mostly high-tech workers. He liked to target them because they work late, and a lot of their wives go off to work also – kind of a competition thing. Hoping for a little extra, he'd go through their bank statements, see if he could find any credit card information, stuff like that, and what he was finding was some of these guys were worth millions. The best he could figure was they made their money with company stock options.'

'No shit,' Danny muttered. I could tell he wanted a joint as badly as I wanted a cig. We both lit up with a silent agreement not to give each other a hard time over our respective bad habits.

'No shit,' I agreed. 'These fuckers were being handed millions while we're scrounging and busting our humps for whatever loose change we could shake out of people's pockets. But here's the kicker. These fuckers have their millions but they don't have a clue how to live like they've got that kind of money. According to Lorentz they're living in the same neighborhoods, probably even the same houses they had before they cashed in. Maybe they might've bought themselves a few expensive toys, and maybe added an addition to the house, but nothing else. And they don't have a clue about security. No alarms, no bodyguards, no security firms, nothing. It's like they don't want to admit they're rich. They want to keep on acting the same way as before.'

Danny scratched his jaw, his eyes a complete blank. He wasn't connecting the dots, probably because of the pot.

'So?' he asked.

'So we're going to snatch one of their kids and collect eight million. A little bit of laundering and we'll end up with four and a half mil of clean cash.'

'You already know who we're going to hit?'

'Yep. Already targeted.'

Danny gave me a dubious look as he rubbed his jaw. 'And you know they've got eight million?'

'They got a lot more than that. This particular fucker made over thirty million with stock options. When companies go public or get bought, they report their top shareholders, and not only that, how many shares each of them were given. And guess what? You can find these reports on the Internet. Not only that, you've got real estate sites now that give you satellite pictures of neighborhoods, even down to the house. I got it scoped out. I know the property and neighborhood. And Lorentz has checked the house. No security alarms. Nothing. He's also been watching it. The fuckers live like they're flower children from the sixties. They leave their kid alone every chance they get.'

Danny took a long deep hit of his joint. He held the smoke in a good thirty seconds before letting it out slowly.

'Lorentz is in on this with us?' he asked.

'Yeah.'

'We can trust him?'

I shrugged. 'As much as you can trust anyone these days. Yeah, as long as he gets his half mil we can trust him. Maybe we can trust him more if he's dead and buried somewhere, but we'll see.'

'How's he able to watch the house without drawing suspicion?'

I couldn't help smiling. It was good hearing Danny ask that. It meant he was thinking it out, trying to look at it from different angles. There was no question I had the old Danny sitting there.

'Lorentz works for a landscaper in the area. One of their customers is doing a big job only three houses over. He's in the area enough to get an idea of the kid's schedule.'

'I don't know, Kyle, I don't like this. The guy's done a stretch. He's working in the neighborhood. You don't think the FBI's going to be looking hard at him?'

'No, I don't. I don't think they'll ever make the connection, but if they do, so what. There'll be nothing to connect him to the kidnapping. He's working as a landscaper, he's keeping his nose clean. It's a stretch to think they'll want to lean on him. And if they do want to they'll have nothing to pick him up on.'

Danny leaned back and took another hit as he mulled it over. 'I'm not killing a kid,' he said. 'I'm only doing this if we don't hurt him.'

'As long as they pay, they'll get the kid back.'

'I need your word on it.'

'You've got my word.'

He nodded, satisfied, his eyes losing their focus as he took one last hit on his now fingernail-sized joint before stubbing it out. When he first rolled it it was the size of his middle finger. I tossed him a beer, took another bottle for myself. So far we were building a nice collection of empties between us.

'Boy or girl?' he asked.

'Boy. Lorentz thinks he's about ten.'

'Where are we going to be holding him?'

'Red Mahoney's cabin.'

Danny's eyes went wide as he stared at me. He drank his beer slowly before wiping the back of his hand across his mouth.

'I always thought that was a myth.'

'It's no myth. And everything you've heard about it is probably true.'

'How come you never told me about it before?'

'Because I was sworn to secrecy. But fuck Red, and fuck any oath I ever made to him.'

Danny listened in awe as I told him about the cabin. Red's cabin was a thing of urban legends, one of the threats mothers in Southie would routinely make to try to keep their boys from being the terrors they naturally were. *You better behave yourself or I'm having you carted off to Red's cabin!* Only three people ever knew about the cabin: me, Red and Kevin Flannery, at least we were the only three who knew about it who were still alive. There were others who came to know about it intimately during the last few hours of their lives, but they have long ceased being around to talk about it. The cabin was in the middle of some godforsaken wasteland in New Hampshire where absolutely no one would ever want to go. Red owned hundreds of acres surrounding the cabin, and last time I'd been up there, there was nothing within miles of it – and there was no reason for there to be anything. The nearest lake was thirty miles away, and there was nothing around the property but woods and swamp. Red bought the land cheap and a dummy name was used for the purchase with enough money put in trust to pay the taxes for a good thirty years. There was not a chance the property could ever be connected to Red.

'You think Red could be living there?' Danny asked after I finished giving him the full scoop on it.

'Unfortunately not. The place wasn't set up for year-round living. And he'd be noticed if he tried buying supplies. But it is a nice thought getting him up there alone.'

'And the feds don't know about it?'

I showed him a half-smile. I couldn't help it. 'If the feds ever found out about Red's connection with that cabin and dug up around there, you'd know about it. Everyone would be reading about what they found.'

Danny had other questions about Red's cabin, then about the kidnapping, like how we were going to handle the ransom note, and more importantly, receive the payoff without being caught, and as drunk and stoned as he was I could see the respect shining in his eyes as I explained it to him. I ended up giving him a complete briefing: when we were probably going to be doing the job, how it was going to go down, and the few details that still needed to be worked. When I was done, Danny leaned back absorbing it all.

'Shit,' he said after a long time, 'you really thought this out.'

'I had the time.'

I also had the desire. I needed a big score. I had ideas where Red was, but it was going to be expensive finding which rock he crawled under. More than that, though, I needed a score to set me up for life. There was no percentage anymore operating in our old businesses, not with all the rats running about. And the fact was, I might've always been flush with cash, but I never made any real money doing all that other shit.

Danny gave me a stoner's smile as he thought over the job. I uncorked the bottle of Bushmills we opened earlier that morning, and we passed it back and forth, mixing shots with beers. Neither of us spoke much after that. It got to the point where we could've just as well been drinking water with the way both of us seemed to be getting more sober the more we drank. We were both letting ourselves get keyed up thinking about the kidnapping, and that was a mistake. All we'd accomplish by doing that this early would be to burn ourselves out. To get our minds on something else, I started reminiscing about when we were kids how we used to jump on the back of trucks – me fourteen at the time, Danny only ten – and then, using a crowbar, steal whatever we could when the driver was in the store making his deliveries. Soap, toilet paper, batteries, it didn't matter. We'd sell whatever we got in the projects. It took a couple of more beers before Danny fully joined in on the reminiscing, but after that we were both relaxing, chilling, and just genuinely feeling good, the pile of empties on the floor between us having grown to something substantial.

I don't think either of us heard Eve when she came into the apartment. It was more that we both felt the chill coming off her. We were well into the second bottle of Bushmills at this point and almost as if on cue we simultaneously turned our attention towards the doorway. There she was, standing there, livid, her eyes first going to the pile of empties on the floor and then to the cig burning between my index and middle fingers. If looks could kill I would've been a dead man, and so would've Danny. I don't want to go into too many details, but needless to say she made it clear she wasn't happy with a number of things; topping the list: me being there, the pigsty we had made of her apartment and the fact that Danny took the day off to be with me. Of course the real reason for her meltdown was her realization that she no longer had Danny on a leash, that the puppy dog she thought she had so well trained had been replaced by another animal entirely. Anyway, the situation escalated to the point where she stormed out of the place with a suitcase in hand, but not without first shedding a bucket of tears and leveling a few choice accusations and words at both of us.

'Christ, the mouth on her,' I said after the reverberations from her door slamming had died down. 'I hope she can do more with it than just bust balls.'

Danny didn't bother saying anything, just tilted back his beer bottle and drained it. I fished through the cooler and tossed him another, and he twisted the top off with a half-hearted gesture.

I continued, saying, 'She ought to grow some tits on her before trying to make those types of demands on anyone. Fuck, the choice she gave you.'

He gave me a look letting me know I'd better shut up, and I did. There was no point pushing it, especially with her already out of the apartment. The two of us sat back and tried to recapture the good feelings from before, but it just wasn't happening – not after that ice storm had laid waste to the place. I suggested to Danny that we go out for some dinner, but he just wanted to order out for pizza so that's we did. After the pizza came and we finished off the pie along with the rest of the beer and the Bushmills, Danny pushed himself off the sofa and told me he was wiped and was going to call it a night.

'You're fucking with me, right? It's not even nine o'clock. Shit, even the assholes at Cedar Junction are still up and about. How about we head out to one of the clubs in Lynn and maybe bring a couple of the more talented and flexible performers back here afterwards.'

'No, bro, after all this drinking it would be wasted on me. You go, have fun.'

He handed me his car keys and stumbled off to the bedroom. I sat alone for a while, but I couldn't shake this edginess. The more I sat there, the more keyed up I got. After a while I realized where I needed to go.

Chapter 5

Janet had moved up in the world. No question. Big English Tudor, manicured lawn, extensive landscaping, ritzy neighborhood, a Volvo and mini-van in the garage. I was impressed. Before leaving Danny's I gave back a good amount of the beer and whiskey I had drunk, but I still had more to return and I figured Janet's front doorway was as good a place as any to make a deposit. After leaving a small puddle I turned and was mostly watering the shrubs when the door opened. I shifted around to see who it was, and the guy standing there must've been Janet's husband. He was a few inches shorter than me, just as broad in the chest, though, and dressed in a polo shirt, short pants and sandals. He had kind of a bulldog look about him, and as he realized what I was doing and what it was that was splashing on him, he started yelling 'Hey!' repeatedly like he was a Russian dancer. I had my hands full trying to get myself back in my pants, and he took advantage of that to grab me and push me over into the same shrubs I'd been pissing in. He was yelling into the house for Janet to call the police. He had some strength to him, but even as drunk as I was I'd still kick his ass. I was picking myself out of the shrubs and planning to do just that when Janet appeared in the doorway. She hadn't changed much over the last eight years. Her hair was cut shorter than I remembered and she was more gaunt in the face, but her body was basically the same as the one I invested all that money into. As our eyes locked, her face turned as white as the moon overhead.

'Go back in the house and wait for the police,' her husband ordered. He was visibly shaking, the adrenaline pumping hard in him. 'This psycho was pissing on our front door.'

'Don't believe a word of it, Janet,' I said. 'I was watering your shrubs. They looked a bit dry to me. Why don't you tell him why I'm here.'

He gave his wife a sideways glance, not wanting to take his eyes off me for too long. 'You know him?' he asked.

She moved in close to him and tried whispering so I couldn't hear. The two of them were going back and forth like that until I had enough of it and interrupted them.

'Chrissakes, Janet. The two of us never kept any secrets from each other before, why start now? And you're not keeping secrets from your new hubby, are you? He knows how we used to fuck three or four times every day, right?'

'That's it,' the husband stated, determined to take charge of the situation. 'I've had enough of this. I'm calling the police myself.'

He had taken out his cell phone, but Janet stopped him. 'Don't,' she pleaded. 'Please, I just need five minutes alone with him. Just go inside for five minutes.'

He was shaking his head, not liking the idea at all. I started laughing. 'Five minutes?' I asked. 'Janet, once we get started we'll be fucking for hours.'

'What do you want?' he demanded.

'I want the ten thousand your wife owes me.'

He turned to her. She shook her head. 'I don't owe him anything,' she said.

'Then why am I here?' I asked.

Her eyes seethed as they held steady on mine. She wasn't going to say anything, but as she stared at me she just couldn't help herself. 'Because you're a sick twisted fuck,' she said. 'You're angry at me for breaking up with you. You want to hurt me because that's what you do to people who dare to stand up to you. How's that, Kyle?'

'A sick twisted fuck, huh? That's interesting. What would you call a woman who flashes men in bars so she can lure them to a hotel room where they get knocked out and robbed, and later, as they're laying unconscious—'

'Shut up!' she screamed over me. 'Shut up! Shut up!'

Janet's husband gave her an odd look, as if he wasn't sure he still wanted to be anywhere near her, then he turned towards me.

'If you don't leave my property now I'm going to physically throw you off of it!'

I smiled then. Because that was what I was after. I didn't care about collecting ten thousand from Janet. Fuck the money. What I wanted was my pound of flesh. I was going to break every bone in his body and leave Janet spending the rest of her life caring for a cripple. That was what I wanted. That was the payback I had in mind for her.

'Go ahead,' I told him. 'I'm waiting.'

He started moving towards me, and Janet seemed too tired to try to stop him. I caught sight then of the girl watching from the second floor window. She looked older than I would've expected for a child from those two given that they couldn't have been together for more than eight years. Janet's a redhead, her husband's hair a dark brown. The girl in the window was blonde, like me. Maybe my eyes were playing tricks on me, but I thought I could see some of me around her eyes and mouth. And there was so much fear in those eyes.

I turned around and headed to where I left the car. Janet's husband started yelling at me, calling me a coward and threatening what he would do to me if I ever showed up there again. The emotion of the situation must've been too much for

Janet. She ran after me then and started punching me in the back and shoulders, screaming like a crazed banshee the whole time. I ignored it and kept walking. At some point her husband must've pulled her off me.

When I got in the car, I drove straight to Danny's as sober as I'd been all day. I tried to forget about Janet. More than anything I tried to get that look from that girl out of my head – that look of pure absolute terror.

Like every other night since my arrest I had trouble sleeping. At first I kept going around in circles thinking about Janet and the girl from the window, and that eventually got my mind racing about the one time Red visited me while I was awaiting trial. I had already been patched up from my bullet wounds by then and had gone through both an arraignment and preliminary bail hearing. The bail had been set at two million, and I needed ten percent – two hundred thousand – to get a bond posted. I didn't have anywhere near that kind of cash. I needed help, and Red, the rat bastard, played me like a violin.

'All me money's tied up now, Kyle,' he told me, as straight-faced and innocent as any choir boy. 'There was Jimmie Clark's funeral to pay for, and his widow and three boys to help. And the feds have been leaning heavily on me. By the time I were to free up the money you're asking for you'll already be standing trial.'

I needed to get out on bail. I knew something was going on with Janet. She was still taking my phone calls then, but had stopped visiting, always giving me one excuse after the next. I didn't dare tell Red any of that, though. I knew what would happen to Janet if I did, Red being the paranoid fuck that he is. So I just sat there listening to Red's feeble explanation about why he couldn't help me. Even back then – at least at some level – I knew he was playing me. Deep down inside I must've known he was laughing his white bony rat bastard ass off at me, but I just couldn't admit it. For years he'd been my mentor, my pal, my protector, my priest. I'd been closer to him than I'd ever been to anyone, even my own brother, Danny. I just couldn't see the obvious, at least not until it was spelled out for me. So I listened to his excuses and tried to rationalize them – that since the feds had me dead to rights, he was afraid I'd skip bail and he'd lose his two hundred grand. In my head that made sense, so I accepted it. I needed to so I could continue to maintain a modicum of respect for him.

I bolted up from the sofa squeezing my eyes tight trying to get that image of him out of my head. If that sonofabitch had helped me back then I would've found out about Janet being pregnant. Things would be different now. I wouldn't have let her pull the shit she did, not with her carrying my child. That sonofabitch smirking rat bastard…

Fuck it.

I knew sleep wasn't even a remote possibility that night. To keep busy, I turned on the laptop, and after double-checking that it had the multimedia software I needed, I deleted any personal files that could've identified the previous owner. I was surprised when I came across some pictures of the guy with a woman who must've been his wife, along with three small children who were obviously his own. Not that I targeted him because I thought he was gay, but still, it bothered me that I was so wrong in reading him. Fuck, if I knew the guy was a family man, I might've gone looking for someone else. But what's done is done. The guy would have a bad headache for a few weeks, and then a story he could brag about the rest of his life…

To Ed.: I don't know what I was thinking when all that happened. I must've gone soft in the head due to the trauma of just finding out that I had a daughter I never knew about, but do you think I'd fucking care whether the guy had a wife and kids? Trust me, something like that has never bothered me before, and I guarantee you it would never have bothered me again. Yeah, I'm going to cry a fucking river over whose head we bash in. Jesus. Anyway, your call whether you leave that in or not. —K. N.

Chapter 6

The next morning I had coffee waiting for Danny when he got up. Christ, he looked like hell stumbling out of his bedroom, barely even grunting out a hello to me. Dark circles under his eyes, red spider webs in the whites of them and his color more gray than flesh. Every little noise while he drank his coffee had him looking up as if he were hoping that his stick figure of a girlfriend had just walked through the door. I suggested we go out for some breakfast but he made a face and said he had to head off to work.

'You're going to have to quit your job soon,' I told him. 'Our own job's going down soon, and it wouldn't look good if you took the day off the day it happened. Not that I think there's any way the cops will be able to connect the dots, but why take any chances? Maybe not a bad idea if you got yourself fired. That way you build some distance between you and the other guys on the job, and even better, you don't have anyone asking what your future plans are. Today's as good a day as any.'

Danny thought about it, nodded, then lumbered to his feet. He cleared his throat, told me he had to head off to work and asked for his car keys. I suggested that I drop him off instead. 'I have some errands I need to run. They could take me all day so take a cab home after you get your ass booted off the job.'

I handed him some cash that he reluctantly took. As we made

our way through the apartment, he noticed I had cleaned up
the living room and stacked all the empties back in the cases.
The room was cleaner than before I'd ever stepped foot in the
apartment. If he had opened his eyes when he stumbled into the
bathroom earlier he would've noticed that it was spotless also.

'Thanks, Kyle,' he said, his face crumbling a bit. For a second I
thought I was going to see some tears, but he clenched his mouth
tight to keep that from happening.

'Chrissakes, Danny, no reason for us to live in a pigsty, is
there?'

He gave me a look as if my real reason for cleaning the place
was to help calm the waters between him and the titless wonder
in case she came back, but that had nothing to do with it. He had
nothing to read in the apartment, so what else was I going to do
in the early morning to keep myself occupied? Besides, I'd gotten
in the habit of keeping my surroundings spotless. It was one of
those little things that helped kill the time while in stir. But I
didn't bother telling Danny any of that. Let him believe what he
wanted to believe.

On the way to Danny's construction site I stopped off and
bought him a bag of doughnuts and a black coffee. When I let
him out at his job, I told him I could be out late with errands and
for him not to wait up for me. He nodded, only half listening to
what I said. The whole morning he'd been like that, acting like
some lovesick dope, and before turning away from me he asked
if I'd have Eve call him if she came back to the apartment. Fuck.
I wanted to knock some sense into him, but what would've been
the point? I told him I would. As I left him standing there I had
an idea of what I was going to do instead.

It was only seven-thirty and I had some time to kill, so I did
what I'd been waiting to do for almost eight years; I drove to
the K-Street Diner in the heart of Southie. The three waitresses
working there were all new, all three of them fresh-faced girls in

their early twenties. I didn't recognize a single one of them from the old neighborhood, but then again, they would've been young teenage girls the last time I was roaming the streets of Southie. Maybe Red would've paid attention to them back then, especially given how they might've looked in their Catholic school uniforms, but I wouldn't have. I did, however, recognize most of the customers. A couple of them pretended they didn't see me – one of those being a cousin of Fred Connor – others either waved cheerfully to me or came over to shake my hand and see how I was doing. A few wanted to know if I had any idea where Red Mahoney was.

'If I did you think I'd be sitting here right now?' I asked them back.

'Maybe he crawled off and died in some sewer like the rat he is,' one of them volunteered.

'Him?' another one said. 'He'll outlive us all. Scumbags like him always do.'

'Trust me,' I said with a wink. 'He's got no chance in hell of outliving me. I'll make sure of that.'

That got a few laughs as if I meant it as a joke. Most of them scattered back to their booths. Eddie Hennessy stuck around. After my dad took off to parts unknown, Hennessy took it upon himself to try to straighten out Danny and me. His method was kindness, though, taking us to ball games and stuff like that as he tried to curb our wild side and get us onto a more law-abiding path. Needless to say the gentle approach with the two of us didn't work. Hennessy had aged tremendously since I'd seen him last. I remembered him as a mountain of a man with a big red face and a gnarled veined nose the size of a normal man's fist. He had since shrunk to maybe half that size, his security guard uniform hanging loosely off his wasted body. In his shriveled state, his nose was absolutely massive, hanging off his face like a big glob of red putty. All I could think was he must be dying, probably getting eaten away from the inside by the big C.

'I believe they're hiring now at my factory,' he said, his voice now a weak imposter of his once booming one. 'Kyle, if you like I could ask around and see if I can scare you up a job.' He showed me a sad smile. 'There should be an opening soon for a security guard, and I could put in a good word for you.'

'I appreciate the offer,' I said, 'but I'm just going to kick back and get used to my freedom for a little while, then try to figure out what to do next.'

He gave me a stern look, which looked ridiculous given how shrunken and wasted his face had become. 'A man needs steady work, Kyle. It's being idle that will send the devil calling.'

'Words to live by,' I agreed.

'It would make your ma so proud of you to take an honest job.'

He had been close to Ma and he meant well, so I said something harmless before turning a deaf ear. Still that last comment annoyed the hell out of me and I sat stewing over the implication. The waitress came and took my order. Before that happened Hennessy must've gone away, but hell if I even noticed. It took maybe three cups of coffee before I started breathing easy again.

The food at K-Street was as good as ever. I had ordered waffles, three eggs over easy, bacon and sausage patties, and it was all as close to perfection as you could ever hope to find. Before too long I was back to my old self with Hennessy's unintentional but nonetheless hurtful insult long forgotten. While I ate I busied myself with the day's *Boston Globe*, looking to see if there were any stories about the guy we mugged in the South End, but didn't find a single one. There'd been nothing on TV or the radio about it either, which meant that no one had witnessed it and there were no police drawings of me or Danny to have to worry about – not that I'd expect one to have much likeness to either of us even if one did exist, not with how quickly the mugging happened and how unreliable police drawings usually are. I still remember one from over a decade ago that made me look like a dark-haired Italian.

After finishing my food, I sat back in my booth and relaxed as I drank more coffee and read the sports section. When the bill came I had to double-check the menu, not quite believing my eyes. The prices had gone up more than double since I had last eaten there. I'd noticed the same when Danny and I had bought beer the other night. It made me wonder whether two million would still be enough to set me up for life, especially since I was going to have to pay a good chunk of that looking for Red. Christ, I still couldn't get over the price of gasoline.

Anyway, I hung around the booth until nine-thirty, then left the K-Street Diner and called Lorentz as we had prearranged. I gave him the number of my new cell phone, and he gave me the number of the next disposable cell phone that I should be calling him on. All of our communications have been with me calling a disposable cell phone of his. There were no phone records for the feds or anyone else to tie the two of us together.

'Still looking good for a week from next Wednesday?' I asked.

'Yeah, I hope so. I'll keep you updated.'

He hung up then. The few calls I'd made to him had been short and sweet.

I still had an hour before I was going to be meeting Timmy Dunn, and then several hours after that before I'd be seeing Kevin Flannery, so I made my rounds visiting the local businesses. A few people snubbed me – not many but a few, and I took note on who they were. Most, though, seemed genuinely happy to see me. As I talked with folks I got a more complete picture than what I had gotten the other night at Scolley's on who was in prison and who was dead, and the list was longer than I would've imagined.

Most I talked to were bemoaning the fact that stand-up guys were on the verge of extinction. Gerald Mulligan, bless his soul, told me in all sincerity that I was the last of a dying breed. 'They're all looking now to cut deals,' he complained bitterly. 'And it's all Mahoney's fault, he was the pied piper of Southie as he led all the rats out of the woodwork.'

At ten-thirty I walked into Scolley's. Joe was working the bar as he always does. Nine in the morning until he closes up, giving him usually less than six hours of sleep at night. At that hour the place was mostly a tomb, only a few hardcore alkies scattered around the bar. Joe, as he always does when he knows I'm there on business, looked through me, but used his head to point out a booth in the back where Timmy Dunn was sitting. Timmy had gotten heavy since I'd last seen him. He used to be as lean as a blade, topping out at no more than a hundred and thirty. One of those wiry types who are a lot more dangerous in a fight than you'd think. Since I'd seen him last he had to've put on at least sixty pounds, making him seem like a caricature of his former self. His face and neck looked like layers of stucco had been slapped on, but even still you could see the hardness in him, and there was no doubt looking in those granite eyes of his that you could trust him. We exchanged pleasantries, he gave me the obligatory but still heartfelt cursing out of Red Mahoney, and after a round of shots and Guinness were brought over, I gave him the list of what I needed. He raised an eyebrow when he came across the UPS uniforms, but he didn't say a word about it. When he was done totaling it up, he told me it would be fifteen hundred.

'Plus or minus,' he added, 'depending on my expenses. When do you need delivery?'

'End of next week?'

'Not a problem.'

'Mind if I give you five hundred now, the rest on delivery?'

'Yeah, not a problem. I know you're good for it.'

I counted out five hundred and slid it under the table, not that anyone else in the place would've noticed or cared if they did. The few patrons sitting around the bar were propped up on their elbows like corpses as they waited to drink the day away and move a few steps closer to their graves.

Timmy Dunn, satisfied with the roll of bills, tucked both the money and the list in his pocket. He finished off his whiskey, then drained the pint in front of him.

'Heard Fred Connor's mouth is a mess right now, almost as broken up as Bill Mullan's skull.'

'Yeah, you probably heard right.'

He chuckled, shook his head. 'What the fuck were those two thinking? They're lucky the both of them to still be breathing.'

'I can't argue there.'

He shook his head some more thinking about it, then started to push himself out of the booth. Before he left, we arranged a time and place for delivery, and he asked me to give Danny his best. After that I kept Joe company at the bar for a spell. I had set up to meet Kevin Flannery at noon near North Station, and since I had a stop I wanted to make along the way, I said my goodbyes to Joe at a quarter past eleven. He wanted to know if he could pack me a few roast beef sandwiches to go, and I told him that would be fine.

Southie to North Station is usually a quick drive up the Expressway, although how quick depends on traffic which can be brutal. At that hour the traffic was light, and I got off at Storrow Drive and navigated to Newbury Street where I double-parked outside of where Nola worked. She was there as I'd hoped, although waiting on a customer. The store manager noticed me first, and he looked away trying hard not to make eye contact. When Nola saw me, she flashed me the same bare trace of a smile that she had shown earlier at Scolley's. She was squatting on her heels by a customer as she took his pant measurements, and as her eyes locked on mine her face heated up as if she were feverish. She let her hand wander too close to the guy's crotch and he jumped from the shock of it. Her eyes burned into mine with unadulterated lust as she apologized to the guy for her slip. When he took a couple of suits into the dressing room, Nola came over to me and grabbed my hand.

'I am so turned on right now,' she whispered in my ear, her voice a husky purr. 'Let's go find someplace to be alone. At least as alone as we can be here.'

She tried leading me towards one of the empty dressing rooms, but I didn't budge. She gave me a puzzled look.

'I don't have time for that,' I told her. 'But I want to see you tomorrow night. That blonde from the other night at Scolley's also. Come by this address around seven and I'll have dinner waiting for the two of you.'

She took the paper I handed her with Danny's address and my cell phone number on it, but she looked uneasy. 'I'm not sure I want to share you,' she said finally.

I couldn't help laughing. 'Nola, darling, you're more than I can handle as it is. The blonde's for my brother. He just broke up with his girlfriend. A fucking witch if I ever saw one. I just want to try to help him move on from that mistake.'

'What's your brother like?'

What she was really asking me was whether Danny was also a bad boy like me. As Joe had warned me, both of them liked trolling Scolley's for Irish bad boys.

'Back in the day no one was tougher,' I said.

That brought out a little smile from Nola. 'I'll see if Sheila's available. If not I've got other friends I can ask.'

I reached down to give her a quick kiss so long, but she moved quicker than me and pushed her mouth hard into mine. When she finally let go I had to check my teeth to make sure she hadn't loosened any.

'Tomorrow,' she said in a breathless whisper.

I nodded and headed out to meet Kevin Flannery.

Flannery was one of the toughest sonofabitches I'd ever met. Two tours of duty with the Marines in Vietnam. Killed dozens there, almost as many here. A crazy motherfucker if ever there was one. He acted mostly as Red's enforcer, but he also did more than his share of truck hijackings and warehouse robberies. Maybe five foot eight, a hundred and sixty pounds. He didn't look like much, but if you bumped into him you'd swear you were bumping into a brick wall. And he was the last person you'd ever want to end up in a fight with. He'd use everything including the kitchen sink to come after you with, and he'd keep coming after you until one or the other of you were dead.

He was waiting for me where we had arranged. He'd turned gray since I'd last seen him, both his hair and skin color. With his blue work overalls on he gave me the impression that he was still in prison. When he saw me, he showed little indication of it other than his eyes following me like a snake's.

'It's been a long time,' I said. I held out a hand and after a moment of contemplation he took it in that vise-like grip of his.

'You're looking good, Nevin,' he said, his lips moving about as much as if he were working a ventriloquist dummy. 'Prison life's been good to you, I see.'

'Gave me time for some quiet meditation,' I said. I didn't bother saying the obvious, that prison life must've really sucked for him. He had just got out five months earlier after four hard years in Atlanta and was now working as a janitor. I offered him a cig, which he took. Then we found a quiet spot on some steps nearby where we could talk. Once we were seated I offered him half of the roast beef sandwiches that Joe had packed up for me.

'You said you'd buy me lunch,' he said flatly.

'These are from Scolley's.'

He gave them a quick look. Satisfied, he accepted them. Neither of us bothered acknowledging the other while we ate. When he was done I told him I was sorry about what happened with his mom.

He stared bug-eyed at me for a long moment, appraising me, his thin lips nearly disappearing as they pressed hard together. 'The authorities made my mom's last few months a living hell once they dug those up,' he said at last. 'You wouldn't know anything about that, would you, Nevin?'

'No more than you.'

He gave me more of that bug-eyed look of his before asking what I wanted to talk to him about.

'About Red. You hear from him? Any ideas where the fucker is?'

'Not a peep.' He gave me a thin lifeless smile. 'About where he may be hiding, it's a large world. You know how he used to always talk about retiring to Galway someday? Not a chance of that, Nevin. They have even less tolerance for rats than we. Of course, you know about his many bank accounts in Europe?'

'Yeah, I know about them.'

'You know any of the names he used for them?'

'A few.'

'Then if I were you, and I had the money, I'd hire private dicks over there to watch the accounts.'

I nodded. It was what I'd been planning to do once I could afford it. 'Your best guess where he is?' I asked.

His eyelids drooped a bit as he thought about it. 'Given his perversion for young girls, if I had to guess I'd say Thailand. I know he took a number of trips to Bangkok during the nineties. But I'd suppose there are many places in this world of ours where young girls can be acquired cheaply.' He stared up at the sky as if he were telling the time from the position of the sun, then pushed himself to his feet. 'You were late coming, and I have to be heading back to work.'

'You're really working a nine-to-five job?'

'I have to. It's a condition to my early parole. And I need the money. Not much waiting for me once I got out.'

'Early parole. Fuck.' I shook my head, not bothering to hide my disgust. 'That's why I served out my full term, so no one would be able to put any conditions on my head.'

A glimmer of light showed in his eyes as he stared at me. 'You had that option, Nevin. You could serve your time and still come out a relatively young man, for all the good it will do you. Me, I'm already on the other side of sixty. If I served my full sentence, I wouldn't have had much left once I finished my fifteen years. But as you'll discover someday, I hope, there's more to life than stealing and whoring. Do give my best to Mahoney if you find him. And fuck any pity you might be feeling towards me.'

'One more question, Flannery. How'd you get parole after only four years?'

He gave me a dead stare. 'Are you suggesting something, Nevin?'

'I'm not suggesting a thing.'

He held his dead stare on me a moment longer before turning and moving quietly away. I watched for a while as the man who had once been part of the holy trinity that ruled Southie headed off to clean toilets. When I had asked around about Flannery I was given a number for a rooming house in Saugus where he lived and was told that he was out of the rackets completely. I didn't fully believe it until I saw him in those work overalls with his hands dirty and stained and grime buried deep under his fingernails. After he was gone from sight, I dusted myself off and found a bar so I could have a stiff drink of whiskey. I ended up having several, holding my own private wake for the man who used to be Kevin Flannery. Then I got back to the car and headed off to Red's cabin in New Hampshire.

It was a three-hour drive to Red's cabin with the last hour bouncing over a dirt road. Not much had changed up there, maybe a few log cabins popping up where I hadn't remembered any, but as I got closer to Red's property it was as desolate as ever. I don't know why, but as I pulled up to the cabin I was almost surprised to see the damn thing still standing. I guess because the place was such an abomination that I had half expected God or some other power to have swept it off the face of the planet. It was still intact, though, none of the windows broken, and from the outside appearing no worse for wear after its years of abandonment. I did a quick walk-around, and the grounds looked undisturbed, even some wild brush growing over our makeshift graveyard. I had the keys on my chain for the deadbolt locks that secured the only door to the cabin, and I used them to find the inside uninhabited and having a strong musty, dead-animal smell to it. After opening the windows, I checked the storage room and found it stocked with five-gallon containers of diesel fuel. I used one of the containers to fill up the electric generator, and it switched on like a champ, not even a hiccup of hesitation.

I next turned on the lights and made a quick inventory of what was inside. The rifles, handguns and ammunition were where they'd always been. I examined the handguns and picked out two of the Smith & Wesson 9 millimeter pistols, loading up the magazines on both of them, and taking two boxes of ammunition with me. After oiling and cleaning both guns, I shoved them in my belt and continued with the inventory. The handcuffs and other tools we used to use to make our guests more forthcoming with their information were as we'd left them. Newspapers from around the time Red had disappeared showed that he had used the cabin as a safe house before disappearing to parts unknown. Shovels, along with bags of lye, were in a storage closet, as was a folded up red-stained canvas painter's tarp. The furniture in the cabin was sparse; a couple of sofas, a card table with some folding chairs around it, and one metal chair with armrests that was bolted to the floor. I closed up the cabin, and after that did some target shooting outside, taking turns with both pistols so I could make sure they were operational and balanced properly. It took a little adjusting of both their sights, but by the time I brought them back into the car with me, they were as good as from the factory.

All told I'd spent no more than two hours at the cabin. By seven o'clock I was off the dirt road, and by nine I was back in Boston. I didn't much feel like being around Danny given his current sad sack attitude, so I first went to one of my other stashes along Columbia Road and found two thousand dollars wrapped in cellophane as expected. Flush with cash in my pocket I headed to one of the strip clubs in Lynn. While the other club patrons were tipping with singles, I used tens which made me an instant favorite among the girls. It was a fun way to blow a grand, especially after all that time in stir. At one point one of the girls must've recognized me from the news because I started catching them out of the corner of my eye whispering to one another and pointing at me. Things got livelier then, with the girls working even harder to impress me. After all, I was as much a celebrity as any that were going to walk through those doors that night. One of the girls, a hot Hispanic number with gorgeous red-painted lips, took me into a back room and got down on her knees for me, but it just wasn't happening. I guess Nola had emptied the well the other day, so to speak, and the booze was keeping me from catching my second wind. Anyway, she offered me a blue pill, suggesting that if I took it in a half hour things would be as good as ever and she'd take special care of me then. I accepted the pill, but decided to store it away for later use. I slipped her a couple of hundred dollars for the effort, and left the place.

It was past one when I got back to Danny's apartment. I was hoping that he'd be asleep, but he was camped out on the sofa with a mostly empty bottle of Jack Daniel's by his side. He gave me an empty stare and asked how my errands went.

'As well as could be expected. Ah fuck, don't tell me you've just been sitting here alone all night?'

'I'm worried about her, Kyle,' he told me, not even hearing what I said. 'I tried calling all Eve's friends. Nobody knows where she is. What if something's happened to her?'

'What the fuck do you think they'd tell you? Your girlfriend's trying to teach you a lesson and get you back in line like the little puppy dog she thought she had. None of her friends are going to tell you shit about where she is.'

Danny hung his head, a look of despair taking over his face. 'I don't know,' he said.

It was depressing being with him. Just when I thought I had the old Danny back, look what the fuck I was stuck with. With the help of Nola and her blonde friend hopefully I'd bring back the old Danny for good, but for the time being I didn't even want to look at him. Still, I asked if he got himself fired from his job. He shook his head, told me not yet.

I was thoroughly disgusted. 'What are you waiting for?'

'I wasn't feeling up to it. I don't know, I keep thinking something happened to Eve. Maybe I should be calling the hospitals?'

I squeezed my eyes hard with my thumb and index finger and muttered under my breath, 'Maybe you should quit acting like a dope.' I felt exhausted just thinking about the way he was moping around. I let out a heavy sigh and told him to go get some sleep. 'She's fine. She's just playing you, Danny, that's all. We'll talk more in the morning, but you're going to have to start acting like you've got some brains in your head. And you have to get yourself fired from that job. Monday, okay? We're running out of time.'

Danny gave me a hard drunken stare, the type you'd see in any bar right before punches are thrown. The moment passed. With his mouth showing all his imagined hurt, he said, 'What a fucking asshole for a brother I ended up with. All I was looking for from you was a little compassion. Go fuck yourself. And give me my car keys.'

'What for?'

He got to his feet, listing badly as he tried to maintain his balance.

'I said give them to me.'

'You're going to start driving around looking for her? Danny, you can barely stand. Just sleep it off, okay?'

'You better fucking give them to me.'

I sighed, nodding to him. 'I'm dead on my feet here, but I'll drive you around wherever you want to go. We'll both be wasting our time, but at least I'll keep you from killing yourself.'

'I don't want your fucking help. It's your fault Eve left. I can't fucking believe I let you stay here. Your last warning, bro, give me my keys now before I take them from you!'

He was giving me that same drunken belligerent stare from before. Slowly, though, his eyes shifted towards my belt, and from the way his jaw muscles hardened there was no doubt that he figured out what I had tucked under my shirt. His eyes dulled as he thought about making a grab for one of the guns. I had two choices: either engage my little brother in an all-out brawl or give him his keys. I debated both before handing him the keys. His eyes shrunk as he gave me one last hard look, then he brushed past me making his way to the door, his body weaving like a punch-drunk boxer. The door slammed hard behind him, and I could hear him cursing me out as he staggered down the back steps. I took his place on the sofa and wondered what the hell I was going to do with him. I wondered if I'd lost the old Danny for good.

Chapter 7

Like every other night for the past eight years, I had a restless time of it. A cell mate of mine at Leavenworth claimed it was due to a guilty conscience. I told him he didn't know shit and if he cared about his health he'd better keep his opinions to himself. We didn't say another word to each other over the next fourteen months. Even when he was being discharged and escorted out by the corrections officers he kept his mouth shut.

What troubled me the most that night was thinking about Danny, wondering whether I could still count on him. Yeah, I still jerked awake enraged whenever thoughts of Red snuck in, and it bothered me thinking how much of a ghost Kevin Flannery had become, but most of my tossing and turning was due to Danny.

By four in the morning I gave up any thought of sleep. I tried vegging in front of the TV, but by six o'clock I was pacing the apartment. I decided the only chance I had was moving things up a week. I'd be rushing the job, but I decided it was the only shot I had. Once Danny's titless wonder of a girlfriend came back – and she was coming back, there was no doubt in my mind that like a bad case of herpes she'd be showing up again – she'd have Danny wrapped so tightly around her little finger that any prospect of pulling off the job with him would be a pipe dream. I had to get the job done before that happened. Thinking about that just made me pace harder. I waited until eight, then called Lorentz and Timmy Dunn. Lorentz sounded concerned when I told him I needed to move things up a week. He was afraid that I was rushing the job and wanted to know whether I was sure I could get everything together by then. I lied and assured him it would be a piece of cake. He sounded like he didn't quite believe me, but he didn't push it, and told me we'd shoot for Wednesday then, that he'd be in touch. Dunn was willing to push up the delivery for an extra five hundred. We agreed and set up a new time and place to meet.

I kicked around for another hour after that, and after still no sign of Danny, I left the apartment and took a walk around the neighborhood. What struck me about the area was how dirty it was, as if there was no pride. The sidewalks were littered with garbage, as were the gutters. There just seemed to be no sense of community to the place. Growing up in Southie everyone knew everyone else, and knew everybody else's business. If someone from outside the neighborhood came in it would draw stares. People I walked past in Danny's new neighborhood barely even noticed me, and most went out of their way to avoid eye contact.

I found a small local market to buy some groceries. The prices in the place were jacked sky high, and when I mentioned it to the girl working the counter, she mumbled some indecipherable gibberish back to me without ever once looking up to see who she was talking to. Staring at her, I could feel the heat rising off my neck. The store was empty other than the two of us, and I thought long and hard about cracking her upside the head and emptying the cash register, but decided not to let my emotion get the better of me. Before leaving, I suggested to her that she buy some lottery tickets, that today was her lucky day. She gave me a look then as if she were wondering whether I was some kind of idiot.

When I got back to Danny's apartment, I put on a pot of coffee, which was going to make my third that morning, then went through the day's *Globe* before starting breakfast. It didn't surprise me when I found an obituary for the guy we mugged in the South End. I saw the way his skull crumpled in when Danny clocked him with the brick. The police were ruling it an accidental death, with the thought being that he tripped and hit his head fatally on the sidewalk pavement. That was one of the tricks I learned from Red, if you hit someone flush with a brick, it leaves the same mark as if they banged their head off of a cement sidewalk. I found a small side story how his widowed wife thought someone must've seen her husband after he fell and ran off with his laptop computer, and how awful she thought that was. She was pleading for whoever did something like that to step forward and return his computer. Jesus, the fantasy world some people live in.

I was frying up ham slices and was just getting ready to break some eggs for scrambling when Danny walked in. He looked about as bad as you'd expect, his hair dirty and matted with sweat, his eyes sunken and buried under dark circles and his skin color pale to the point of showing shades of green. He spotted the coffee I had brewed, and without a word to me poured himself a cup. I asked if he wanted some scrambled eggs and ham, and he nodded. I mixed in a few more eggs, and after the food was ready I divvied it up onto two plates.

We sat at the small butcher block table that was set up outside the kitchen and ate quietly. Danny was halfway done with his food before he acknowledged the other night. 'I was drunk on a quart of Jack Daniel's, bro,' he said. 'I wasn't thinking too clearly. I said some things I shouldn't have. Things I didn't mean.'

'Any luck finding her?'

He shook his head, showed me a sheepish grin. 'Fuck, was I a mess last night. I drove around pounding on doors like a lunatic, and none of her friends were too happy about it. None of them would tell me shit, except when they threatened to call the cops on me if I didn't shut up. I'm not even sure I got all the addresses right. Around four I settled back in my car and closed my eyes to take a short nap. I didn't wake up until a half hour ago when some guy knocked on my window to make sure I wasn't dead in there.'

'You're lucky the cops didn't run you in.'

He shrugged at that, and picked up his fork and continued chewing half-heartedly on his scrambled eggs.

I waited until we both finished our breakfast, then asked, 'What about your girlfriend?'

'What do you mean?'

'Are you going to keep acting like an asshole?'

He shook his head, half-grimacing, said, 'Come on, bro, that's not fair. I was drunk out of my mind last night.'

'Danny, you've got to make her be the one to come crawling back, otherwise you're lost, little brother. She'll have you by your short hairs for the duration.'

'Excuse me, bro, if I don't take any relationship advice from you too seriously.'

I lit a cig and held the smoke in as I considered him. He tried grinning back at me but had trouble meeting my stare.

'The job's been moved up to this Wednesday,' I said. 'I have to know if I can still count on you, 'cause Danny, I'm having some serious doubts.'

A shadow fell over his eyes as they shifted upwards to hold steady on mine.

'For two mil you can count on me,' he said, the hurt once again showing on his mouth.

'And you're going to lose your job Monday.'

'Yeah.'

'Alright then,' I said, as if the issue was settled. In my mind it wasn't, but I was willing to give him the benefit of the doubt. I got up and took one of the handguns out of the hallway closet where I hid them, and tossed it to Danny. He tested the gun in his hand for balance, then snapped out the magazine, and after making sure there were no bullets left in the chamber, squeezed the trigger slowly so he could test its action. He slid the magazine back in place and handed the gun to me so I could hide it again.

'Why do we need guns for this?' he asked. 'It's supposed to be a quick snatch, right? No one gets hurt, right? That's what you've been telling me.'

'That's the plan, and I'm hoping we don't have to use them, but any job you go on you have to be prepared for the worst. I shouldn't have to be telling you this.'

'The kid doesn't get hurt. That's the deal.'

'That's the deal,' I agreed.

Danny accepted that. He was smelling kind of ripe, so I suggested he take a shower and clean off while I did the dishes, and he nodded and trudged off to the bathroom. As I scrubbed the frying pan and then the plates and utensils, I was feeling better about things. Wednesday was only four days away. If I could keep Danny from going crazy again worrying about that titless wonder of his, I should be able to keep him together enough to do the job. After that with two mil behind him, I knew I wouldn't have to worry about him. Whatever hold she had on him would be history. That type of money has a way of opening people's eyes wide and clear.

When I finished with the dishes I sat on the sofa and closed my eyes and played out the kidnapping in my head. At this point I had all the details worked out. As long as the kid and his family stayed on the same schedule they'd been on, it should work fine. The trick was having the kid alone in the house. That way no one would get hurt, and there'd be no reason for the feds to be called in. An eight-million-dollar payoff would still leave the parents with more than enough money to do whatever the fuck they wanted for several lifetimes. As long as no one acted stupidly there'd be no reason for anyone to get hurt.

It was a relief knowing Red's cabin was still standing, and even more, that no one had discovered it yet. Not that there was much chance that that would have happened, but it was key that the cabin was isolated and unknown to the rest of the world. The ransom payoff was also key, and without wanting to sound too full of myself what I came up with was close to genius. There was no reason why the kidnapping wouldn't go off like clockwork. As long as Danny could hold it together until Wednesday. And as long as the kid and his family stayed on the same schedule...

Danny looked better after he had cleaned up and put on some new clothing. The two of us decided to take it easy that day. Shoot some pool, drink some beers, and for the most part hang loose. I didn't tell him about Nola and her friend coming later for dinner. I figured I would leave that as a surprise.

The pool hall Danny took me to was around the corner from Fenway Park, and it was night and day's difference from the back room of O'Callaghan's bar where we used to play. Here it had the feel of some kind of posh private club with maybe a hundred tables, all nine-foot jobs with the felt looking new and stretched tight across the slate. You could've held a tournament in the place. And the girls waitressing the tables, Jesus! Each one of them gorgeous, all wearing the same style micro-mini shorts, and T-shirts so tight they looked like they would bust loose right out of them. At O'Callaghan's, you had a typical six-foot bar-sized table with the felt loose enough that you could scrunch up a handful of it. And Peggy who waitressed there, you wouldn't want to see her in those type of shorts, at least not unless you were trying to cure yourself of a bad case of hiccups. Back in the days when we'd hang out there she was close to sixty with biceps almost as thick as mine.

I hadn't picked up a stick in years and wasn't used to that size table or one in that good a condition, and Danny kicked my ass. We were playing nine-ball which can give any shmoe a chance, so I got lucky in a couple of games, but Danny still took me ten games for every one I pulled off. It lifted his spirits to kick my ass like that, so it was worth it. Around five in the afternoon I told him we should be heading back to the apartment, that I was going to be cooking him Ma's lamb stew for dinner. I leaned in close and asked if the guy he was scoring weed from could score us some coke, maybe a couple of grams.

He gave me an amused look. 'I thought you didn't do that shit?'

'What the fuck, one night.'

Danny was still smiling at me as he took out his cell phone and made a quick call. He nodded to me when he got off. On the way back to his apartment, he double-parked in front of an apartment building a half-dozen blocks from where he was living. I gave him two hundred dollars and he went in to make the purchase. While I waited for him a little girl, maybe no older than four, rode her big wheels up to the curb and stared intently at me. For the love of God, I couldn't see any parents around and I couldn't imagine letting something that tiny out alone in that neighborhood. I tried asking her where her mommy was, but she just kept staring at me. After a minute or so more of our staring contest, I stuck my tongue out at her. Her eyes narrowed into a look of inscrutable fury, and then she returned the favor before riding off, her wire-thin legs pumping like crazy on the pedals.

When Danny came back out of the building, he gave me a dead-eyed stare to let me know things went as expected. Later we made a quick stop at a liquor store, and then back to his apartment.

By seven I had the lamb stew simmering with the aroma of it filling the apartment. The only alteration I made to Ma's recipe was adding several bottles of Guinness to it. As I stood there breathing in the smell, it made me think of Ma, and I started feeling a bit nostalgic. From where I was standing I could see Danny in the living room as he sat slumped on the sofa nursing a bottle of Guinness. I guess he'd been hopeful that his girlfriend would be waiting for us when we returned, and his mood just seemed to be souring by the minute. I didn't want to do any of the coke until Nola and her friend showed up, but in an effort to shake Danny out of moodiness the two of us did a couple of lines each. It didn't help any, he brooded more than ever after that. When the intercom buzzed at twenty past seven his eyes jerked towards mine, his face frozen with anticipation.

'Maybe that's about Eve?' he said.

I shook my head. 'I invited a couple of friends over.'

'Who?'

'Relax. I'm not violating your plea agreement. It's a surprise, okay?'

I buzzed open the lobby door, and while I waited for the girls I found the blue pill that I had stored away from the other night and washed it down with some Guinness.

Danny had been watching me, and when he saw the blue pill his lips pulled back into a hard grin that showed teeth.

'I should've figured that's why you wanted the coke. What did you do, bro, invite a couple of strippers to come over? You're really trying to fuck me up with Eve, huh? Nothing's changed between her and me, and I'm not going to start banging some stripper.'

I gave him a couple of light brotherly slaps along his jawbone.

'Danny, first off these aren't strippers. Second, while you're moping around like some lovesick dope, your girlfriend right now is probably boning one of her old boyfriends. Chrissakes, we're only talking one night here, and when you see these two you're going to be thanking me. Just don't embarrass me.'

'Eve's not with an old boyfriend.'

'How do you know?'

He opened his mouth to answer me, but couldn't come up with anything.

'Just have fun tonight, okay, Danny?' I said. 'All I'm talking about right now is some dinner, a few drinks, a few lines. See where it leads. If you don't want it to go any further, then don't. But just give yourself a break here.'

Danny moved off to the side, a darkness muddling his face. He nodded. 'Sure, bro, we'll have some fun,' he said without too much enthusiasm.

Nola and her friend were outside the door knocking. I let them in, and they were both breathtaking. Nola had on a sleeveless belly shirt and a pair of micro-mini shorts that would've made the waitresses at the pool hall we'd just left blush. The pumps she wore did a nice job of accentuating her calves, and for the first time I noticed the rose tattoo along her ankle. Her friend, who Nola introduced as Sheila Fenn, was the same blonde from Scolley's, and while she may not have had such an obvious *please rip my clothes off and fuck me* sign on as Nola, she was dressed just as much to excite, in a skirt that went maybe a third of the way to her knees and a shirt that looked painted on. After short introductions, Nola wrapped her arms around my neck and kissed me intensely as she pressed her body hard into mine so I could feel every curve and every point of it. Either the cocaine or the blue pill had started to do its job, and Nola's eyes flashed as she felt the hardness down there. There was a question in her eyes, and I shook my head and whispered to her don't even think it, that she'd have to wait until later.

We all went into the living room where we took turns doing lines. When Nola's turn came, she hesitated, but she did hers like the rest of us. Laughing at the sight of it, I licked some residue off the tip of her nose. After that we had a few drinks while the lamb stew continued to simmer. I had bought Coronas and lime for them, along with a bottle of Tequila, but they wanted to drink the same as Danny and me – Guinness with shots of Irish whiskey. I could tell both girls found the apartment a dive, but that only seemed to add to the excitement of being with a couple of dangerous mobsters, both of their faces showing a jittery nervousness. As we sat enjoying our drinks, Nola moved close enough to me that she was halfway up my lap. Sheila was also flush up against Danny, and he didn't seem to mind when she rested her hand casually on his thigh. He tried to hide it, but I could see the hunger in his eyes when he caught glimpses of her tanned and gorgeous legs.

It didn't take long before they asked about Red Mahoney. Nola started it off, asking if I knew where he was, or better yet, if he was even still alive. I gave her my stock answer, that if I knew where he was he wouldn't still be alive. Sheila was next, asking what Red was really like.

I smiled at her. Jesus, I found her attractive with her little overbite and all those tiny faded freckles scattered along her nose and under her eyes. But I had to get those thoughts out of my mind. She was there for Danny, and I'd have to be satisfied with what I had.

'I used to think the man could walk on water,' I said. 'Christ, was I wrong. The honest truth. He's nothing but a scumbag who conned us all.'

'Were you really his right-hand man like the papers said?'

I nodded. 'Yeah, before he set me up for an armed robbery bust. But I don't want to talk about those days.'

'Why?'

'You wouldn't like my answer.'

'Go on, try me,' Sheila said, her piercing blue eyes challenging me.

Danny let out a laugh. Both Nola and Sheila looked over at him, curious, and he gave them the type of harsh open-mouthed grin that you might catch on a rattlesnake before it strikes. He told them how if I got careless and let something slip that I'd have to spend the night looking for a place to bury the two of them.

I don't know what the fuck he was trying to do, whether he was just trying to be a prick or scare them away, but whatever he was attempting it didn't work. All he did was make the two of them hotter. I could see it in Sheila's eyes, and I could feel the heat coming off Nola as she moved closer. I made a feeble joke about how I'd find a more creative way to keep them both quiet, then told the girls to sit back and enjoy their drinks while I checked on dinner. As I went to the kitchen, I eyeballed Danny to join me.

'What the fuck was that?' I asked when we were alone.

'I don't know. It just came out.' He pushed his hand through his hair, leaving it sticking up. 'I guess I was just trying to shut them up from talking about Mahoney. One of the nice things about moving out of Southie is not having to hear anything about that cocksucker. Nola's the same girl from that clothing store that you banged?'

'Who said anything about banging her?'

'Come on, she's the same one, right? The one you had that business card from?'

'Yeah.'

'So they're not hookers?'

I couldn't help laughing at that. 'Nope. They're here because they want to be here.'

'Then what the fuck is it with them?' he asked.

He looked perturbed. I handed him my comb and told him to fix his hair. While he did that, I told him how those two get turned on being with bad boy Irish mobsters. Keeping my voice low so there'd be no chance of Nola and Sheila hearing, I said, 'The more dangerous the guy, the more turned on they get. Joe Whalley told me how they routinely troll for bad boys at Scolley's. So far they've only been getting bottom-feeders like Tom Dunleavy, with us they're getting the real deal.'

Danny absorbed that, asked, 'They're just freaks then?'

'A bit harsh, but yeah, that about sums it up. They're not alone, though. You wouldn't believe the letters I got in prison from chicks wanting to marry me, some of them as hot as these two. And the pictures they sent me. Jesus. But fuck it, if rock stars and big Hollywood muckamucks can have their groupies, why not us? Anyway, grab some plates and I'll bring out the stew.'

When we came out of the galley kitchen, the girls asked if they could help set the table, and I told them to just relax and conserve their energy for later. At this point what I had in my pants was rock hard and I just wanted to finish dinner so we could get down to business. As Danny and I set the table, I told the girls that they were in for a treat, that my ma's lamb stew recipe was known throughout Southie and has been a closely guarded family secret for over a hundred years, that even his holiness, Red Mahoney, came knocking a few times when we were kids to join us for Sunday dinner when Ma had the stew cooking.

With the big pot of stew centered on the table, we all took our seats. I have to admit, I would've made Ma proud. With the added Guinness, the stew was even better than I remembered. I wish I could have bought a nice loaf of Irish soda bread, but they didn't have any at the grocery store I stopped in, so I had to settle for rye. Still, the dinner was a big hit. While we ate I told a few stories of when Danny and I were kids, just some penny ante stuff, nothing that could come back to us, but the girls were eating it up as much as the stew. After dinner we took it back to the sofa.

First thing, we each did one more line to get the juices flowing. I settled back on the sofa, and Nola was all over me with her tongue driving into my mouth and her hands digging into my pants. I kept her from pulling it out. I mean, Christ, my brother was right next to me, but with the coke and the pill I'd taken,

I was throbbing down there. I kept eyeing Danny, hoping he'd take Sheila back to his bedroom and give Nola and me some privacy. She was on him the same as Nola was on me, but he was only half-hearted at best in the way he was reciprocating. Yeah, he was kissing back and feeling around a little, but I could tell he was slipping into that sullen moodiness of his. To try to keep that from happening, I separated from Nola enough to ask Sheila what proof we really had that she was a blonde. She laughed at that and pulled on a handful of her honey-blonde hair.

'Look at my roots,' she said.

'It doesn't mean anything. You could've had a professional dye job.'

'How about my eyebrows?'

'Same thing. Only one way for you to prove to us you aren't a brunette by nature.'

'It wouldn't do any good,' she said, a shit-eating grin spreading over those beautiful soft lips of hers. 'I had a full Brazilian a few days ago. Nothing down there anymore to prove whether I'm a blonde.'

'I don't believe you. I think you've got a little brown patch growing down there. What do you think, Danny?'

Danny just grunted out something in response, both a sullenness and hard intensity fighting it out over his face.

When I started all this, it was nothing but a lark, and Sheila responded in kind, but as we sat there I could see the subtle change come over her eyes. I could see it in her smile too as she stood up and lowered her skirt and panties to prove that she didn't have a trace of hair down there, blonde or otherwise. Nola let out something that was a combination of a gasp and a laugh. 'Sheila, you slut!' she exclaimed. Danny came to life then, jumping off the sofa making a beeline out the back door. I sat in shock watching him leave, not quite making sense of it until I heard him on the back steps. He was almost down to the street level before I caught up to him. I grabbed him hard by the shoulder, spinning him around and asking him what the fuck he was doing. When he faced me his eyes were resolute.

'What I should've done an hour ago,' he said. 'I love Eve, and I'm not going to start banging other girls, no matter how hot they are. It's all part of growing up, bro. But you know what, I don't have to explain myself to you. You go up there and have fun. I'll find a place to crash for the night.'

I couldn't argue with him the way he was. I watched as he made his way down the rest of the stairs, and then out the building. I went back upstairs. Sheila looked both a little frightened and confused as she stood half naked in the living room. Nola didn't look too happy either.

'Did I do something wrong?' she asked, her voice sounding more like a little girl's.

I shook my head. 'He's got some issues right now,' I told her. She stood awkwardly for a moment, then started to pull her skirt and panties back on. I put an arm around her waist, and without too much effort, guided her back to the sofa. 'No need for that, darling,' I said. 'I'll just have to make up for my little brother.'

Nola's dark eyes were seething. She whispered in my ear, her breath hot against me, 'I'm not sharing you.' I gave her a hard look back in response, letting her know that if she wanted any piece of me that night she was going to have to share. I could tell she didn't like it, but I could also sense some excitement from her about the idea of it. Anyway, she was perceptive enough not to try fighting it, because I would've tossed her ass out the back door if she did. After we finished off what was left of the coke, we went at it. Since Nola was my date – and also what I had building down there wasn't going to go away anytime soon – I let her take her turn first, although I had some of Sheila while I pounded on Nola. Nola, bless her heart, tried wrapping her legs tight around me to keep me from taking my turn with her friend, but I broke free and went at it just as hard with Sheila. The coke and the blue pill left me throbbing all over – not just with the hard brick between my legs, but my head, my chest, my fingers, my toes, everything. It was like I couldn't have enough of them and they couldn't have enough of me – like the rhythm and pounding of the sex just swallowed me up. That pill held up its end of the deal. Or maybe it was the coke. It didn't matter. For hours it was like I was thirteen again and it was past three in the morning before I rolled off Nola for the last time, both girls as spent as I was. I didn't see much point in them spending the night so I said my goodbyes, then after they left, crawled back to the sofa and collapsed dead to the world. I didn't open my eyes again until Monday morning, losing all of Sunday.

To Ed.: I swear to God, this is the only place in the book where I'm taking 'artistic license'. I figure if I can come clean and admit that I left that hot Hispanic stripper working away on nothing more than a limp piece of rigatoni, than I can embellish things a little here so I don't come across like a total schmuck. Up to the point where that crazy fuck Sheila showed us how she was clean as a whistle between the legs, everything happened exactly as I said. After that, though, things went a little different. Mixing the coke and that pill was a bad idea. Doing those last lines left me feeling like my heart was being ripped apart. Fuck, it was embarrassing, both girls screaming like I was dying, and then the EMT workers carting me away to Boston City Hospital with my dick as hard as a piece of oak and pointing straight to the moon. It turned out it was nothing serious and after a day's observation they let me go. Only a handful of people know about this – Nola, her blonde friend, the EMT workers, and a few people at Boston City. So far none of them have said word one about it, and I don't think they're going to. Still, after the shitstorm that hit me smack in the face with my first book, I don't want to see this one crucified over one small exaggeration. If you think there's a chance of this book being given the 'James Frey' treatment because of the above, then take it out. But I don't want what really happened to be mentioned. —K. N.

Chapter 8

Not much happened during the days leading up to the kidnapping. As I mentioned before I was mostly out of it Sunday, and what time Danny came back to the apartment was anyone's guess. When I saw him Monday morning, he had turned mostly surly with his moping around for his girlfriend, and I decided the less I had to do with him until we did the job the better. At least he got himself fired from his job as we agreed. He ended up picking a fight with his supervisor, and when the supervisor tried giving Danny a second chance, Danny, bless his heart, pissed in the guy's coffee mug. That pretty much sealed it. Later that night I met Timmy Dunn at the Revere Mall parking lot. I paid him what I owed him and he handed me a canvas bag with all I ordered. I checked it over quickly and everything was in it. Yeah, I could've gotten all of it myself, but it was better not to have any salespersons out there who could tie me to anything that might end up being reported in the news. And since Timmy stole the stuff himself, there'd be no one to tie him to it. As far as he went, I took it as gospel that he wasn't going to say word one about it to anyone.

After leaving the Revere Mall, I went straight back to Danny's apartment. I was still feeling too shaky from Saturday to want to go to Scolley's for any sort of socializing and drinking. When I got back to Danny's apartment, he was there moping around.

I told him things went well with Timmy Dunn, but he barely acknowledged me. If I wasn't feeling so out of sorts, I might've had it out with him, but instead I just had him move off the sofa so I could call it a night. Even with the stereo blasting and the lights on, I was out before my eyes closed.

Tuesday was more of the same. That morning Danny and I didn't bother saying more than a dozen words to each other. I left him staring sullenly into space, then drove to Southie where I spent most of the day searching out Red's old childhood friends, but none of them knew anything – and with the way I leaned on them, I believed them. I was feeling more like my old self with the shakiness from the other day mostly gone, feeling strong enough to have a few shots and pints at Scolley's where I made some calls trying to chase down Red's younger brother, Tommy. Tommy Mahoney owned one of the biggest auto dealerships in Boston, with all of the early money used to finance it coming from Red. It didn't matter that the money was as dirty as if it had come straight from the sewer and that men had been murdered for it – or for that matter that the dealership had been used for years to launder Red's stream of dirty money – as far as the city of Boston was concerned Tommy Mahoney was a success story. The sonofabitch was even made a board member of Boston's Chamber of Commerce. The guy thought he was a big deal, and in the old days he'd be off limits. But these weren't the old days.

Anyway, it wasn't easy chasing him down, but I eventually got word that he was at a restaurant a few blocks from the State House that was popular with the pols, lobbyists and other insiders; one of those places where beers were eight bucks, mixed drinks started at twenty and state legislators could be had for ten grand and up. When I got there he was still sitting where I was told he'd be, having drinks with a group of business associates with maybe some state senators in the mix for all I knew. Tommy had to be close to his mid-fifties. He looked a lot like how Red used to look, except thicker and with a rounder and softer face. Same slicked-back red hair, and like Red, same rosy color in his cheeks that made you think he used rouge. When he saw me approach he gave me a bland smile as if I were a lackey there to relay a message to him. His smile faded when he recognized me. He froze trying to decide how to play it. His options weren't great. He knew me well enough to know how dangerous I could be and what could happen if he started yelling for the police. Even if he thought he could get away with it, it would mean having to explain me to his friends, and even more awkwardly, how we knew each other. Also, Tommy was never one for a scene. He liked to do things quietly, softly, with as little attention as possible. He ended up excusing himself from the table. As he got next to me, he grabbed me by the arm and tried to steer me away. I let him walk me away from the table before I shook him loose.

'I wouldn't recommend touching me again,' I said. 'Not unless you want to lose your hand.'

'Are you looking to go back to prison?' he asked.

'No, not at all.'

'Then my advice is for you to leave quietly,' he said sternly, his voice low while his eyes darted from left to right to see who was watching us. 'It would be awfully messy if the police were called.'

'More for you than for me,' I said.

He studied me carefully, indecision showing in his pale blue eyes. He could only guess how much I knew about his money dealings with Red.

'You wouldn't go against the code, Kyle,' he said. 'Not with how it would affect your standing in the neighborhood.'

'Guess what? I couldn't care less about the old neighborhood,' I said. 'Not after what your brother did to it. You want to test me, Tommy, go right ahead.'

His eyes again darted left to right. Sweat was building on his upper lip and along his forehead. 'What do you want?'

'To talk with you.'

'I'm not leaving here alone with you, Kyle.'

'We'll find a private booth then.'

He nodded, some relief showing on his face. He must've thought that I was there to kill him, not that the idea hadn't crossed my mind. There weren't too many funerals Red would show up for, but there was a chance he'd try to find a way to attend his beloved brother's, in disguise of course. Even if Tommy's death didn't flush Red out, it would hurt him deeply. Taking care of Tommy was one of the things I was considering, but now wasn't the time for it.

Tommy first went back to his table to explain his absence, then to the maitre d', and after that we were shown to a private booth. No one else was sitting close enough to overhear us.

'What do you want?' he demanded, some boldness back in his voice.

'First, why don't you buy me one of those twenty-dollar martinis? I'm curious about them. And while you're at it, a tenderloin steak, rare.'

'Kyle, I don't have time for this. I really have to be getting back to my table. Why don't you just say what you came here to say.'

I shook my head. 'Sorry, Tommy. Because of your dear brother I lost eight years of my life, and quite a bit more than that to be honest. We're going to do things the way I want to do them. The quicker you order me a drink and steak, the quicker you can get back to your friends.'

Again, I could see him considering his options before he waved over a waiter and ordered me a martini and tenderloin, along with a double scotch for himself. He waited until the waiter was out of earshot, and then again asked me what I wanted.

'Relax,' I said. 'I'll tell you after I get my food.'

He sat fidgeting, losing his patience.

'If you think you're going to shake me down, you must know that I have enough on you to send you back to prison.'

'You'd make your rat bastard of a brother proud if you did,' I said. 'And who knows, maybe the two of us could end up as cell mates. Nothing that I would enjoy more.'

Whatever rosy color had been left in his cheeks had long since bled out. He opened his mouth to argue with me, but I held up a finger warning him to be quiet, and he complied.

Our drinks came quickly, but I didn't touch my martini and he didn't touch his scotch. We just sat staring at each other while we waited for my steak. As we waited, his face turned red with forced indignation.

'Whatever you think you're trying to pull here—'

'Shut up,' I ordered.

He closed his mouth. Eventually my steak came out. I took a few bites of it, then sampled the martini.

'Forty bucks for this steak, huh? A waste of money. I can get better on West Broadway for half the price.'

'What the fuck do you want?'

I gave him a hard dead-eyed stare. He tried to match it but his eyes wavered.

'You know what I want.'

'I have no idea where my brother is,' he said.

'Bullshit.'

'It's true, Kyle. The FBI's been watching me for years. I can't afford any contact with my brother. He knows that as well as I do. Red has made no attempts to contact me since he left.'

'You're lying to me, Tommy,' I said. 'I know the two of you, and I know you must be funneling him money.'

'I'm not, Kyle. I swear on my mother's grave. Red was well-prepared financially for what he did. You know him, you know how he plans out every little detail of what he does. He knew the

FBI would be watching for any money transfers from me. If you insist, I'll open my books to you.'

He was lying. I knew he was lying. I took a few more bites of my steak and chewed it slowly.

'I'm going to find Red,' I said. 'There's not a chance in the world I won't. I don't care where the fuck he is, I'm going to find him. When I do, I'm going to take my time with him. I'm going to make him tell me everything, Tommy. I'll find out if you've had any contact with him since he went into hiding. This is your one chance to come clean with me about it, because if he ends up ratting you out I'll find a way to take you someplace quiet and do exactly to you what I'm going to do to him. Do you think I'm lying about that?'

He almost told me something then. I could see it in his eyes as he almost ratted out his own flesh and blood, but I guess everyone has their limits and that was his. All color drained from his face, and as he faced me he looked as lifeless as a mannequin.

'Kyle, now that you're out of prison you have an opportunity to make a new life for yourself, something good, something you can be proud of, but this bitterness driving you is only going to lead to destruction. Maybe you'll find my brother, maybe you won't, but if you do you'll be no better off for it.' He paused, his eyes faltering as he tried to look at me. With an artificial benevolence, he continued, 'I'm willing to help you. I'm offering you a job right now as a salesperson at my BMW dealership, which is a plum position. With your toughness and persuasiveness you could easily earn two hundred thousand your first year. What do you say?'

I pushed my steak away. My hands were shaking I was so angry. 'What do I say? How about go fuck yourself. Your business was built on money made by me and Kevin Flannery and dozens others just like us, and you're going to sit here and lecture to me and act as if you're worth two shits? Maybe someday I'll take you up to your brother's cabin and show you first-hand the types of things we did up there so you could have the money to buy this business of yours you're so fucking proud of.'

He had turned ashen. He dropped a hundred dollar bill on the table, then sucked in his gut and pushed himself out of the booth. He hesitated before walking away, then forced himself to meet my stare, his mouth grim and his blue eyes like steel. For that moment he could've been his older brother.

'It would be a mistake for you to try to see me again,' he said. 'If you think I don't have the resources to take care of the likes of you if need be, then you are sorely mistaken.'

I sat thinking about him and Red after he left. He'd been in contact with Red, there was no doubt about that. How much he knew was another question. There were two ways that I could see to play this – either use him to flush Red out of hiding, or coerce Tommy to spill whatever information he had. After a while of spinning my wheels I decided to wait until later to make a decision. I had too much on my plate as it was with the kidnapping. Tommy Mahoney could wait, and as far as his threat went it was meaningless. The next time I saw him, he wouldn't know about it until it was too late.

On the way back to Danny's, I stopped off and bought a hibachi grill, along with some charcoals, chicken pieces to barbecue, and a couple of six packs of Michelob Light. If things worked out as planned we were going to have a busy day on Wednesday and I didn't want either of us getting hung-over, but I wanted to try to lighten the mood. Danny was sitting alone on the sofa when I got back. He looked as sour as he had when I left.

'You haven't been sitting here all day, have you?'

He shrugged. 'I had nothing better to do.'

'I bought some stuff to barbecue chicken. How about we get started?'

I expected an argument out of him, but he surprised me and

agreed to it. It took several trips up and down the three flights of stairs but eventually we had things set up in the parking lot with the chicken barbecuing and the two of us sitting on beach chairs with a cooler of Michelob Lights between us. As the chicken cooked, a few of Danny's neighbors returned from work and stopped to chat with us. I tossed them Michelobs and shared the potato chips and some other snacks I brought. With the way they were introducing themselves to Danny, I don't think any of them had a clue who either of us were. It was as if we just a couple of normal guys. I invited them to bring hotdogs or whatever else they wanted grilled, and I would put it on the hibachi. A couple of them took me up on my offer, bringing down their own beach chairs and food. During one of the brief moments Danny and I were alone, I made a comment that it seemed as if he were meeting his neighbors for the first time.

He shrugged, said, 'Eve's got her circle of friends from work and college and isn't into socializing with people from the building, so I guess I haven't been either.'

It was hard to believe Danny living like that. In the old days he was as well-liked as any in the neighborhood. Jesus, his girlfriend had done a number on him. Anyway, the party grew over the next few hours with maybe a dozen of Danny's fellow renters joining in. Several beer runs were made, and a couple of girls who lived above Danny brought down pitchers of homemade sangria, but Danny and I watched how much we drank and mostly stuck with the beer. The chicken came out about as well as I could've hoped, and it turned into a nice evening where I was sampling chorizo sausage, monkfish and a few other things that I had never tried before that people had brought down. For a few moments I even forgot about Red. These moments didn't last long, they never did, but it was nice to get him out of my head for a few minutes. After the party died down Danny and I stayed on the beach chairs and just sat deep in our own thoughts as we stared up at the sky. It would've been nice if we could've seen some stars, but there was too much haze in the air. Around midnight I suggested we get some sleep, that we had a long day ahead of us. Danny didn't bother arguing, and the two of us headed back upstairs.

I didn't sleep that night, my mind racing too much with thoughts of Red and his beloved brother, Tommy. Around three I gave up trying. I sat for a couple of hours lighting one cig after the next, then at five o'clock I headed to Logan Airport so I could take a couple of license plates off cars from the Central Parking lot. The guy working the gate seemed suspicious that I was paying for only ten minutes of parking, but he took my two dollars and didn't ask any questions. When I got back I walked around Danny's neighborhood looking in apartment building lobbies until I found what I needed. By six o'clock I was back in the apartment cooking breakfast, and twenty minutes later I had Danny out of bed and joining me for ham and cheese omelets and fresh-brewed coffee.

He seemed more his old self than he had in days. I don't know whether it was relaxing the night before at the barbecue or being able to gear himself up for what was coming or simply not having time to mope around, but whatever was behind his attitude change I was glad to see it. By seven o'clock we were out the door and heading towards Malden.

One of the items I had bought from Timmy Dunn was the address of an older model van for us to steal and dispose of in a manner in which it wasn't going to be recovered. The owner wanted it stolen for the insurance – most likely his claim would have it loaded with expensive items, all of which I'm sure he'd have receipts for. He paid a guy who paid Timmy to have it done, so Timmy was making money from both ends, but hell, you can't blame someone for being enterprising. Me, I needed an older model van because I needed to be able to boost it without the key

– these days the newer ignition systems are almost impossible to hot-wire.

The van was where it was supposed to be. The doors were unlocked, and while I used a screwdriver to pull out the ignition wires, Danny exchanged license plates with one I had taken earlier from Logan. Less than a minute later we were ready to go. I took off in the van while Danny followed behind in his Honda. We drove out to the Nashua Mall, about thirty miles from where the kidnapping was going to take place. While I sat in the driver's seat, Danny transported what he needed to the back of the van. Then he took the passenger seat.

I checked my watch. We had less than an hour before we'd find out if the kid and his family were sticking to the same schedule they'd been on for the past month. Wednesdays had the kid staying at home in the morning while the mother took off at ten for either a yoga or aerobics class, at least that was Lorentz's guess based on how she dressed. From what Lorentz was able to figure out, the dad still worked. The guy cashes in thirty million dollars and he's still on the job. It takes all kinds.

I gave Danny a quick look and asked him if he was ready.

'For two mil, yeah, I'm ready.'

I swung the van out and headed back to Massachusetts. Thirty-five minutes later I pulled into a small nature preserve off the Assabet River, maybe ten miles from the kid's house. The nature preserve was for shit like canoeing and kayaking, and its small dirt parking lot could hold maybe a dozen cars. Danny and I were the only ones there. We sat and waited, both of us as quiet as stone. It was a half hour later when I got the call from Lorentz that we were on. Danny went into the back of the van to change into his UPS uniform, then I took my turn. Fifteen minutes later I was pulling into the kid's driveway. The street the family lived on was sparsely populated and had kind of a country feel to it. Before it got developed the land was probably used for farming.

Most of the houses there were small and fairly modest, but the one the kid lived in was like some weird three-dimensional jigsaw puzzle gone awry, as if they kept adding additions to the house without any thought as to how everything would fit. Anyway, the house stood out on the street like a sore thumb. I pulled the van in close enough to the side entrance that Lorentz and the other landscapers working three houses over wouldn't be able to see what was going to happen.

Danny and I both put on rubber George W. Bush masks, then pulled our Boston Red Sox caps down low and added sunglasses. The masks were actually pretty realistic looking, at least realistic enough that if you got a quick look at either of us through a window or a door peephole you wouldn't realize we were wearing masks. According to Lorentz the family had an Audi and a Mercedes SUV. Before going to the side door, I checked the garage to make sure both cars were gone. I had the delivery package that I had taken from Danny's neighborhood in one hand, a rag balled up in my other. I waited until Danny was hiding in the bushes to the side of the door, then I knocked and announced that I had a delivery.

A minute went by and no answer. I gave Danny a look. Just our luck the kid would be out of the house. I tried it again. Still nothing. I was trying to decide whether we should give the house a search when I heard some movement inside. I tried one more time and the boy told me from inside that his parents didn't want him opening the door to strangers. Christ, this was the suburbs. There was supposed to be some trust here.

'Son, UPS,' I said. 'I need someone to sign for this.'

He had the chain on the door as he opened it a crack. I put my shoulder into the door – hard enough to break the chain off, but not hard enough where the force of the door would do any real damage to the kid. The next second I had the rag in his mouth and was carrying him under one arm back to the van with him struggling like a fish pulled out of the ocean. While I took care of him – wrapping masking tape around his ankles and wrists – Danny ran into the house to leave preliminary instructions. Seconds later I heard the noises from inside the house. It was like a pack of wolves were going after Danny. I rushed inside and found Danny on the floor wrestling with a German Shepherd. The dog was massive, at least a hundred and fifty pounds. It was all fury, teeth and snarls as it went after Danny's throat, while Danny tried to ward it off with his forearm. I hit the damn thing as hard as I could on its skull with the butt of my pistol but all it did was make the beast go after Danny with more ferocity. I hit it again with everything I had, and still nothing. The damn skull must've been as hard as cement. I put the muzzle of the gun against its side and fired until the animal dropped. I helped Danny to his feet. He was breathing hard. His sunglasses had fallen off and his eyes were as hot as coals. I found the glasses and handed them back to him.

'Why the fuck didn't you tell me they had fucking Cujo here?'

'You think I knew they had a dog? Let's get the fuck out of here.'

Danny looked kind of shaky as he ran out of the house. He got in the back of the van with the kid while I pulled out and tried hard to maintain the speed limit. I was checking the rear-view mirror to see if anyone was rushing out after those gunshots, but I didn't see anyone. Before I drove too far I found a quiet spot to change license plates in case any neighbors wrote down the one I was using. Even still, as I got onto Route 3 I was expecting to see a cruiser pull up behind me with its lights flashing, but nothing. Fucking Lorentz. How the fuck could he not tell me about that dog? It took every bit of self control I had to keep the car at a steady pace and not race to Nashua. When I got back to the Nashua Mall, I found Danny's car and pulled up to it. Danny got out of the back of the van wearing his street clothes and moved quickly into his car. He had a makeshift bandage wrapped around his forearm. It was stained through with blood. I got out of the van and tapped on his window, asked him how bad it was.

He was too mad to look in my direction. 'Pretty fucking bad,' he said.

'Did you leave any blood in the house?'

'I don't know.'

It was too late to do anything about it if he did. If Lorentz were there I would've ripped his heart out where he stood. I gave Danny's car door a couple of taps, told him it didn't matter if he did.

'With all the blood left from that dog, I don't see how they could separate it out,' I said. 'Even if they did, unless the FBI has your DNA in their system it won't make any difference. When you took your plea arrangement, you didn't have to give them a DNA sample?'

He shook his head.

'Then it doesn't matter.'

He gave me a look to shut up, and that's what I did. No one was around. I changed quickly into my street clothes, then got back in the van and led the way to Red's cabin. We stopped a half dozen times before we got there, once so I could buy anti-bacterial ointment and bandages to fix up Danny's arm, the other times so we could give the boy water and keep him from dehydrating on us. The bite marks on Danny's arm looked ugly. Fortunately the dog didn't as much tear his flesh as puncture it, but still they looked deep and the wounds just kept bleeding.

'It better not get infected,' he said.

'It's not going to get infected.'

'Shit, I probably need a shot or something.'

We both knew we couldn't see a doctor about this. The FBI would be all over us if we did.

'You'll be fine,' I said.

'How can you say that? That dog sank its teeth into the bone. Fuck knows how much saliva and other shit it got into me. I'm going to lose my arm.'

'You're not going to lose your arm. I cleaned out the wounds with some anti-bacterial shit. You'll be fine.'

I watched to see if blood was going to keep seeping through the cloth bandage wrapped around his forearm. He sat stewing, his lips pressed hard into thin bloodless lines.

'Your buddy didn't mention word one about a dog?' he asked.

'What do you think?'

I needed to wrap another bandage around his wound. He winced as I pulled on it, wrapping the cloth bandage as tight as I could.

'I'm going to cut his fucking arm off,' he said. 'It won't make us even, but it will get us closer.'

I nodded in agreement. I was furious with Lorentz also. How could he check out the house and not know they had a hundred and fifty pound German Shepherd roaming around in it? Before leaving us that surprise I had mostly settled on paying him his cut. Not now, though. I finished up as best I could with Danny and we continued on.

It was an hour after the kidnapping when I got a call from Lorentz as we had prearranged.

'What was with the shooting?' he asked.

'Any of the other landscapers hear it?'

'I don't think so. I was working in front, they were all in back with enough equipment on to cover the shots. At least I hope so. If they heard them, no one's said anything. But maybe one of the neighbors did.'

'The police show up?'

'No.'

'Then no one heard anything.'

'So what was with the shooting?'

'I'll tell you what was with it. They had a full-grown German Shepherd in the house waiting for us. The damn thing nearly tore my brother apart.'

'Fuck. You're kidding me?'

'What do you think?'

'Oh, fuck. Kyle, there was no dog in the house when I checked it over before. No sign of one either.'

I didn't believe him for a second. If he did his job he would've found a food or water dish or something, and Danny and I would've been prepared. But he fucked up and Danny was paying the price, as was I, because that fuck up put us all at risk. But I still needed the cocksucker, so I played along that it was just one of those things.

'Your brother, he's okay?'

'Yeah, he'll live. We'll just have to call him lefty from now on. Did the mom show up?'

'Yeah, about fifteen minutes ago. No police yet. I'll drive by in a couple of hours and see what's going on. The merchandise still in one piece?'

'Still kicking and breathing.'

I got off the phone then. It wasn't going to do us any good for him to call me back in a couple of hours since by then I'd be far outside the range of any cell phone service, but I didn't bother telling him that. Fuck him. I was still working out in my mind how I was going to deal with him when I pulled the van up the dirt path to the cabin with Danny trailing right behind. He held his arm gingerly as he got out of his car. I asked him how his arm was, and he shook his head and told me it hurt like hell.

'I think Cujo also broke a couple of bones.'

Shit. What could I say? We both knew there was nothing we could do unless we found a doctor we could trust, and these days I didn't know any. Fuck it. For two million dollars he could wear a prosthetic arm if he had to.

'I don't know what to tell you. You're just going to have to deal with it for now.'

He nodded, still angry as all hell. He was looking around. 'So this is it, huh?'

'Yeah, this is it. Let me set things up, then we'll take him inside.'

I took care of business inside the cabin, turning on the generator, stuff like that. The cloth painter's tarp had been cut in the middle so it could be pulled over the metal chair bolted to the floor. As I did this, Danny asked me why we needed the tarp.

'We probably don't. Just an old habit. Let's go get the kid.'

He gave me a wary look, but he didn't fight me on the tarp. Before getting the kid we put our disguises back on, then the two of us carried him from the van to the cabin and set him down in the metal chair. I ended up using masking tape to secure his hands to the armrests since his wrists were too small for handcuffs. There wasn't much to the kid, probably less than five feet tall and eighty pounds. Thin enough that it looked like you could break him in two like a stick if you wanted. He trembled as he stared at us, his eyes huge, his skin color unnaturally pale – almost like he'd been dipped in wax. I wanted to get this over with quickly. I went back to the van, got the camcorder out of the canvas sack that Timmy Dunn had given me and returned back to the cabin. Danny was standing holding his injured arm, looking away from the kid. I went over to the kid and told him what he was going to say to the camera. He acknowledged me with a scared nod and I took the gag out of his mouth. When I put the camera on him he started stammering out some gibberish.

'Say what I told you to or I'm putting that gag back in!'

In a weak faltering voice he stammered out most of what I had told him to say.

'Please, please, I–I'm—'

'Shut up,' I ordered.

I gave the camera to Danny and told him he needed to videotape what was coming next.

'What are you talking about?' he asked.

I didn't answer him. I went over to the *drawer of persuasion* as Red used to like to call it and took out a pair of pliers.

'What the fuck are you doing?' he demanded.

'It's either a tooth or a finger. Your choice.'

'Bullshit. We had a deal.' He put the camera down. 'I'm not letting you do this.'

I grabbed Danny by his injured arm so he wouldn't be able to fight me, and dragged him out of the cabin. I let go of his arm and he bent over cradling it, in too much pain to talk. When he could he told me if I ever did something like that again he'd kill me.

'Look, you want to collect your two mil? We need to impart real fear in the parents. They need to be convinced that if they don't pay their kid is dead. That's not going to happen with him only stammering out what he did.'

'We…had…a…deal!'

'Yeah, well, as long as the parents pay the kid's going to be returned back in mostly one piece. So he loses a tooth? Big fucking deal. Maybe they'll replace it with a gold one. It would give him a cool look and maybe help him get laid when he gets older. But if you don't want me pulling a tooth I'll cut a finger off. It's going to be one or the other.'

Danny stood cradling his arm for a long hard minute before giving in and telling me to pull the damn tooth then.

'Make sure to videotape it,' I said. 'I don't want to have to pull a second one.'

We went back in. The boy was blubbering about something, his voice high and breaking apart like a dog whine. I wanted to get it over with quickly. What the fuck was the big deal? When I was eleven I had three teeth knocked out of my own when my dad rapped me in the mouth with a beer bottle. Danny picked up the camera and gave me a nod that he was ready. The boy tried fighting me. It was almost like opening up a clam, but I pried his mouth open and ripped out one of his front teeth. I held the tooth up for the camera.

'He's bleeding a lot,' Danny said.

He was right. It was almost as if someone had opened up a spigot. I found the gauze I had bought earlier and tried pushing it into the open hole, but it didn't do any good. The blood just kept coming. My hands were getting soaked in it as I tried applying pressure to stop the bleeding. If the boy was pale before, now it was like he was a sheet of paper. He had absolutely no color. His eyes fluttered, he made a kind of a gurgling noise, and then I think he died. I couldn't fucking believe it.

'What the fuck happened?' Danny asked.

I ignored him. I found an old towel, wiped my hands off best I could, took off my mask, then left the cabin and lit up one cig after the next. I was on my fourth cig when Danny came out. He had taken his mask off also, his face muddled with fury.

'That kid's dead!'

I shrugged and let the smoke out slowly through my nose.

'We had a deal!'

'I don't know what happened,' I said.

'Fuck you! We had a deal!'

I didn't bother saying anything. What was there to say? For a minute I thought Danny was going to take a swing at me, but I guess he was even too angry for that. He stormed off into the woods. I stood where I was and smoked the rest of the pack, then I went back into the cabin and wrapped the boy up in the tarp. When I was cutting the masking tape off his wrists I saw the bracelet identifying him as a hemophiliac. Sure enough there was a hypodermic needle and medication in the backpack we took off him. I grabbed a shovel and a bag of lime and dug a four foot deep hole a hundred yards away from where the other bodies were buried. When I was done I was sweating all over. I stood catching my breath for a minute, then went back to the cabin and carried the tarp and what was rolled up inside of it to the hole and placed it inside of it. I stripped myself of the bloody clothing I had on and tossed that in the hole also, along with the backpack and the rubber masks that we used. After spreading a bag of lime over all that, I filled the hole and spread around the rest of the loose dirt. There was a stream a couple of hundred yards away. The mosquitoes made a buffet out of me, but I ignored them and washed the kid's blood off me. Fortunately I was thinking ahead and had brought a change of clothing along. When I went back to the cabin I sat outside on a tree stump and ate the turkey sandwich that I had brought to feed the kid, then found a fresh pack of cigs and smoked them until Danny came back.

He hadn't cooled off much, if at all. He stood next to me steaming. I kept smoking my cig.

'You promised me we weren't going to hurt him,' he said.

'What do you want me to say? Shit happens.'

'Shit happens, huh? We killed a kid, God damn you!'

'Chrissakes, Danny, he's not the first person you killed, is he?'

He stared at me as if I had grown horns. 'Anyone in the past, they were in the game. They were fair target, just as I was. This kid was innocent. How old did you say he was? Ten? Bro, if you don't realize how wrong this is then you're one heartless sonofabitch, and I really feel nothing but pity for you.'

I could've mentioned that the guy's head he cracked open with a brick hadn't been in the game either, but Danny obviously didn't realize that the man had died, and in the state he was in I figured it was better not to bring it up. So I swallowed the comment back, along with a crack for him to save his goddamn pity.

'Kids die all the time,' I said. 'Even younger and more innocent ones than this kid. It's the way the world works. I'm not crying for any of them and I'm certainly not going to cry for this one. Besides, it was an accident.'

'Yeah, fuck it was an accident. You had to use those pliers on him.'

'You think I had any idea he was going to bleed out like that?'

I was starting to get a little hot under the collar also. Danny got quiet after that. I smoked two more cigs before he asked what we were going to do.

'We're going to go on as planned and collect our money.'

I tossed the cig on the ground and stubbed it out with my heel, then got the laptop from Danny's car and brought it back to the cabin. Danny followed me in.

'You took care of the body already?'

'Yeah, why? You wanted to say some words over it?'

He didn't say anything but from the expression on his face I had the idea that that was exactly what he wanted to do. Christ. I ignored him and went to work then, first downloading part of the videotape to the laptop and formatting it as a file that could be included in an email message, then using a multimedia software package to alter the background shown in the video in case there was anything in it that could've helped the FBI figure out the location of the cabin. I also made sure that the only voice present on the video was the kid's. When I was done I played it back a few times. The video ended with the kid pleading for his parents to pay the ransom. There were no shadows or reflections of me or Danny in it. Nothing that could be used to identify us, which was more important now that the two of us were candidates for the federal death penalty.

When I was done and we were walking away from the cabin I was struck with the thought of lighting a match to it. It would've been stupid and rash; a pointless thing to do and it could've easily ended up drawing attention to the cabin and all the bodies buried around it, but the thought still overwhelmed me. I guess the place was just such a goddamned fucking abomination.

I ended up driving back since Danny's arm was bothering him too much. He didn't look too good either, but I didn't feel like talking to him about anything. I was maybe a half hour from Nashua when I got a call from Lorentz.

'I tried calling you before but you weren't answering,' he complained, some nervousness edging into his voice.

'I was out of range. What's up?'

'I drove by the house around three o'clock. The husband's car was there, but nothing else different. No cops yet. We still good for tomorrow?'

'Yep.'

He hesitated, asked, 'The merchandise still in working order?'

'Still in one piece. Unless you hear from me otherwise, tomorrow as planned.'

I put the phone away. Danny slid his gaze towards me. 'Was that the cocksucker whose arm I'm going to cut off?' he asked.

'Yeah.'

'I'm not kidding about that.'

'I know you're not.'

When we got to Nashua I drove down Main Street slowly until I found a coffee shop that had a Wi-Fi signal strong enough that I could pick it up in the car. I pulled into an empty parking spot in front. The directions we had left in the house included an anonymous email account for the parents to log into for further contact with us. As spelled out in the directions we left they sent a message to it giving me a cell phone number that I could reach them at. They also pleaded with us not to hurt their son. That they would pay us whatever we wanted, but that their son suffered from Type B Hemophilia and any injury could be fatal to him. Lousy timing getting that information from them. I sent them a response that included the video I made and the directions for making the payoff. I wasn't giving them much time to get the eight million dollars together, but I figured with thirty million in the bank they'd find a way to get it by noon, and the less time they had to think, the less chance they'd try something clever like bringing the police into it. When I was done I pulled back onto Main Street.

'No one's going to be able to figure out you sent that?' Danny asked.

'Not a chance.'

'How about that you sent it from that coffee shop?'

'Yeah, they'll be able to tell that. But we never stepped inside of it. And no one's going to remember us sitting in that parking spot for thirty seconds.'

He was quiet after that until I got onto Route 3 and was heading back to Boston. 'Unless one of the stores around there has video surveillance,' he muttered.

I didn't bother responding. That was just paranoia talking. The rest of the ride as far as I was concerned he wasn't even there.

When we got back to the apartment I asked Danny if he wanted to go out for dinner but he had other ideas for the night. He made a call to his dealer and left. I thought about heading out to Southie but decided I wasn't in the mood for it. I gave Nola a quick thought – a real quick one – since I decided I wasn't much in the mood for her either. I ended up walking around the neighborhood and buying some Chinese takeout. When I got back to the apartment, Danny was there smoking a joint with a full baggie of pot next to him. I joined him and we shared the food and pot, but neither of us said a word to each other. I doubt either of us would've wanted to know what was on the other's mind.

Later that night after Danny had gone to bed I cleaned the laptop of any prints by scrubbing it down with vinegar, then took a drive to get rid of it. The laptop might've been worth three grand, but I wasn't going to keep any evidence around that could tie us to the kidnapping.

Chapter 9

It was at ten past four in the afternoon when Lorentz called to tell me that the mark had just driven past him. 'No one else in the car with him that I could see, and no one behind him,' he said.

Danny and I were on a small hill overlooking a two-lane road up in the lake region of New Hampshire. The reason I picked the road was that it was within ten miles of two major highways and, as I knew from past experience, at this time of day traffic would be light. Over the last half hour only two cars passed us, both filled with families. Danny and I were hidden behind trees so they weren't going to see us, nor were they going to see our car where we had left it on a dirt road a quarter of a mile away.

Lorentz was calling from twenty miles down the road. He was hidden like we were, and if he spotted any cops or FBI he would call back and the mark would never know where to drop off the money. After hanging up I told Danny what Lorentz had said and that it wasn't going to be much longer. He nodded, his face shiny with perspiration. He didn't look like he was doing too well. I couldn't tell with the bandages wrapped around his arm how his wounds were, but his arm looked more swollen to me. Before we left I offered to do this alone but he insisted on coming along. Maybe he didn't trust me – afraid I was going to run with the money, or maybe it was just nerves and it was easier for him to come along than to wait at home, but whichever it was I didn't fight him on it.

'When this is done we're going to take a trip up to Canada and find a clinic up there to get you taken care of,' I said. 'We'll get you a fake ID, pay cash, and the FBI will never know about it.'

'Yeah, sure.'

Danny's face looked wooden as he stared at the empty road. I didn't bother saying anything else to him. I just sat back and waited and tried to ignore the black flies buzzing around my face.

When I spotted the Audi coming around the bend I nudged Danny. 'Payday,' I whispered softly. I took out a small tape recorder and used a disposable cell phone to call the mark.

'Is Jason okay?' the mark tried asking.

Earlier I had used the laptop to prerecord a message with a synthesized voice. I played the message over the phone, which directed him to drop the money on the road and to keep driving. That if he did anything other than that his son would be dead.

'Please, is he okay?'

I hung up.

The car slowed down to a crawl and a duffel bag was pushed out of the passenger door. The car fishtailed for a moment as the driver reached over to close the open door, then it sped off.

I waited a couple of minutes listening for the sound of helicopters. You just never know what the Feds might try. It was quiet, not a sound of any kind other than an occasional tree frog chirping and the flies that were buzzing around my ear. I tried calling Lorentz to make sure things still looked good from his end but he didn't answer.

'He's not answering,' I told Danny.

'Fuck that. Let's just get the money.'

We started down the hill. At that moment a car turned the corner and raced down the road. Danny and I scrambled back to where we were hiding. The car was a beater, an old Chevy Nova, not the type of car any Fed would drive. It stopped near the duffel bag and Lorentz got out. It took a moment for me to register what was happening, and when I did I was scrambling down the hill with my 9 millimeter out taking potshots at the sonofabitch. I hit some wet leaves and my feet flew out from under me and I slid down most of the way on my back. Danny ran past me firing at the car. He knocked out the back windshield as Lorentz made a quick U-turn and raced back from where he came. If Danny hit Lorentz it wasn't fatal because the car drove out of sight.

'Shit! Shit! Shit!' Danny yelled. He ran down the road firing more shots but the car was already long gone. When he turned around he looked like a dead man walking. Like he couldn't believe what just happened. Shaking his head, Danny kept repeating how the sonofabitch had double-crossed us.

I had picked myself up from the ground and was trying to think of what we could do. My head was buzzing as I stood there. 'Let's get the car,' I finally said.

'He's already got too much of a head start on us.'

'We're not chasing after him. We just have to get the hell out of here.'

Danny didn't like it anymore than I did, but what the fuck else were we going to do? The place could be swarming with Feds any minute now. We ran the quarter of a mile back to where we had left the car. Before driving off, I wiped off both guns and chucked them into the woods. Driving back I headed in the same direction Lorentz had gone but I took the first right turn I could, then some back roads and eventually found Route 93 heading back to Massachusetts. Danny sat fuming as I drove. Me, I could've killed the first sonofabitch who gave me an excuse.

'What are we going to do?' he asked, already knowing damn well what the answer was going to be, but I told him anyway that I didn't have a fucking clue.

I tried thinking what we could possibly do to get back the money. If Lorentz had any family I could try to use them to get at him, but Lorentz never struck me as someone who'd care about that. He'd let me torture and murder his own mother for all he'd care. How the fuck was I supposed to chase after him? He had eight million dollars. If I were in his shoes I'd already have my escape route planned and within hours I'd be on a flight heading to the Bahamas or South-east Asia or God knows where. I punched the steering wheel and kept punching it until my knuckles were bloody.

'If you fuck up my car you're going to fix it,' Danny said. 'I don't have a job anymore, and guess what, whatever money had been promised me just got pissed away.'

I ignored the crack. Anyone else and I would've pulled them from the car and beaten their last breath out of them, but Danny was my own flesh and blood and he was hurting as much as me.

'What a fucking brilliant plan,' he muttered. 'Bringing in some double-crossing piece of shit onto the job.'

Again, I tried hard to ignore his crack. Out of the corner of my eye I could see the veins bulging in my hands as I gripped the wheel. It took every ounce of self control I had left to keep from ripping the steering wheel off its base. My muscles bunched along my shoulders and neck as I drove, a cold fury filling me up. Danny sensed he'd better keep quiet. He didn't say another word until we were approaching the Storrow Drive exit ramp.

'You killed a kid for absolutely nothing,' he said. 'Christ, I hope you're fucking proud of yourself.'

I slammed on the brakes. Tires squealed out behind me, then people yelling and blasting their horns as I raced around to Danny's side of the car. By the time I got there he had his door locked and window up. I kicked the window out with my foot, then unlocked the door and pulled Danny onto the pavement. Everything went red for an instant. Through a haze I could see

Danny trying to stare defiantly back at me but all his imagined hurt showed on that weak mouth of his. I had my arm cocked above him as if I was going to start pounding away. I was about to kill him. My own brother. Right there in front of dozens of shocked motorists. I got my knee off of Danny's chest and staggered back to the driver's seat and continued on Route 93, leaving Danny lying where he was.

I was shaking like a leaf. I was still filled with a murderous rage, but I was shaking and scared out of my wits with what I almost did to my own brother. As I drove I felt the rage inside choking me. It was as if my head was being held under water and my lungs were about to burst. There was so much pressure building up inside. My first stop was at Flynn's Liquors. John Flynn was working the cash register. I could see in his face that he had planned to argue with me, but he understood immediately how dangerous that would be. He told me he'd be right back with my Bushmills and he moved faster than he'd probably moved in years. He was red-faced and breathing hard when he came back carrying the remaining half a case of whiskey.

'It's going to be three bills a week from now on, John, to keep you and the store safe,' I said.

Without a word of argument, he counted three hundred dollars out of the cash register and handed it to me. I took the money from him somewhat half-heartedly. I was hoping for any excuse from him, but he wasn't going to give me any. I told him to carry the whiskey out to my car, and he did it without a word. Didn't even raise an eyebrow at the shattered window. After I left Flynn's I went straight to Scolley's.

People at Scolley's cleared a wide berth for me. They knew better than to do anything other than that. Joe poured me shot after shot without saying a word. The whiskey wasn't helping though. It was like I was slowly being strangled to death. I just couldn't breathe right. The place had gotten deathly quiet. Then someone clapped me on the shoulder, and there was Tom Dunleavy grinning drunkenly.

'Kyle Nevin, just the man I was hoping to see,' he said, his voice booming and echoing throughout the bar. 'You and me, Kyle, I have plans for the two of us. Something monumental I have in the works. Let me buy you a drink first.'

I was off my barstool and staring him down. 'You're going to insult me like that in front of my own people?' I asked.

His drunken grin started to weaken as he looked around uneasily. Others sitting nearby started to scatter.

'Wha—? I didn't mean any insult, Kyle—'

'You didn't mean any insult? It sounded to me like you were implying I was just a two-bit punk.'

'What? Jesus. I wasn't trying to say that.'

'You weren't? Why the fuck else would I ever work with a bottom-feeder like you?'

'I swear, Kyle, I didn't mean anything. Christ, you know that.'

'Every time you say my name it's a fucking insult. Where the fuck do you get off calling me by my first name?'

'I'm sorry, I didn't mean any disrespect.'

He was backing away, his eyes shifting from left to right as he looked for an escape route.

'What the fuck you doing? Running away from me? How the fuck is that showing any respect?'

His goofy grin slowly came back. He looked around the bar as if he were in the middle of some practical joke. 'This is a joke?'

'You think it's a joke that you fucked my girl?'

'What? Fucked your girl?'

'Now you're going to start acting like you don't know what I'm talking about?'

A hint of light showed in his dumb eyes as he remembered me sitting at a table with Nola. Also some anger started to show in them. You can only jab a person in the chest for so long before they snap back.

'What the fuck are you talking about? You were still in prison when I banged her.'

'It's a joke to you that you stuck your two inches into my girl?'

Color had gotten back into Dunleavy's cheeks. He was just drunk enough to still think he was a tough guy and he had already forgotten who he was standing in front of.

'Why don't you go suck my two inches like all the other prison cocks you sucked, and leave me the fuck alone,' he said.

I went at him like a buzz saw.

Less than a minute later I was being pulled off him. I turned on the person who had put their hands on me and saw it was Joe Whalley. Anyone else I would've done the same as I did to Dunleavy. With Joe I froze until I got some control back. At least I was breathing easier.

'Kyle, you're going to kill him.'

He was right. Dunleavy was a mess. His face was broken and bleeding badly, his eyes buried under swollen flesh. He moaned softly as he curled up into a fetal position.

'Maybe you should call it an early night,' Joe suggested.

I nodded and gave Joe a few hundred dollars to handle the ambulance ride for Dunleavy and any damage caused to the bar.

I felt better leaving Scolley's. It was as if a weight had been rolled off my chest. It didn't make up for losing eight million dollars to that cocksucker Lorentz but it helped and I could breathe easier again. After leaving Scolley's I stopped off at a 24-hour auto glass shop and had a new side window put in. The guy who did the work told me from the way the glass was spread around the interior of the car that some asshole must've kicked in the window. I let it slide.

When I drove back to Danny's apartment, I saw my brother hoofing it maybe two miles away from his building. I slowed down to a crawl, lowered the passenger window and told him to get in. He didn't even bother looking at me and just kept walking.

'Chrissakes,' I said. 'I apologize. I'm sorry. I completely lost it back there.'

'Fuck you.'

'I'm sorry. I'm sorry. How many times do I have to say it?'

He gave the car a quick sideways glance and noticed that I had the window fixed.

'You were going to kill me back there,' he said.

'I told you I lost it. But shit, Danny, you're my brother. There's no fucking way I'd ever hurt you. You gotta know that.'

He started laughing then. 'No way you'd ever hurt me, huh? That so? Let's look at what I've lost since you've been back. The girl I love and wanted to marry, my job and any future I might've had.'

Drivers behind me were blasting their horn and giving me the finger as they slid into the other lane to pass me, but I didn't let them affect me. I kept at the same crawl pace so I could keep even with Danny.

'Come on, for Chrissakes, get a grip, okay?' I said. 'All we had was a temporary setback. I'll figure out a way for another ransom drop. We'll get our money one way or another.'

'You're fucking delusional, bro.' Danny spat on the side of the street. He wiped a hand across his mouth, his eyes shining like a rabid dog's as he looked at me. 'No fucking way are they going to pay another ransom. But that's the least of our problems. What happens if your piece of shit buddy gets picked up by the Feds?'

'That's not going to happen.'

'You're sure about that, huh, bro?'

Of course I wasn't sure about it. The only thing I was sure about was if he did get picked up he'd sell me out in a second. But I had to hope that if he was smart enough to double-cross me the way he did, he'd be smart enough to keep from getting picked up. I had to hope he was smart enough to check the duffel bag for a GPS tracking device, because if the family had contacted the FBI that minimally would've been hidden in the bag. All I could hope for at this point was that he was smart enough to do that.

'Come on, Danny. You're sweating like a pig out there. Besides, I'm following you back the rest of the way. You might as well just get in the car.'

He was sweating pretty badly and his gait had turned more into a shuffle than anything else. He hesitated for a moment, then got in the passenger seat.

'What happens if Lorentz gets picked up and rats you out?' he asked.

'It's not going to happen.'

'What if it does?'

'If it does, then I'm leaving you out of it. What I'll tell them is you had no idea what I was doing.'

He laughed again. It was kind of a hollow and hopeless laugh. 'Bro, I'm sure some of my blood must've been left in the house, at the very least a drop or two in that dog's mouth. They have my DNA. I'm fucked.'

'It's not going to happen, Danny. I know in my heart it's not going to happen.'

'Yeah, what makes you so sure?'

I tried to explain it to him but I knew it didn't come out right. To me, though, it was as clear as day. There was a reason I survived prison without a hitch and was now on the streets. It was so I could hunt down Red and pay him back. Not just for me, but for making a mockery of our code, of our very lives. It just didn't seem right for it to happen any other way. I lost Danny with my explanation, though. I could see his eyes glaze over as I tried to make him see what was so obvious to me.

'Whatever you say, bro,' he muttered under his breath.

I didn't appreciate that comment, the dismissive tone of it, but it had been a long day and I let it slide. Anyway, sometimes it's just a matter of faith. Some people have it, some don't. I knew I didn't get out of prison only to go right back there to rot.

When we got back to his apartment building I had to help Danny out of the car. Touching his skin I could tell that he was sick. It had an unhealthy rubbery feel to it. I took the Bushmills up with us while he had to rest after every half dozen steps or so to catch his breath. As we stood outside his apartment door I could hear noises from inside. I felt my heart jump in my throat and tried to signal to Danny to back away, but he seemed resigned to the situation and opened the door and walked in before I could stop him. Inside was his girlfriend watching TV. Her face looked like some kind of hard plastic mask as she watched us, almost as if her eyes were buried deep behind it.

'Where have you been?' she asked, more of a demand than a question.

Danny broke into a large broad smile. 'Eve, Jesus, I've missed you. Thank God you're back.'

'I've been waiting for you all day,' she said.

'We've just been out, Kyle and me. Nothing too interesting.'

Her eyes shifted towards me for a second before going back to Danny. There was nothing but utter contempt in the look she gave me.

'He hasn't gotten you into doing heroin, has he?'

'No, baby, I'm not on anything right now.'

She got up and moved cautiously to him. When she put her hand on his forehead she shot me an accusatory look before asking him what was wrong.

'You're burning up, Danny,' she said, concern flooding her moon-shaped face.

'I just caught something, that's all. I'll be fine.'

'What happened to your arm?'

He lifted his forearm up and laughed bitterly at it. 'Just some stupid accident. Nothing to worry about.'

She was saying something about his job, but both Danny and I had stopped paying any attention to her. Our focus was on the TV. The news was on and there was a story about a shoot-out in a Providence motel room between the FBI and an unidentified man. The reporter didn't have much more information than that. The FBI wasn't divulging the name of the suspect or the crime he was supposed to have committed, nor would they say how seriously he was injured. An ambulance was shown in the background. As was Lorentz's Chevy Nova.

Danny's girlfriend kept rattling on asking about his job, about why he was fired. Neither Danny nor I paid any attention to her, both of our eyes glued on the TV. I opened up a bottle of Bushmills and took a healthy swig of it, then passed the bottle to Danny. When I lit a cig, the titless wonder went a bit nuts, first yelling at me that she didn't want anyone smoking in her apartment, then trying to grab it from out of my hand. At one point she got in front of me and I had to move her away so she wasn't blocking the TV. I guess she ended up on her ass, but it wasn't intentional on my part.

'Danny!' she yelled. 'Your thug brother just threw me to the floor!'

The story ended and Danny's eyes slid from the TV to his girlfriend. His eyes were blank for a few moments until he made sense of what she had said and realized why she was sitting where she was.

'Don't ever lay a finger on Eve again,' he warned me.

'I didn't mean it, Danny. She was in the way of the TV.'

The titless wonder was fuming. I could almost see the steam coming off her.

'I want him out of my apartment! You get him out now or I'm calling the police.'

Danny nodded slowly. 'First thing in the morning, okay?' he asked her.

She was staring at me with pure hate. 'I want him out of here before I wake up,' she said.

'You hear all that, bro?' Danny asked.

'Yeah, I heard it,' I said. 'Let's go outside and talk for a minute.'

Danny pushed himself off the sofa that he had sunk into. The titless wonder tried complaining that there was nothing for him to talk to me about, but Danny held out a hand to stop her. The two of us walked out of the apartment in silence and down the steps. We got in his car and turned the radio on so no one could overhear us.

'It's over, Kyle,' he said. 'We're fucked.'

'We don't know that. Lorentz could've been taken out in a body bag for all we know.'

Danny shook his head. 'It's over, bro. As soon as his lawyer gets a deal together, we're both fucked.' He wiped a hand over his eyes. He looked exhausted, but more than that, defeated. I knew then that he had given up. 'We're both going to burn in hell for what we did, Kyle.'

I grabbed him by the shoulders and tried to shake some sense into him. 'Don't give up yet,' I told him. 'If we have to we can run, but we don't know yet whether that cocksucker is alive or dead. My gut's screaming at me that he's dead. And if he's dead there's nothing to tie us to him.'

I wasn't getting through to him. I could see it in the way his eyes drifted away from me.

'What we did was worse than evil,' he said more to himself than to me. 'We butchered an innocent kid, and almost as bad, we're not even letting his family give him a decent burial.' He hesitated, and again wiped a hand across his eyes, then stared bleary-eyed at me as if he barely recognized me. 'Maybe we should just do the right thing here. Maybe it's about time we just do the right thing,' he said.

The silence between us grew until I asked him if he was thinking of ratting me out. He shook his head, but he couldn't meet my eyes.

'Okay, then,' I said, trying hard to ignore the obvious. 'Let's both try and get a good night's sleep. I'm sure that cocksucker's dead, and I'm sure we'll both be feeling better about things in the morning.'

He nodded, looking as glum as any condemned man who knows there's no reprieve coming.

'How's your arm?' I asked.

He gave me a weak smile. 'It hurts like hell.'

'You have anything to take the edge off?'

'Yeah, I got some pills yesterday when I got the pot.'

'Take some. Get a good night's sleep. Things will look better tomorrow. I promise.'

He nodded, said, 'Kyle, I'm serious about you leaving tomorrow morning. I might only have a few days left with Eve, and I want them to be good days.'

'Jesus, you're being a pessimist, but I'll be out before you two wake up. When I squeeze more money out of the mark, you're still getting half of whatever I get. Danny, trust me on this. Things aren't over.'

He nodded again as bleak as before, and the two of us walked back upstairs. Danny and his girlfriend disappeared into their bedroom, leaving me alone on the sofa with my Bushmills and cigs. At one point the titless wonder came out to give me an earful about smoking in her apartment, but I pointed a thumb towards the open window and ignored her. It didn't take me too long to empty one bottle of Bushmills and open another. I had CNN on and was trying to focus on the TV and any more stories about the shoot-out in Providence, but I could hear Danny and his girlfriend through the walls. She had gotten him to take the bandages off his arm, and was going on and on about how bad his arm looked. With all her harping on it, he finally told her that a dog in the neighborhood bit him. She wanted to take him right away to the emergency room, but he convinced her that he could wait until morning for that, that he was dead on his feet and needed to get some sleep. Eventually it got quiet in there, but not before she let him know how I was no good – nothing but a rotten influence on him and that he'd be better off without any further contact with me. The last words I heard from Danny were his agreeing with her.

I tried giving Danny the benefit of the doubt. It had been a hard day and I could understand his saying just about anything to shut her up so he could get some sleep, but the last thing he said to her kept echoing through my head. *I wish he had died in prison. Fuck, I wish I had never laid eyes on him again.* Those words just kept playing back and made it tough for me to follow what was being shown on TV. As far as I could tell no new information was being given about the Providence shoot-out, but I couldn't swear to that. Danny's words haunted me. They made me go through the cigs and Bushmills even faster. I didn't even realize when I blacked out, cig in hand.

I woke thinking I had died and gone to hell. It was so damn hot, like I was on fire. My mind just couldn't comprehend anything else. It was probably also due to the lack of oxygen I was getting. Eventually my lizard brain took over and screamed at me that I was on fire, and not only that, I had to get the fuck out of there.

I was fully conscious then and realized my shirt was burning up. Not just my shirt, but the whole damn apartment. I opened my eyes for a second but then had to squeeze them shut. Flames were shooting up everywhere and a thick black smoke was choking off the air in the apartment. I rolled off the sofa and pulled my shirt off. My arms were on fire also. It was too late to do anything about Danny and his girlfriend. If I tried getting to their door I'd be dead before I reached it. Even if I managed to wake them, they wouldn't get out of there alive. The only thing I could do was crawl to the back door. Somehow I got to it. I was half falling and half crawling down a flight of steps before firemen were putting an oxygen mask over my mouth and extinguishing the flames that were burning me up. I must've blacked out then.

I woke up in a hospital bed suffering from smoke inhalation, and with second and third degree burns over my chest and arms. I was going to live. Danny and his girlfriend both died, along with six other tenants in the building. The cause of the fire was careless smoking. It didn't help that half a dozen of the apartments had dead batteries in their smoke detectors. In Danny's apartment it was even worse – at some point the batteries were taken out, not even giving them a chance in case of a fire. So yes, I caused the fire when I passed out holding a lit cigarette. The last few days I had stopped keeping things orderly and the apartment had kind of become a pigsty with newspapers and pizza boxes all over the floor. Of course, if Danny's girlfriend had cleaned up the place when she got back instead of just sitting there waiting to bust his balls, the fire probably wouldn't have started. While I was ostensibly to blame for the fire, I had to put some of it on her.

So Danny was dead. The only person other than Ma who ever gave a rat's ass about me. What a fucking lousy night to cap off an equally lousy day.

To Ed.: Some people are probably thinking that I set the fire intentionally. I don't think that's true, at least not at a conscious level. At a subconscious level, who the fuck knows? Yeah, I took the batteries out of the smoke detectors, but that was only because my cigs kept setting them off. It doesn't explain why I threw them out in one of the dumpsters

by the Chinese restaurant. Who the fuck really knows about these things? Yeah, I knew Danny was lost to me. I knew he was planning on giving up and confessing all so the family could have some relief by being able to bury their kid. But fuck, if you're going to go on a job you have to accept the consequences of what happens. You can't be such a fucking pussy about it. I heard other shit between Danny and the titless wonder. She was three months pregnant, blah, blah, blah – not that that was any surprise to me. Given how thin she was I could tell from the size of her stomach that something was in there. So there you had it. The reason Danny went on the job – to make enough money to buy the suburban dream. The fact was he no longer had what it took to be in the game. I had no doubt that if he had lived to see the morning he would've ratted me out so he could cut a deal for himself. I had no choice. I couldn't let that happen to my own flesh and blood. Nothing in the world's lower than a rat. I had no choice; I had to save him from himself.
—K. N.

Chapter 10

I was in the hospital four days when the FBI, State and Boxboro Town Police all came to my bedside as a small mob to officially charge me with kidnapping, among other crimes. I was too hopped up on painkillers to really care one way or the other, and I told them I wasn't saying squat to them without a lawyer. The state and local police left, but the FBI investigator hung around pretending not to hear me. Even though I refused to say anything else he kept asking me questions, mainly where the boy was being held. I guess he was planning later to lie under oath and claim I never asked for a lawyer. Who knows? Maybe I didn't. Maybe I was too hopped up on drugs to get the words out right. Anyway, I closed my eyes and drifted off under the influence of the narcotics I was being given. After a while his voice faded. Even when he pinched an area along my arm that had suffered second degree burns, I kept my eyes closed and pretended he wasn't there. Throughout it all I didn't make a peep. Damn, I was grateful for those narcotics.

I ended up staying in the hospital for three weeks before the Feds got medical clearance from my doctor to transport me to FMC Devens. During my remaining time at Boston City they manacled my ankles to the bed. The Feds probably would've handcuffed my wrists also, but because of my second degree burns covering them I don't think the hospital would've stood for it.

It took over a week after I was charged before I met my lawyer. Before that happened the FBI came every day to ask me where the boy was. Mostly it was the same two agents, one in his fifties who looked like when he was younger he could've played linebacker in the NFL, the other a woman in her early thirties who would've been attractive if she wasn't such a goddamned frigid piece of ice. They kept talking about how if the boy died I'd be up for the death penalty but if I helped them return him safely to his parents I could end up with a life sentence instead. I didn't say word one to them. When they tried getting in my face, I stared through them as if they didn't exist. I think it was the fourth day after my arrest that the FBI brought the dead kid's parents to see me – although it's kind of hard to tell because I was losing track of time then due to the drugs I was on so it could've just as easily been the fifth or sixth day for all I knew. The agent who brought them in was one I didn't recognize; a stocky guy with a military-style buzz cut wearing a cheap suit that was too tight on him. The parents were in their forties and both looked like they had aged a lot recently. The husband was thin and lanky with a large forehead and the kind of soft wispy brown hair that was a strong indication he'd be going bald soon. His wife had the look of someone who had probably been attractive at one time but had gone to pot almost overnight. Both their eyes were red and puffy from crying and their faces were filled with dread. Even without that I would've known who they were. I could see the resemblance in them with the kid Danny and I took. The husband was fighting to keep a stiff upper lip so he wouldn't break out bawling. He started things off, begging me to tell them where their son was.

'Please,' he went on. 'Jason has a severe form of hemophilia. Any internal injury could cause him to bleed to death. Please let us bring him back home.'

Before I even had a chance to say anything his wife let loose with the waterworks. It was like something medieval the way she wailed. As I looked at the two of them all I could think was *fuck the both of you, you cocksuckers*. I would find out later that the FBI had sewn a GPS tracking device into the lining of the duffel bag that the husband dropped for us, but even without knowing that I knew they had brought the FBI in from the start. After doing that they were going to have the fucking balls to expect any help from me? Thank God for the drugs the hospital had me on. Without them taking the edge off I would've been out of my mind with rage. I composed myself as best I could and explained to them that I had no idea why the FBI arrested me and I had nothing to do with what happened to their son. When they kept pestering me I told them that as they could clearly see I had problems of my own; that I was suffering second and third degree burns and had just lost my only brother, his fiancée and their unborn baby in the same fire that almost killed me. I asked them as politely as I could to leave me the fuck alone.

They wouldn't take no for an answer. I turned a deaf ear to them. When the wife physically went at me, the FBI agent corralled her and escorted the two of them out of the room. When he came back, he pulled a chair up to my bed and studied me like I was an insect.

'We have you dead to rights, Kyle,' he said.

I didn't say anything. I pressed a button for the nurse, then another button to increase my dosage of painkillers.

'Manuel Lorentz gave you up,' he said. 'He cut a deal and sold you out. As it stands now, you're in line for an injection of potassium chloride. Your only chance for a life stretch is to start cooperating with us.'

I pressed the button again for a nurse.

'We found the shell casings by the ransom drop-off point,' he went on. 'What happened? Lorentz double-cross you? He show up unexpected? Must've pissed you off when he grabbed the money and ran. So now this double-crossing rat is going to skate with only a five-year stretch while you'll be heading to death row. Doesn't seem fair to me. If I were you I'd be pretty damn pissed. I'd want to get my side of the story out there—'

A nurse came into the room. I told her that I thought my dressings needed changing. The FBI agent clammed up while she checked on them.

'I want it on record that I've been asking for a lawyer for four days now and for whatever fucked-up reason they have the FBI keeps ignoring my fundamental constitutional rights. They're insisting on questioning me not only without my lawyer present but while I'm high on painkillers.'

The nurse exchanged glances with the FBI agent. He got up off his chair and left the room. I didn't expect to be able to count on this nurse to repeat what I said in a courtroom but the message got out nonetheless. No one else bothered questioning me after that. A few days later my lawyer showed up. A young black woman named Lorraine Jackson. After she introduced herself to me I told her I'd been asking for a lawyer for over a week.

She checked through her paperwork and told me the request to the public defenders' office came in only that morning. I gave her a quick look up and down and wasn't impressed with what I saw. The suit she had on couldn't have cost more than two bills, and shit, I had bullet-wound scars that were older than her. Plus, she was just a wisp of a woman, maybe ninety pounds soaking wet. There just wasn't enough substance to her. I told her no offense, but she looked like just a kid to me and I asked if I could get a more experienced lawyer, maybe a Jewish one. My request didn't faze her one bit.

'We were told that you're indigent. Do you have the funds to hire your own attorney?'

I shook my head, gave her a half-grimace, half-smile. 'I'm a little cash poor right now.'

'Then I'm afraid you're a little stuck with me right now. If it will make you feel any better I graduated fourth in my class at Boston College Law.'

Boston College is a Catholic school run by the Jesuits. I flashed her my pearly whites and told her she finished fourth only because there weren't any Jews in her class. She smiled then – the only time during any of our dealings that she smiled in front of me – and told me that there were a number of Jewish law students in her class, none of whom finished ahead of her.

I didn't have much choice in the matter. I had fifteen grand still scattered around Boston which would buy me maybe two weeks from a top-notch defense lawyer, so Lorraine Jackson and I got down to business. She had just gotten the assignment and didn't know much yet other than that there was an arraignment hearing scheduled in two days. I told her how I had asked for a lawyer right away but that the FBI ignored my requests and continued to question me.

'Did you say anything to them?'

'I don't think so,' I said. 'I've been doped up on painkillers so it's hard to say, but I think the only thing I've been saying to them is that I want a lawyer and that I don't want to talk to them.'

A scowl creased her smooth angular face as she glanced over her paperwork. 'According to what I have you weren't officially charged until yesterday. I think they've been taking advantage of your being in the hospital and have been playing some games here. Have they given any indication of the case they have against you?'

'Yeah. A couple of days ago they were telling me that one of the kidnappers implicated me.' I stopped to make a show of trying to remember a name. 'I think they told me the guy's name was *Laurent*?'

Lorraine Jackson frowned at that. 'I see there's no TV in the room. Have you been able to read the paper since you've been in the hospital?'

I shook my head. 'I think they've been trying to keep me in a news blackout.'

'They obviously have been,' she said. 'The story has been heavily reported over the last week that one of the kidnappers, a Manuel Lorentz, was killed in a motel room shoot-out with the FBI. Everything that I've read had Mr Lorentz dying at the scene. Did you know this person?'

I scratched behind my ear as I thought about it. 'The name doesn't sound familiar,' I said.

'I wonder if the FBI's hiding the fact that he really died,' she said, distracted, her gaze moving away from me as she pondered this. She shifted her gaze back to me, her eyes holding steady on mine. Jesus, they were beautiful eyes. 'Or if he gave a deathbed confession. Why do you think this person would implicate you?'

'I doubt he did,' I said. 'I think the FBI's trying to frame me for this.'

'Why would they do that?'

'How much do you know about me?' I asked.

Her face weakened a bit as she remembered fully who she was dealing with. 'Only what's been reported in the news,' she said.

'So you know that I was once an associate of Red Mahoney's and that I just finished an eight-year stretch for armed robbery. The Feds were pissed at me for not giving them anything on Mahoney when they arrested me nine years ago, and this is now payback for that. Any case they have against me now is being manufactured.'

She didn't seem too convinced of that, but she nodded and told me she'd be seeing me again soon. She gave me a card with her cell phone number and, as if she were talking to some green wide-eyed kid, warned me about saying anything to anyone. I watched her as she left. There may not have been much to her but what there was was nice to look at.

Of course, I knew Lorentz was dead the moment that FBI agent shot his mouth off about him making a deal with them. Up to that point I was worried he might've still been breathing, but not after that. If they had Lorentz they would've moved quickly to get me lawyered up so they could cut a deal to get the kid returned. They knew the kid was probably dead but they still wanted to return his body to the parents. If they didn't have Lorentz I had a good idea what they did have. When I went into the federal prison system for the failed bank heist, I was forced by the courts to provide the FBI a DNA sample for their CODIS system. They must've found some of Danny's blood in the house and it probably matched my DNA enough where they thought they could try this shit. They had to know the match wasn't exact, but that wasn't going to stop them from trying to convict me with a bogus DNA case. Or maybe they thought they could use it to leverage a deal with me about Red's old operations. Either way, they were trying to railroad me.

It left me in a tricky situation. I didn't want to volunteer anything to my lawyer. I wanted her to at least think I was innocent. If I started mentioning to her that they probably had DNA evidence that was a close but not exact match to me because it matched my brother it would open up a can of worms I didn't want to get anywhere near. Who knew where it would lead if the FBI connected Danny to the kidnapping? My first day in the hospital after the fire, Joe Whalley had come by. He was raising money at Scolley's to have Danny taken care of, and I told him Danny's preference would've been to be cremated, especially given the condition of his body and not being able to have an open casket. I had no idea where that was in the process, and the last thing I wanted was the FBI getting to his body for a DNA sample before it hit the ovens. All I could do for the next couple of days was lie in bed fuming over what the FBI was trying to do to me. Yeah, they might think I was involved, but they still knew their evidence against me was no good. So here I was, my only brother having just died and instead of being able to grieve, I had to deal with this shit?

I was in no shape to attend my arraignment hearing so I stayed in my hospital bed. After the hearing, Lorraine Jackson visited me and told me that I had been indicted on all charges and that bail was being denied. And as it turned out I was right on target about the supposed DNA evidence.

'Their case against you consists of DNA evidence found at the child's home that matches a sample you provided to the FBI when you were previously incarcerated. Also, they have that you and the dead kidnapper, Manuel Lorentz, served time together at Cedar Junction.'

'What kind of DNA evidence was found?'

She consulted her notes. 'Blood drops.'

'They're not mine.'

She gave me a tired look, not even considering there was a remote chance I was telling her the truth. How old was she – twenty-five, twenty-six? She had probably been out of law school for less than a year and was already as jaded as any twenty-year seasoned veteran from having to listen to one lying con after the next insisting on their mother's grave that they were innocent even though they were caught with enough evidence to convict them ten times over.

'Mr Nevin, DNA evidence like this is nearly impossible to counter in court. I strongly suggest we explore a deal if one's available.'

'Ms Jackson, I swear any blood found there's not mine. The FBI's either manufacturing the evidence or doing a sloppy job with their matching. I'd bet my life on it that if you could get a real DNA test done it would show that that blood's not mine

– assuming the evidence wasn't planted by them. Who knows, maybe with the level of testing they did it would match anyone of Irish descent. As far as Manuel Lorentz goes, if I served time with him I don't remember. But there were over six hundred inmates at Cedar Junction. Most of them I wouldn't have a clue who they were. I kept mostly to myself there, trying to be a model prisoner.'

There was a slight spark in her eyes; like maybe, just maybe, I was the one guy out of a hundred who wasn't lying out of his asshole to her. She consulted her notes again.

'The two of you were in MCI Cedar Junction together from May 20th, 2003 until Mr Lorentz was released on June 1st, 2004.'

I made it look as if I were giving the matter serious thought. 'I can't place him,' I said.

She had brought the last two weeks' worth of newspapers for me to go through, hoping that I'd spot something in one of the articles about the kidnapping that could help. The fire dominated the front page for several days, then the kidnapping took over. As far as the fire went, because of the injuries I sustained and the evidence they were able to find of both my heavy smoking and drinking that night and my blood alcohol level being at 0.46 percent when they brought me in, the fire was ruled accidental and no charges were being brought against me. Lorraine Jackson found a picture of Lorentz on the front page of one of the papers, the sonofabitch looking as smarmy as ever. She showed it to me and asked me if I recognized him. I stared at it and shook my head slowly.

'I don't know,' I said. 'I don't think so.'

She left the newspapers for me. As she gathered her stuff together, I repeated myself about whether we could have our own DNA test done.

'I promise you,' I told her. 'If they found blood there, any accurate DNA test will prove it's not mine.'

The slight spark that was in her eyes earlier had turned brighter. She was starting to take me more seriously, maybe even thinking there was a chance I wasn't just jerking her around.

'I'll look into it,' she told me. 'In the meantime I'll do some research on DNA testing and see if I can understand their report better.'

There were no handshakes between us when she left, not that I would've minded if there were. I was finding her more attractive each time I saw her. I watched as she walked away and soon found myself daydreaming what she'd look like bent over my bed with her skirt pulled up over her waist. Fuck, what I would've given for a chance at that.

I tried to hold onto that thought but it faded quickly. It was the one moment of relative peace I'd had since the fire. Lorraine Jackson had left the newspapers stacked up on the table next to me. I grabbed them and went through the obituary pages for each one and found that Danny's memorial service was held four days ago. I didn't even have a clue about it since the FBI had taken away my hospital phone before Joe had been able to schedule it. When I had tried asking the FBI agents before, they used it as an opportunity to barter with me, the pricks. *A memorial service being held for your brother? Sure, Kyle, we can find out about it and bring you there as long you're willing to help us. What are you willing to do to help us?* I told them what they could do with their fucking help.

I closed my eyes for a while and thought about Danny. It was already getting hard to remember the way he was before the fire. Whenever I tried thinking about him, I could only see him the way he was when he was a kid, the way he'd tag along when we'd jump on the back of trucks, or when the two of us shoplifted whatever we could from stores, or when we'd break into apartments for stereo equipment and TVs, then later when I was sixteen and he was twelve and we'd roam Southie on Saturday nights and beat the hell out of guys in their twenties who thought they could walk our neighborhood uninvited. I thought about all those moments and said a few silent prayers for the old Danny, then went through the articles in the newspapers.

They had all the stuff you'd expect about my association with Red Mahoney and used several pictures of when I was being led out of court eight years ago after my sentencing, all showing a mean motherfucka scowl on my face as I looked as badass as I probably ever have. Christ, they were doing a number on me, trying to make me look like some psycho. How would anyone have looked under the same circumstances? Anyway, the articles had a lot of information about the family and the ten-year-old kid, but not much about my possible involvement other than I had served time at Cedar Junction with Lorentz and that someone in the FBI leaked that they had physical evidence tying me to the crime. Good way to prejudice a jury pool and give me an automatic appeal. One columnist who always had a hard-on for me during my days with Red hinted that maybe the fire was more than an accident, that maybe I used it to destroy evidence. He didn't come right out and say it, but he hinted at it. There was a time when Red was so fed up with this very same cocksucker that he ordered me and Kevin Flannery to take him out. If it were just up to Flannery it would've been done but I convinced Red that it would be bad business and wasn't worth the publicity we'd get. Reading that smug sonofabitch imply what he did, all I could think was I wish I had kept my mouth shut and had just butchered the guy and his family like Red wanted us to.

Lorentz had been all wrong about where the wife had been going each Wednesday morning. It wasn't to yoga or aerobics classes. If he hadn't been so fucking sloppy and had followed her he would've known that she was suffering from kidney disease and was going for dialysis treatments. If I had known that maybe I would've handled things differently. I would've known I wouldn't have had to lean so heavily on the parents to get them to pay off. Fuck Lorentz. All I could think was that I was glad to hell he was worm food now.

The rest of my stay at Boston City wasn't too eventful. They wouldn't let me have any visitors other than my lawyer, and she came by only once to tell me that the medical staff had cleared me to be transferred to FMC Devens. When I asked her if we were going to have our own DNA test done, she got vague about that, simply telling me she was still studying the report. It didn't really leave me feeling very warm and fuzzy. The next morning I was transported to Devens. I was still in rough shape at this point and had trouble walking, but I guess they decided they'd rather have me in a prison hospital than a real one.

I was in Devens for six weeks, supposedly for physical rehabilitation, but it was more like torture. I didn't hear from my lawyer once during that time. I was getting kind of edgy, nervous, but at the end of those six weeks I was walking more normally and lifting light weights. They wouldn't let me have any cigs at Boston City, and I used that to quit them for good. When I had a chance to get some at Devens I refused. Quitting cold turkey like that was part of the reason I was so edgy, but it was also just not fully trusting my lawyer to deal with the bogus blood evidence the FBI was planning to use against me.

After Devens they transferred me to MCI Plymouth, kind of an old fashioned jail that was a cakewalk compared to Cedar Junction. There were several guys from the old neighborhood that I knew and had always been friendly with, and no one that was about to give me any trouble even given the weakened condition I was in. The second day there my lawyer came by for a visit, her eyes sparkling like black diamonds as she sat across from me.

'Pre-trial hearings are scheduled for next month,' she told me, 'with the trial scheduled for October 2nd in Federal District Court.'

That put it from indictment to trial in four months. That was unheard of. Any major federal felony would usually take twelve to fifteen months to end up in court. I knew damn well why the Feds had put this on the fast track. They were hoping to slip their bullshit DNA case by before anyone had time to notice it.

'What about the blood?' I asked her. 'Are we doing our own test?'

She shook her head, her eyes dazzling as anger hardened her facial muscles. She lowered her voice, said, 'The test that they performed to match your DNA to the blood found at the scene is a weaker test than what they're required to use for a positive match. This is technical, and if you don't understand it that's okay, don't worry about it – but the weaker test that they used for you matched your core DNA loci, which all it does is prove that the blood is from someone with a similar genetic makeup to you, possibly a blood relative. Their internal policies require them to perform a more extensive test to see if something called STR markers match. I don't want to let them know that I'm aware of this. They probably think that you got stuck with some inexperienced and overworked public defender that they can slide this past. I want them to keep thinking that and then hammer their DNA expert on the stand.'

'Shit,' I muttered. 'Those fucking bastards.'

She nodded. 'Don't mention a word of this. We want the element of surprise. As far as I'm concerned what they're doing by trying to pass off a weaker test as genuine amounts to falsifying evidence, and I want to hit them hard and set a precedent for them ever trying this again.'

At that moment I don't think I ever thought anyone was ever more beautiful. Jesus, she just left me speechless. When I could I promised her I'd keep this to myself.

A week after I was brought to Plymouth I was able to contact Joe

Whalley and he came by a few days later for a visit. He looked sober sitting across from me. His normally large ruddy face looked so damn pale, almost like his skin had been replaced by wax paper. I realized this was the first time I'd seen Joe outside of Scolley's.

'I am so sorry about Danny,' he told me.

'I know. It breaks my heart to think about him. It's just like with my ma all over again, not being able to be there for Danny's funeral service.'

Joe wiped a finger across his eye. 'You would've been proud of the service, Kyle. We held it at Scolley's. The place was stuffed to the rafters. We finally brought Danny back home where he belonged.'

'You had his ashes at the service?'

Joe nodded and turned away to wipe another tear from his eyes. 'I poured in a couple of shots of my best. We sent Danny out in style.'

It was a relief to know that Danny had in fact been cremated. Even if the FBI started to strongly suspect Danny of being involved in the kidnapping, it would make it harder for them to prove it. Hopefully at this point impossible, because if they were able to tie Danny to it, they'd have a better chance of tying me to it. Joe mistook the reason for the relief showing on my face.

'It really was a beautiful service, Kyle,' he said. 'Near everyone paid their respects.'

'I owe you,' I told him.

He reddened a bit with modesty. 'How about you, Kyle? You look like skin and bones.'

'Yeah, I lost a lot of weight. Believe it or not, I'm about ten pounds heavier than I was a week ago.' I showed him my arms, then lifted my shirt so he could see the burn scars on my chest. Pain showed in his eyes as he looked at them.

'That fire was a terrible thing,' he said.

I nodded.

'The kidnapping of that young boy they're claiming you're part of...'

'It's a frame-up, Joe. They're trying to use it so they can hold a lethal injection over my head and make me finally talk about Red Mahoney's operations. I'm not saying word one to them. And I'm going to beat their frame. I'll be walking Southie again soon. Any cocksuckers who think otherwise are going to be in for a surprise. Get the word out about that.'

He nodded, accepting my explanation without question. A slight smile cracked his lips. 'The brunette you hooked up with during our small celebration party – the same one you damn near sent Tom Dunleavy to an early grave over – she's been asking around at Scolley's about you, about whether anyone knows where you are. Would you like me to tell her you're being held here?'

I thought about it, nodded. 'Yeah, why not. Wait a couple of weeks, though. See if I can hit the weights enough to put back on a little more muscle mass.'

We were informed our allotted ten minutes were over. Physical contact with prisoners was forbidden, which was fucking insane since I hadn't been convicted of anything yet. The two of us weren't even allowed to shake hands. Joe stood up awkwardly and gave me kind of a sad smile as he walked away. He looked smaller and older than he'd ever looked outside of Scolley's. I ended up returning the same sad smile.

Two weeks later, almost as if on cue, Nola came by to visit me. By this time I had gained another twelve pounds of muscle. I was still twenty pounds lighter than when she'd seen me last, and I could see the alarm in her eyes as she noticed the scars on my arms and how much thinner I was.

'Nothing like having flesh burned off by a fire and then being on only liquids for two months to lose weight,' I told her. 'Don't worry, darling, I'll be back to my old fighting weight soon enough now that I'm hitting the weights again. And these scars on my arms mean nothing except for a few ruined tattoos.'

'Kyle, I wasn't thinking anything like that. Only how sleek you look. Like a cougar.'

She was dressed in jeans and a T-shirt. It made her look younger, more innocent. I found myself more attracted to her than I'd been at any other time.

'I'm glad you're here,' I told her.

'So am I,' she said. She looked away for a moment, an uneasiness showing in her eyes. 'I know things got kind of crazy the last time we were together.'

I showed her my palm to hush her. 'Let's not talk about that. I'm just glad you're here now. I've missed you more than I realized.'

Her eyes met mine and before too long her skin was glowing a warm pink and her lips twisting into a bare trace of a smile. The old Nola was back in force. The sexual heat came off her in waves. If she could've she would've fucked me right then and there.

'I heard about what you did to Tom Dunleavy,' she said, a soft throaty purr rumbling in her voice. 'He meant absolutely nothing to me.'

Jesus, she thought I beat him near to death because of her. Good, let her.

'The thought of that cocksucker being with you was more than I could take,' I said.

She reached for my hand. A guard cleared his throat and warned her about physical contact. Reluctantly, she pulled back.

'I'd like to do a lot more right now than hold your hand,' she whispered.

A big surprise there, let me tell you.

'How are things at work?' I asked. 'Your boss better not think my being arrested means he can get away with firing you.'

'He hasn't done anything yet. I think he's waiting to see whether you get convicted.'

'Smart man, because I'm beating this charge.'

The heat in her eyes was near boiling over. At that moment I wouldn't have needed any blue pill or coke to take care of business. But all I could do was sit there and feel the heat from her blasting over me.

The guard broke the spell by telling her that her time had run out. Nola walked hesitantly away. I felt a dryness in my mouth as I watched her.

After that visit, Nola became a regular, making the two-hour drive for every allotted visitor slot I had. Each visit she wore skimpier clothes. Each visit the sexual heat coming off her was hot enough to scald. It damn near took my breath away. It's funny though, as gorgeous as Nola was, I would've given just about anything to have had Lorraine Jackson visiting me like that. Still, it didn't change the fact that every time the visit ended and Nola had to walk away, I could see the guards licking their lips over her and glaring at me with a mix of hate and envy.

'Why a girl like that would be interested in a cold-blooded piece of shit like you is beyond me,' one of the guards said to me as he escorted me back to my cell.

'Yeah, well, if it wasn't beyond you, you wouldn't be working a minimum wage job as a prison guard, would you?'

He wanted badly to take a swing at me, but he held back – probably more because I was now closer to my pre-fire weight having spent every hour I could in the weight room.

'They'll be sticking a needle in you soon enough, Nevin. You'll be nothing but a bad memory to her soon.'

I let that slide, but I made a note of remembering his name. It was only two weeks before the pre-trial hearings were scheduled to start. I spent whatever time I could hitting the weights, trying to burn off whatever nervous energy I could. At night I still wasn't sleeping, but I was able to relax enough where I could drift off into daydreams, usually about Nola and Lorraine Jackson – both naked and doing things to me that would make a porn star blush, at other times about me and that smart-assed guard where I'd be smashing his fucking face into pulp.

It was the day before my pre-trial hearings were to start when my lawyer came to me to tell me that a Timothy Dunn was on the government's witness list. 'What is he going to say?' she asked.

I couldn't talk for several seconds. I don't know whether it was outrage or shock, but whatever it was it had me damn near choking on my tongue. Timmy Dunn. One of the last stand-up guys in Southie now turned rat and ready to fuck me ten times over. That sonofabitch had changed a lot more than just becoming fat. My mind raced as I tried to think about what he had on me.

'You know about my background,' I said finally, my voice catching in my throat and not sounding quite right. 'I've done armed robberies in the past. Maybe I was planning to do more heists in the future. This still has nothing to do with any kidnapping.'

A film fell over her eyes as she stared at me.

'What is Timothy Dunn going to say?'

I rubbed a hand across my jaw, shrugged. 'He sold me some stuff.' I gave her the full list, leaving off the mini-van. The insurance fraud that Dunn was running was a lucrative business for him and I was guessing that he wouldn't tell the Feds about it.

'Where are these items now?'

'They were in my brother's apartment. They must've been burned in the fire.'

'Did he sell you a 9 mm handgun?'

'No.'

'You're sure about that?'

'Yeah, I'm sure. There were no guns involved.'

'How about a laptop computer?'

'No, nothing like that.'

'Any chance the FBI could've found a laptop in your brother's apartment?'

'I don't think so. I don't think he had one.'

'Any other surprises for me?'

'Look, all that stuff was for a planned jewelry store heist. I had nothing to do with the kidnapping. What difference does this make as long as you can prove that blood's not mine?'

She gave me a look cold enough to freeze. 'The government can establish that you knew the dead kidnapper, Manuel Lorentz. You're by no means a sympathetic defendant. You have a long history of violent crimes behind you. Even though you've only been convicted of that one lone bank robbery, the government can still establish your past relationship with John "Red" Mahoney. The jury is going to want very much to believe the DNA evidence against you, and this is only going to make them want to believe it all the more. If you were planning a jewelry store robbery, how come you didn't ask Mr Dunn to obtain a handgun for you?'

I tried smiling at her, but it was hard with the way she was looking at me. 'It was going to be a quick smash and grab,' I said. 'If I got caught I didn't want it to be an armed robbery bust, not after just finishing eight years in stir.'

I don't know whether she bought my explanation or not, all I knew was I was far from her favorite person at that moment. That night was maybe my worst. Not a second of sleep. All I did was lay on my prison cot frozen with rage. I should've tried counting rats, there'd been so many of them in my life of late.

The next morning I was put in shackles with my ankles and wrists chained together, and brought by bus to the Federal District Courthouse in Boston. While I waited with my lawyer, Timmy Dunn walked by. Sonofabitch even tried to smile at me.

As soon as we were brought into the courtroom, Lorraine

Jackson moved quickly to file a motion to exclude Timmy Dunn as a witness. That brought fireworks from the federal prosecutor, a thin pasty looking man in his late thirties. My lawyer talked over him.

'Your honor, Mr Dunn is going to testify that my client bought from him a list of items that include UPS uniforms, Halloween masks and a camcorder. Unless the government is prepared to show that these items were used in Jason Newman's abduction, then it would be highly prejudicial to allow his testimony.'

The prosecutor was on his feet with a smug smile spread wide across his face. 'Your honor, I believe the jury will be able to reach their own conclusion why these items were obtained by the defendant only days before Jason Newman was violently abducted from his home.'

The judge, a large thick man in his late fifties with rubbery looking skin and heavy-lidded eyes, asked, 'What was the purpose of your client obtaining these masks and UPS uniforms, if not for the kidnapping?'

'Your honor, it is not up to my client to explain this. It is up to the government to show that these alleged items were used in the crime, not to theorize that they could've been.'

The judge's eyelids lowered a bit as he turned to the prosecutor. 'Well?' he asked, frowning and looking a lot like a bullfrog.

'We've all seen the video made of a frail ten-year-old boy suffering from hemophilia begging for his life. The camcorder was obviously obtained for making this video.'

'I would've guessed that that video was made using a laptop computer camera,' Lorraine Jackson said. 'Unless the government can show that the video was made with the same camcorder Mr Dunn claims was provided to my client, there is no relevance to him telling the jury about it.'

The judge continued to peer at the prosecutor through his

heavy-lidded half-closed eyes. 'Mr Stevens, is this the substantive nature of Mr Dunn's testimony?'

'Yes.'

'Has the FBI lab been able to determine whether the video we all saw was made with the same brand of camcorder that Mr Dunn claims he provided the defendant?'

The prosecutor hesitated for a moment before shaking his head.

'Do you have any witnesses who saw men in the vicinity of the victim's house wearing masks or dressed in UPS uniforms prior to the abduction?'

'Not yet, but we're still interviewing potential witnesses.'

'I suggest strongly that you interview them with extreme caution. If I discover that any interview is done improperly and witnesses are unduly coerced, I will see that appropriate charges are filed. At this time do you have any evidence showing that these items were used in the commission of the crime in question?'

The prosecutor lowered his eyes from the judge and back to the papers he was shuffling. His large ears tinged red as he appeared absorbed in studying the papers in front of him.

'Not at this time, your honor,' he admitted after looking back up, 'but we're working on it.'

'I'd suggest you work harder. You have until the start of the trial before I make my ruling.'

The rest of the hearing was not that interesting and I mostly tuned out what was being said. I thought about Dunn and how I was going to have to get word back to Southie about what needed to be done with him. Even with the judge's warning, I didn't put it past the FBI to convince one of the neighbors about what they might've seen. Or who knows, maybe one of them actually did see a UPS truck the day before or the day after the kidnapping and ended up confused as to when they actually saw it. If that were to happen and Dunn was still around to testify, then I'd get linked to the kidnapping. As far as Dunn went, it didn't matter whether or not any of that happened. He still turned into a rat and there was only one thing to do with rats.

After the hearings ended and my shackles were put back on, I was led out of the courtroom by a federal marshal with my lawyer walking briskly at my side. In the hallway waiting for me were a dozen or so guys from the old neighborhood. I guess they had found out about the hearing and came to offer their respects towards Danny. The marshal seemed overwhelmed by them and they ignored his warnings and pushed forward to shake my hands and tell me how sorry they were about my brother. As Martin Foley pumped one of my shackled hands with both of his, I told him about Timmy Dunn being a rat.

'No kidding,' he said, a hard glint in his eyes.

'No kidding.'

I was pulled away by the marshal, and some Boston Police had joined in to separate me from the crowd. My lawyer got alongside me and scolded me in a low voice so that no one else could hear that she would not tolerate me intimidating or threatening witnesses.

'If I see you doing that or find out about it, I am under an obligation to report you to the courts,' she said.

'How the fuck did I intimidate Dunn? I didn't say word one to him. As far as the guys in the neighborhood go, they have every right to know what he is. It doesn't matter that his testimony against me is bullshit, there could be others in the neighborhood doing business with him, and they need to know the guy's a rat. Nothing in the world's lower.'

She stared hard at me, matching my intensity. Jesus, she was beautiful.

'Leave Mr Dunn to me,' she said. 'Do not get involved any further. And do not use that type of language in front of me in the future.'

I was separated from her at that point and taken onto the bus. I knew I didn't have to worry anymore about Timmy Dunn, at least not unless he was put in protective custody. There were others in Southie who had a lot to lose if Dunn was talking, and if someone's willing to rat on one person, they're willing to rat on anyone. As far as Southie goes, Dunn was a dead man.

I was calmer than I would've expected during the week leading up to the trial. I spent most of the time in the weight room. I think my lawyer would've liked me to have stayed at a hundred seventy pounds for the trial so I'd appear less threatening to the jury, but the hell with that. We met the day before the trial to go over strategy. She was as intense as I'd ever seen anyone, including Red. There was going to be a lot of national media coverage for the trial. This was a big case for her. It was going to put her in the spotlight. If it didn't appear like such a slam-dunk loser, I'm sure one of the high profile criminal defense lawyers around town would've taken it on pro bono for the publicity.

The jury selection took longer than the trial. You wouldn't believe all the fuckers who were already convinced I was guilty and claimed that nothing could change their mind. I guess most of these fine citizens wanted to avoid being picked and were willing to say anything to make sure that happened. The jury that ended up being selected was certainly not a jury of my peers. Forget Irish, there wasn't a single white person on it. Lorraine Jackson was pleased by that. During one of the breaks she told me that minorities would be more sensitive to the evidence manipulation being done by the FBI.

After the jury was selected, the judge had them cleared. Once it was just me, my lawyer, the prosecutor and the other courtroom personnel, he asked the prosecutor whether the government had been able to connect any of the objects Timmy Dunn had supposedly sold me to the kidnapping. The prosecutor had to admit that they had come up empty. The judge's eyelids drooped a bit more as he suppressed a yawn and ruled that Dunn's testimony could not be used.

The prosecutor's face reddened as he accepted that. 'A more serious matter, you honor,' he started, his voice cracking a bit, 'is that Timothy Dunn seems to have disappeared. My office will be looking into whether a witness tampering charge, or worse, will be pursued against Mr Nevin.'

That got the judge's attention. His eyes still mostly closed, he asked the prosecutor to tell him what he had.

The prosecutor's face reddened a bit more. 'A federal marshal overheard Mr Nevin relay a message to an associate that could've been an order to have Timothy Dunn taken care of.'

The judge turned his gaze towards me. 'Is that true, Mr Nevin?'

'No, your honor. This so-called associate I talked to is a school bus driver who's never been involved in any criminal activity that I know of. All I told him was that Dunn was planning to testify against me. I didn't ask that anything be done to Dunn, or imply that anything be done to him.'

The judge looked annoyed as he turned back to the prosecutor. 'Did the federal marshal hear anything that contradicts Mr Nevin's statement?'

The prosecutor had to admit that he didn't. The judge stifled another yawn, told him he hoped the upcoming case against me had more merit than this last accusation.

The next day the courtroom was mobbed. Nola had fought her way in and had a seat in the second to last row. Her face looked paler than anytime before – even when she was doing coke. There was kind of a brittleness to it, as if she wasn't sure what she was doing there. I guess my whole bad boy routine was finally becoming real to her. I gave her a quick wink and then focused my attention on the proceedings.

That first day was mostly bullshit, just smoke and mirrors as the prosecutor brought in forensic witnesses to reconstruct the crime and to show photographs of the dead dog lying on the floor and the door frame splintered after it had been kicked open. One of the forensic experts testified that the puddles of blood on the floor shown in the photographs were dog blood but that they were able to scrape human blood from the dead dog's teeth. This same witness gave his conclusion that the dog must've attacked the kidnapper, who was then able to shoot the animal several times in the side. After that the prosecutor wanted to play to the jury the video I made of the kid. My lawyer tried to argue that unless the prosecution could tie me to the video it would be highly prejudicial to play it. The judge overruled her and they played it on an almost theatre-sized screen. Without looking in their direction, I could hear several members of the jury weeping while it played. The judge adjourned for the day after that. Half the jury refused to look at me as they filed out, the other half glared openly at me.

'Going great so far, huh?' I remarked without bothering to hide any of the hostility I was feeling. 'You didn't say a hell of a lot in my defense.'

Lorraine Jackson looked unperturbed by the day's events.

'There wasn't anything that needed to be said. So far all the government's case has proved is that a kidnapping occurred. They offered no evidence yet to tie you to it. Just try to stay calm and be prepared for tomorrow,' she said.

The next day was when the government presented their real case against me. Like the other day, Nola had fought her way in and was sitting in one of the back rows but I was in too rotten a mood to bother acknowledging her. The government's first witness was the superintendent at Cedar Junction who was there to testify that my stay at the prison overlapped with Lorentz's. When my lawyer cross-examined him, she brought out how my time also overlapped with 1,429 other prisoners. He nodded and admitted that was probably true. None of it seemed to have any impact on the jury. The government next brought out their DNA expert. The guy looked like a college professor, complete with bow tie, thick-rimmed glasses and an unnaturally pink face that looked like it had been scrubbed for hours. He testified that blood found at the scene matched a DNA sample that I had been required to provide the FBI's CODIS system when I had previously been convicted of a federal crime. According to him all thirteen of my core loci matched, which was what led the FBI to identify me as being involved in the kidnapping. The prosecutor was brief in his questioning. None of the jury at this point could even face me. When my lawyer's turn came to cross-examine the witness, she asked whether fluids from the dog could've contaminated the blood evidence found. The guy without as much as a blink insisted that they couldn't have. Lorraine Jackson left it at that one question, but reserved the right to cross-examine him later.

The prosecution finished their case, then it was our turn. Our only witness was the doctor who had treated me at Boston City. Under oath he testified that when I came in with second and third degree burns, he found no evidence of any recent dog bites. That seemed to get the jury's attention. A few of them were even looking at me now as if I could possibly be something human. My lawyer then presented into evidence photographs of me that showed there were no recent bite marks.

The prosecutor didn't take this lightly. He tried his damnedest to get the doctor to admit that my burns could've hidden the bite marks. While the doctor wouldn't bend at all on his conclusion, he did hesitate enough at one point to make the jury think that maybe there was something to this. Then for good measure the prosecutor went over each scar on my body to ask whether it could've been made by a dog bite, and for each one the doctor gave his opinion on what was the most likely cause of the scar. I don't think he missed with a single one as he identified old bullet and knife wounds. I had a lot of scars and it took the doctor and prosecutor over a half hour to go over each one. It left the jury with no doubt about my violent past. All in all, I'm not sure the doctor helped me at all.

Lorraine Jackson looked unconcerned by it and I was grateful for that. It helped me hang in there. She next called the government's DNA expert for readdress. She waited until he took the stand before making a show of studying her notes and appearing overwhelmed. When she walked towards him, though, she glided in like a shark.

'Mr Harrison, you testified earlier that my client's DNA matched the blood found at the scene. Is that correct?'

'Yes.'

'What exactly matched?'

He cleared his throat, said, 'Thirteen of the core loci.'

'Is that what the FBI typically requires to make a DNA identification?'

'It's sufficient, yes, if that's what you're asking.'

'That's not what I'm asking. Don't the FBI's internal regulations call for a far more stringent test when identifying a suspect by their DNA?'

The guy wasn't dumb. He knew what was coming before he ever walked back to the stand. He cleared his throat again as if something stubborn was lodged back there, and said, 'Usually, yes.'

'In fact, don't their internal policies call for something called STR markers to be matched before a positive DNA identification can be considered?'

He coughed, nodded. Lorraine Jackson asked him to repeat his answer, and he acknowledged that those were generally the FBI's policies.

'Was a test done to match the STR markers in the blood found to my client's DNA sample?'

'We felt the dog saliva might've compromised the sample for doing that level of testing—'

'Please answer the question, yes or no.'

He wiped his brow and generally looked harried as he consulted his notes.

'Y-Yes,' he said, his voice faltering and sounding even more harried than he looked. 'I believe a more extensive test was done.'

'What did the test reveal?'

He blinked for the first time since she had brought him back on the stand. 'I don't have the results with me,' he said.

The judge cleared the courtroom while we waited over two hours for the FBI to fax over the more extensive DNA test results. When the results came in the expert looked them over and admitted that the STR markers didn't match, that according to the FBI's own internal policies the DNA did not identify me.

The judge was livid as he stared first at the witness and then at the prosecutor. The expert tried to explain how while the dog's saliva might've compromised the DNA for the more extensive test, he was sticking by the results of the other test. My lawyer spoke over him, demanding from the judge that due to the government's complete lack of any evidence linking me to the crime he provide an immediate not-guilty finding. The judge agreed. The case was over.

Fuck me.

That was all I could think when the judge ruled me not guilty. Fuck me.

It was over that fast. One second I was sweating for my life, the next I was a free man. My lawyer was gathering her papers and files together. While I was only half-kidding, I told her I should marry her for what she did for me. She didn't seem to hear me. I moved closer to her and asked if she'd like me to take her out for a celebratory dinner. That it was the least I could do.

Her large dark eyes flashed as she raised her head to look at me. She moved even closer to me and talked low enough so no one else could hear her.

'I am required to provide my clients a vigorous defense not only because of an oath I took but to keep the prosecution honest,' she said. 'If I see the government trying the tricks they did with you I have to fight it no matter how repugnant I might find my client. If they're willing to falsify evidence to send a guilty man to prison, they could just as easily do the same to convict an innocent one. But Mr Nevin, I'm not stupid. I know why the blood found at the crime scene was genetically similar to yours. I know why you *accidentally* set that fire in your brother's apartment, and why you had his body cremated. Where the government made a mistake was thinking the two UPS uniforms were for you and Manuel Lorentz, but Mr Nevin, to me it's clear who those uniforms were for. If you have even a shred of human decency in you, I pray that you contact that family – anonymously if needed – and let them know where to find their son's body. Please do not ever speak to me again.'

'You're wrong. None of that happened—'

She tuned me out and moved quickly to talk to the prosecutor and to offer a handshake. I sat clenching and unclenching my fists, waiting until I thought it was safe for me to move. When that happened, when the heat coming off my neck started to fade and I could see normally again, I left the courtroom as fast as I could.

Nola saw me first. I guess word hadn't gotten out yet about the outcome and the reporters weren't looking for me. She moved awkwardly towards me, her face scrunched up in a kind of a puzzled question.

'The FBI had to admit the blood found wasn't mine,' I told her. 'Their case against me was a sham, and the judge ruled me not guilty. It's over.'

I had her in my arms, lifting her and pressing her body

into mine. A hot moistness came off her. As we kissed her lips parted and her tongue pushed hard into my mouth. It was like swallowing fire. The rest of the world disappeared. My heart was pounding, I could feel hers also. For a long moment I imagined that Nola was Lorraine Jackson, that she was the one who I was holding and kissing. I know that probably sounds crazy after the verbal attack I'd just suffered from her, but that's what was going through my head.

Word must've gotten out about me being found not guilty. I could feel the buzz of it in the hallway and hear the footsteps running towards us. I put Nola down, and the two of us stood with arms around each other's waists, red-faced and breathing hard. Within seconds we were surrounded. Cameras flashing blinded me, making me squint. I held up a hand to stop their questions and to stop those cameras from flashing in my face.

'No more pictures,' I said. 'Until they stop not a word from me.'

There were a few more flashes before they stopped.

'The FBI admitted that their DNA evidence against me was a fake,' I said. 'The judge dismissed the case against me with a finding of not guilty.'

'Are you saying you had nothing to do with the kidnapping?' a woman TV reporter asked. Jesus, she was tiny, her hair looking like it had a layer of shellac over it. I gave her a grim smile. 'Yeah, that sounds like what I'm saying. The Feds never had any evidence linking me to the crime. This was a frame-up from day one. Payback for me not ratting out Red Mahoney nine years ago.'

'What about the fire that killed your brother along with seven other people?'

That question came from the sonofabitch newspaper columnist who had implied in his column that I had set the fire intentionally. I turned my back on him and answered a question from another TV reporter about what I'd like to say to the Newmans.

'What can I say? I'm like any of you. I feel for their loss, I pray that their son is miraculously still alive and is returned to them safely. But Christ, just because the FBI manufactured a case against me doesn't mean I had anything to do with it.'

The questions kept coming rapid-fire. I answered a few more until I spotted my lawyer leaving the courtroom. I pointed her out to the media jackals, then Nola and I made a run for it.

After months of moving outside only in shackles it felt odd not having any chains on my wrists and ankles. I squinted off into the horizon against the sun. At that time of day it seemed as big as my fist and a brighter orange than Red's old dye job. I stood transfixed by it. I didn't want to move, but I knew the jackals would be on us any minute now.

'I'm going to have to go find a place to stay tonight,' I told Nola.

'Kyle, honey, you can stay with me as long as you want.'

I nodded. It was what I was expecting. We hailed a cab to take us the three miles to Nola's waterfront condo.

Chapter 11

Nola's condo was just a one-bedroom but it still looked like it cost some bucks. Top of the line everything in the place and a view of the Boston harbor from her balcony that was close to spectacular. As she continued the tour I mentioned how she had the same blue-silver granite in the kitchen and bathrooms. She laughed and told me that it was Norwegian, that her father insisted she have a piece of Norway in the condo.

'You have to be making a lot more than I would've guessed selling suits to buy this place,' I said.

'Not really. I probably make less than you think. My parents bought it for me.'

'They're loaded, huh?'

I could see the nervousness creeping into her eyes as she fumbled with some noncommittal answer to that. What, she thought I was that much of a scumbag that I'd try to rip off her own parents? Anyway, I let it drop and we continued our tour to the bedroom. It didn't take either of us long to get out of our clothes. As I went at it with her, I closed my eyes and tried to hold the image of Lorraine Jackson in my mind. Nola, though, had to keep saying things to break the spell. I ended up finding creative ways to shut her up, and I did okay, lasting longer than I would've thought possible, at least long enough to leave her moaning and apparently satisfied. I couldn't help feeling a slight jolt of disappointment opening my eyes and remembering who I was with.

When we were done we both took long showers, then dressed and headed off to Scolley's. A large crowd from the neighborhood had gathered. I guess they were expecting me to show for a celebratory party. There were probably as many people there as when I showed up after getting out of Cedar Junction. People were buying me drinks and wishing me well and shaking my hand, but it wasn't like it was before. It was as if my shine had been tarnished. Before I was one of the holy trinity that ruled Southie, now I was some sad sack who passed out drunk and set his brother's apartment on fire, killing him and others. Yeah, I beat the government's case, but if I were really the mastermind behind the kidnapping, I was also the dumbass who let myself get ripped off and out-smarted by a lowlife like Lorentz. Worse, I was the guy who ended up with nothing but trouble for my efforts. I don't know, there was some sadness and maybe even a touch of pity behind their smiles and well wishes; kind of like I was a washed-up prize fighter, a guy who used to be a champ but was now just a punch-drunk bum. The only person who still looked at me as if I were the old fearsome Kyle Nevin was Joe, bless his heart. Nola also sensed the change in mood from before, and after a couple of hours seemed anxious to leave. Around midnight she told me she had to get up early for work. I told her to leave without me, that I'd catch up after an hour or so. When she walked out of the place she gave me this funny look, like she wasn't so sure anymore I was the man she thought I was.

I moved to the bar where I slowly sipped on a pint of Guinness and exchanged some small talk with Joe. I felt this uneasiness creeping into my chest, like things just weren't quite right and I had no idea what to do to fix them. Yeah, finding that rat bastard,

Red Mahoney, would go a long way in setting things right, but how the fuck was I going to do that now? Bill Nealy came over to offer his best wishes, and when I asked him if I could borrow his car, he hesitated for a moment before giving me his keys. That's how low I'd sunk, that someone like Bill Nealy would hesitate and have to think about something like that.

'Will the car be back to me by morning?' he asked, one eyebrow raised as he stared at me with alcohol-glazed eyes.

'What if it isn't?' I asked.

His eyes fell from mine as he realized that there was still plenty of violence left in me. He mumbled to keep it as long as I needed it. I ignored him, shook hands with Joe and told him I was calling it a night. I thanked him again for Danny and for looking out for me. He gave me a wink and told me to have fun with the rest of my evening.

'You've got a breathtakingly beautiful girl waiting for you,' he said.

I nodded and waved a few farewells as I left. I found Bill Nealy's seven-year-old Volkswagen Jetta where he told me it would be. He was going to give me a hard time over this piece of junk? Made me think for a moment of torching it. Instead I got in it and drove to an alley where I had money hidden under a sewer grate. It was still there. After that I drove to an area of Dorchester known for having hookers walking the streets at this time of night. Nothing had changed. They were still out there. Maybe more subdued and less aggressive than in the past, but they were standing on the street corners barely covered in their hot pants and halter tops. Most of them were black; a few fat white girls scattered among them. None of them looked too happy. I drove slowly until I found one that I wanted. She was black and skinny and reminded me of Lorraine Jackson. I waved her over. After she got in the passenger seat I realized she didn't really look at all like Lorraine. Her eyes were yellowish and had a drugged-out diluted look to them and her skin was a mess. She was also much skinnier than Lorraine, almost like a skeleton.

'Fifty dollars,' she said.

I showed her a fifty. She reached out for my zipper. I stopped her, told her I wanted to fuck her instead.

'Whatever you want, sugar,' she said.

She directed me to a crumbling brownstone a couple of blocks away and had me park on the street. We sidestepped garbage and filth as we walked up two flights to an apartment that made Danny's old place look like the Taj Mahal. Jesus, the place was a dump, far worse than any cell I'd been in.

'If anyone tries sneaking up on me to rob me I'll bust their heads,' I told her.

'No one's going to try that, sugar.'

She took me to a small room with a single mattress on the floor covered by a stained sheet. I folded my clothes carefully, hoping I wasn't picking up any livestock. I had her get on her knees with her back towards me and went at her from that end. It wasn't very good. Up close with her clothes off she looked more like a hospital cadaver than a live woman and she had this smell to her, kind of like bad chicken soup. When I penetrated her she made noises that made me think of a cat crying in the night. Still, I went at it until I was done. I was just hoping it would help get Lorraine Jackson out of my system.

I wanted to wash off, but I didn't want to see what a bathroom in that place would look like. I dressed quickly, and so did the whore I just fucked.

'That was nice, sugar,' she told me. 'Anytime you want a piece of my snatch, you come looking for me at that street corner. Now, would you be a dear and drive me back to that same corner?'

I gave her a sideways glance as I slipped on my shoes, but didn't bother answering her. As I headed to the door she started to give me some lip. When I turned towards her, though, she shut up pretty quickly. Outside Nealy's car was still in one piece, not that it would've mattered much to me if it wasn't. I drove back to Nola's condo with the expectation of returning Nealy his car when I was good and ready.

When Nola heard me in the apartment, she called out in a drowsy voice to join her in bed. I yelled back to her that I was going to take a shower first. The bathroom was big enough that there was a separate shower stall next to a Jacuzzi tub. The vanity in the bathroom was the blue-silver I had noticed earlier, the walls and floor of the shower were a white marble. It was like something you might see in a Trump Tower suite. It was the way I used to live before all the shit came raining down on me after Red set me up for that bank robbery. I turned the water on as hot as I could stand it and stood there for close to an hour trying to collect my thoughts and figure out what I was going to do next. I just couldn't shake this uneasiness filling me up.

When I left the shower I was feeling too antsy to want to go to bed. Jesus, what I would've given for a cig! I almost went out to a 24-hour store to buy a pack, but I fought back the urge. I sat for a while on a sofa in Nola's living room pounding a fist into an open palm, trying to figure out what to do to kill the rest of the night. I ended up finding some paper and a pen and wrote a long scathing letter about how the FBI tried to fuck me. Most of what I had in there was the truth, about how they knew the DNA evidence against me was phony but still tried to pass it off as genuine, and all the other shit they tried to coerce me into a deal. I exaggerated some with their reasons for this: to get back at me for refusing to give up Red's operations before and to try to force me to talk about them now. The gist of my letter was that I had just served my time and paid my debt to society, but I was targeted simply because of my past, and that if the FBI could do this to me they could do it to anyone. When I was done my letter was six pages handwritten, back and front.

I reread the letter several times, made some changes, added more outrage and indignation to it and then decided where to send it. At first I was planning to send it to one of the Boston papers, but after the way they had portrayed me over the past four months, screw them. I decided to go to the top. The *New York Times*. It felt good addressing the envelope and folding the pages into it. It was as if I was paying back those FBI cocksuckers, even if only a little. After that I turned on the TV and vegged. The early morning local news had stories about me, including video footage of me and Nola with our arms draped around each other. Something to make her parents proud, I'm sure. A little after six-thirty I could hear the radio alarm go off in the bedroom. Nola came out a short time later wearing a negligee but looking kind of disheveled, her face somewhat craggy as she squinted against the morning light. She asked me if I'd been up all night. I told her that I was feeling too antsy to try to get any sleep. She made an attempt to smile, but it was hard, though, against the light, and it fell apart. She asked if I wanted to go back to bed with her and work off some of my nervous energy. *I'd love to*, I told her, *but I wasn't feeling quite up for that*. She gave me a funny look again, sort of like when she was leaving Scolley's the previous night, but she didn't say anything.

While she took a shower and blow-dried her hair, I cooked her breakfast, French toast and sausage. She didn't have any maple syrup, so I made a sauce by first melting some brown sugar, then melting butter and squeezing lemon and orange into it. I had the food on the table and the pots and bowls already scrubbed and cleaned before she came out of the bathroom. She looked surprised when she noticed the food, then showed that bare trace of a smile of hers.

'A stud who can also cook,' she said. 'I think I hit the jackpot.'

'Yeah, you got the whole package with me, baby.'

She seemed to enjoy the food – at least she told me enough

times she did. When she was done she hesitated a bit, then suggested that she could take the day off and spend it with me.

'That would be something special,' I said. 'But I've got some things I need to do. We'll do it another day, okay?'

She exaggerated a pout as she came over and sat on my lap. While she wrapped one arm around my shoulder and kissed me, she snuck her other hand down my boxers to try to get a rise out of me. It just wasn't working and I stopped her.

'I'm not feeling up to it right now,' I told. 'Later I'll be as good as new, promise.'

She nodded and tried to smile to let me know it was okay. 'Why don't you come by at noon? We don't have to make love or anything, but it would be nice just to go out to lunch with you.'

'We'll see. I've got things I need to do, but I'll try to fit it in. If I'm not there by twelve, don't wait for me, okay?'

'I understand, but try to show up. Please?'

I told her I would, knowing full well there wasn't a chance in hell I would show up. Seeing her at night was about as much of her as I think I could take. She got up to change and later, before she headed off to work, stopped by to give me a long kiss goodbye. As her hips gently pushed into mine, what I had down there felt as dead as the rest of me.

I spent most of that morning visiting Ma and telling her how sorry I was that I wasn't able to take better care of Danny. After that I did some shopping for new clothes, then spent the rest of the day at Carson Beach, sitting and watching the ocean and trying to figure out what the fuck I was going to do next. How I was going to get enough money to find that rat bastard, Red.

Chapter 12

When I woke up two mornings ago I caught Nola staring at me as if I were a mistake that she wanted to get rid of. Once she realized I was awake, she forced an artificial smile, but there was no hiding what had been troubling her only minutes before. It had been four weeks since I moved in with her, and over the past week I started to pick up vibes that maybe she didn't want it to go on for too much longer. Until she worked up the courage to say something about it, I certainly wasn't going to. Her apartment was a nice place to come home to each night. It was comfortable, had a nice view of Boston Harbor, and the sex when I was up to it wasn't bad. There was no question Nola was nice to look at, and now that she was getting moodier and quieter, all the better.

The first few days things were pretty good between us. I had a couple of TV interviews with the local news channels, some write-ups with the papers, and even an appearance on one of the national talk shows, in all of which I played up being the injured victim but making sure to still give a wink to what a tough motherfucka I really was. The *NY Times* printed my letter as a guest editorial, and Nola and I celebrated that. For a few days I was riding high and Nola was as hot as a furnace and beaming as brightly as any Christmas tree. I didn't need any pills to get the job done with her then. Last week, though, I bought a few dozen.

I hadn't used any yet, but I figured it would be better to have some on hand to shut her up in case she started the *maybe it's time for you to find your own place* speech.

I guess the depression hit me shortly after the rush of making my TV appearances. Those first few days I thought things were going to work out differently, that I was going to sue the government for millions. I saw a string of lawyers and the results were the same with each. After they checked things out they all called back to tell me that I didn't have a case. It didn't make sense to me, but they seemed adamant that the case was a loser – and that the last thing I would want to do would be to take the stand, which I would have to in their opinion if I wanted any chance of winning a large judgment. I started to accept that I was going to have to rob banks again. With Danny gone and the way things were in the old neighborhood, I didn't trust bringing anyone in with me. I was going to have to do the jobs solo and without any inside information. Those types of jobs I'd be lucky to net a few grand. Thinking about all the banks I'd have to hit to make up for the two mil I lost depressed the hell out of me, and I must've let it show. Anyway, Nola picked up on it, and I could tell she was losing respect for me. I could tell she was beginning to doubt whether I was the same man she thought I was. Maybe even thinking that I wasn't much better than a bottom-feeder like Tom Dunleavy.

I had parked near a stand-alone ATM kiosk with a newspaper and a large Dunkin Donuts coffee in hand. I decided that if I was going to do these robberies by myself, it made more sense to hit ATM machines while they were being reloaded with cash. That way I'd end up with a few thousand in already circulated twenties and wouldn't have to worry about cleaning the money, plus it was the kind of job a single person could do easily. So I was spending my time camping out at several of these kiosks, trying to pick up their drop-off schedules. I still had Bill Nealy's Jetta. A few days earlier I was at Scolley's shooting the breeze with Joe

Whalley when Nealy walked up to me and asked if I was going to be needing his car much longer. I gave him a sideways glance, pretended not to hear him. He cleared his throat and asked again.

'What was that, Nealy?'

'I was just wondering how much longer you're going to be needing my car,' he said.

I gave Joe a wink, said, 'Wasn't that generous of Nealy to loan me his car like he did? Helping me to get back on my feet after a wrongful imprisonment.'

'Hell of a gesture,' Joe conceded.

Nealy was sober. If he'd been drunk he might've said something he would've regretted; instead he cleared his throat again and mentioned how he was having to rent a car each day to drive to work.

'You might want to be looking into a long-term lease,' I said. 'Or maybe find someone to carpool with.'

That got a chuckle from Joe, then the two of us continued our talk without any further interruptions. As far as I was concerned Nealy wasn't even there.

I sat reading the paper until an armored truck showed up, noted the time and wrote it down in a notebook. Four oh five. Three days ago a drop off was made at four fifteen. Only one driver in the front, an armed guard in the back. If I took out the guard I might be able to empty out the truck. That would be a hell of a bigger score than simply ripping off the guy bringing more cash to the machines. I worked out in my mind both scenarios, how long each would take and what would be needed. I was parked a few hundred feet away and tried to act as nondescript as possible as I observed all this. After they left I drove eight miles to the next kiosk that I was watching. When the time was right I wanted to hit five or six ATMs within a couple of hours before word got out and they tightened security.

I watched the other kiosk for over an hour. No delivery of new cash. I still didn't have the schedule worked out for this one yet. I had three more ATMs I wanted to watch, but I just wasn't in the mood for it. I thought long and hard about spending the evening at Scolley's, but instead I took out the bottle of blue pills I bought. It had been over a week since I'd tried anything in the sack with Nola and tonight was as good a night as any. I needed to keep her happy for a few more weeks until I was ready to pull these jobs. The last thing I wanted to worry about was finding a new place to stay. I swallowed one of the pills with cold coffee.

My heart just wasn't in it as I drove back to Nola's waterfront condo, but you do what you have to, right? When I walked in the place, she was there ahead of me but instead of the apprehension that had been ruining her mouth the last couple of weeks there was something more like a giddiness in her face. She broke out into an odd smile as she watched me.

'There's a message for you,' she said.

The only people who knew I was there were Joe and a couple of others from Scolley's, so all I could think was someone was calling me in for a job. When I played the message back there was a man's voice I didn't recognize. Somewhat effeminate, kind of a nasal whine. The guy introduced himself as Michael Bennett, senior editor and Vice President at Harleston Books. He wanted to let me know how fascinating he found my *NY Times* editorial, how he thought my writing was filled with a raw vibrant energy and showed literary talent, and that he wanted to talk to me about my writing a book for his publishing house. He left me his cell phone number and asked me to call him anytime. My first thought was that this was some sort of FBI sting, a way to trick me into a confession. I looked over at Nola and she broke out giggling.

'Wow,' she said.

'Have you ever heard of Harleston Books?' I asked her.

She nodded. 'They're big. I looked up Michael Bennett. He's very big in publishing.'

She had bookmarked a number of pages and I went through them with her. One of them showed a picture of Bennett. He was my age, tall, skinny, a lightweight with a big head, not much hair and a closely-cropped and well-manicured mustache and beard. The picture tried to make him look literary, I guess, with him wearing a sports jacket with leather patches on the elbows as he leaned against a large globe. It also tried hard to de-emphasize his thin neck and pronounced Adam's apple, but didn't do a very good job of it. Several of the articles mentioned a wife and kids, and maybe he was straight, but he looked as effeminate as he sounded. I read more of the articles, and all of the book deals mentioned in them were for millions. I still thought there was a chance that this was a set-up – that he might be doing this in conjunction with the FBI – but I called the cell phone number he left.

Bennett picked up quickly and started telling me in that same effeminate nasal whine of his how thrilled he was that I called back. I shut him up quickly.

'How'd you get this number?' I demanded.

'Why, through the *NY Times* of course,' he said. 'You did provide them a contact phone number and address.'

That was true. I did.

'What do you want?' I asked.

'Direct and to the point,' he said, some amusement highlighting his voice. 'As I would've expected from your brilliantly written editorial. What I want is for you to write a novel. A two-book deal offering a six hundred thousand dollar advance.'

'This is a joke, right?'

'No joke, Mr Nevin.'

I scratched my forehead, thinking. Nola's eyes had grown large with her mouth pressing into a crooked line as she tried to listen in. Our bare arms touched and it was as if she was burning up with fever.

'What type of book do you expect from me for that kind of money?' I half-heard myself asking him.

He paused at his end, and I had a vivid picture in my mind of him sitting behind his desk with his lips pursed and his palms pressed together so that his fingers formed an apex under his chin. I would've bet my last dollar that was how he was looking.

He broke his silence, saying, 'That, Mr Nevin, is something I'd like to talk to you about in person. Do you have time over the next few days to come to New York? We will of course pay your expenses.'

'Yeah, sure.'

'Wonderful. I will have my assistant, Tammy, call tomorrow morning to make the arrangements. I look forward to meeting with you, *Kyle*.'

I stood staring at the phone, not quite believing the call I just had.

'Fuck me,' I said.

Nola was staring at me breathless with anticipation.

'Did I hear right?' she asked. 'He offered you six hundred thousand dollars to write a book?'

I nodded, said, 'Unless this is all some elaborate scheme on the FBI's part to get a confession out of me.'

I think the idea of that excited her even more than a possible big money book deal. She bit her lip and gave me a shy hesitant look. As she moved forward, her hand *accidentally* brushed against my groin. At that moment I wouldn't have needed the blue pill I'd taken earlier, but with it I was more than ready to go. We melted into each other and didn't make it more than a few steps towards the bedroom before we were rolling on the carpet, a hot kind of craziness taking us over. It was a long time after that that I was carrying her to the bedroom, and even much longer

after that before we were finished, both of us on our backs, wet
with perspiration and breathing as if we'd just run a marathon.

'Wow,' she said.

'That's two *wows* in one night,' I remarked.

She smiled at me, then got up to take a shower. As I watched
her walk away without a stitch of clothing on I couldn't help
admiring how beautiful she really was. For the most part I had
gotten Lorraine Jackson out of my system. It had been days since
I trolled Dorchester for any skinny black hookers to fuck.

Nola turned the water on in the shower. It was comforting
lying there listening to its soft drone. I felt more relaxed than I'd
felt since Danny's death. Longer actually. It had probably been
over nine years since I'd had this sense of calm and peace. Six
hundred thousand dollars would go a long way towards finding
Red. Yeah, it was possible this was a scam cooked up by an
overzealous FBI agent, but I didn't think that was too likely. As
Nola took her shower I lay there wondering what type of book
they would want me to write. In the meantime, I decided to
postpone my plans to rob ATM machines.

Later that night the two of us were walking into Scolley's, and
from the shine on both of us people knew something was up. A
grin stretched across Joe's face as we approached the bar.

'What?' he asked.

'What do you mean *what*?'

'Kyle, don't keep me in suspense. Spill it, lad.'

'I don't know what you're talking about, Joe.'

He gave me a suspicious look. After he poured me a pint of
Guinness and Nola a glass of white wine, I commented how I
might've been contacted by a book publisher.

He raised an eyebrow at me. 'No kidding?' he said.

I drained half my ale before looking back at him, my own
smile growing as wide as his own. Nola let loose with a giggle
next to me.

'A two-book deal,' I said. 'A six hundred thousand dollar advance.'

Joe's jaw dropped. Then I swear, tears of joy popped up in his eyes. He reached over the bar to hold my hand in both of his.

'That is wonderful news, Kyle,' he said. 'With this you should be able to put the old days behind you and have a fresh start.' He turned to smile at Nola. 'And what a beautiful young lass to start a new life with.'

Nola's tiny fingers squeezed my hand tight on hearing that. I nodded to Joe and played along. Of course that wasn't what it meant. Me, a new career as a writer? What a fucking joke. But if some dumbass publisher wanted to pay me that kind of money, let him. Six hundred thousand would get me started in my hunt for Red and what was left of it would be a nice stake in getting me back in the game. I had no plans to leave my old ways behind, at least not until I found a way to make up for the two mil I lost.

Bill Nealy was sitting at a corner table slouched over as he nursed a beer, his head so low to the table that his nose nearly dipped into his glass. I excused myself from Joe so I could give Nealy his car keys back. He nearly broke out blubbering as I handed them to him.

'Oh, Jesus, Kyle, bless you, you have no idea how much I appreciate this.' He wiped a hand across his eyes and bit down hard to keep his emotions in check. 'I didn't know how I was going to handle the lease payments if I was going to have to do something like that.'

I slipped him a hundred. Fuck, in the mood I was in, why not?

'Chrissakes, Bill,' I said. 'Don't you know when a guy's joking with you? Anyway, you did me a solid loaning me your car like you did. I won't forget it.'

Nealy looked like he wanted to kiss me full on my lips. I

moved away before something embarrassing like that happened. When I rejoined Nola and Joe, word of my upcoming book deal had spread and folks within Scolley's were coming over to offer their congratulations. During it all I noticed one guy sitting at a table across the way staring bullets at me. I'd never seen him before. He was in his late thirties, had kind of a stocky build, wire-rimmed glasses, dark messy hair and a thick stubble that showed he hadn't shaved in days. I asked Joe about him and he shrugged, told me he was one of the gentrified newcomers who'd been coming to Scolley's off and on for the last couple of months. I tried to ignore the guy and simply enjoy the moment but I kept feeling his angry stare on my back. I finally had enough and walked over to him.

'What the fuck's your problem with me?' I asked him.

He seemed startled by that. He lowered his eyes and tried to act as if he hadn't been openly glaring at me.

'Oh, no, nothing,' he mumbled uncomfortably. He shifted in his chair and brushed his hand through his hair, leaving it even messier than before. 'Did I hear right? Did you really just get a two-book deal with a six hundred thousand advance?'

'Yeah.'

'Do you mind if I ask who with?'

'Harleston Books.'

He nodded as if he knew about them.

'That's a good publisher,' he said. 'Do you mind if I ask what your book is about?'

'I don't know. They haven't told me yet what they want.'

He blinked at me several times. He must've thought I was joking. When he realized I wasn't, he frowned severely, asked, 'You haven't written your first book yet?'

'Fuck no.'

'Then why did they make you this offer?'

'You don't recognize me?'

He shook his head.

'Kyle Nevin,' I said. 'I'm the guy the FBI tried to frame for that kidnapping in Boxboro.'

He stared at me blankly, then nearly doubled over laughing. Watching him laugh like that I could feel my throat tightening and the heat rising from my neck. I clenched my fists and moved closer to him.

'What's so fucking funny?' I asked.

'Jesus, I'm sorry.' He wiped some tears from his eyes and tried to control himself but still broke out with a couple of snorts. 'I'm not laughing at you. Just my own sad sorry situation. I have an MFA in creative writing and spent three years working on my first novel. After a year and a half of sweating I was able to find an agent who has since gotten my novel into a number of houses, including Harleston Books, where editors have wanted to acquire it only to be shot down by their marketing boards because I wasn't a *name*, and they didn't want to risk spending the money to promote a book by someone who wasn't a *name*.'

'What does MFA stand for – Motherfucka?'

He laughed. 'It could just as well stand for that. Makes as much sense as anything else.'

I gave him a hard eye before backing away.

'Here's a suggestion,' I said. 'Instead of bitching and moaning to strangers about your problems, why don't you go out and make a fucking name for yourself. Rob a few banks. That will do it.'

He nodded and pushed himself to his feet, drunk enough that he wobbled a bit as he stood. As he studied his feet, his smile faded and his face turned darker and grimmer.

'Solid advice, but I think instead I'll go home and fill the tub with hot water and slit my wrists,' he said.

I nodded, told him that would get his name in the papers also. I watched as he stumbled out of Scolley's. Always has to be some fucker trying to rain on your parade. I rejoined Nola, Joe and the rest of my well-wishers and made a night of it.

I was dead to the world later that night – maybe my first decent night's sleep in over nine years. When the phone ringing woke me and I stared bleary-eyed at the clock next to the bed, I couldn't quite believe it was as late as nine-thirty in the morning. I reached over and felt for Nola and realized she was gone. I rubbed my eyes for a few seconds, then pushed myself out of bed and caught the tail end of Bennett's assistant, Tammy, leaving me a message.

Nola had left a note for me in the kitchen to let me know that she had gone off to work. She also wanted to tell me how much she enjoyed the previous night and how happy she was both about my news and that I had spent the night sleeping with her. She sounded as if we'd reached a new level in our relationship, and I guess we had. I'd been spending most of my nights driving around looking for armored trucks as they made their ATM delivery drop offs. Later, when I'd get back to the apartment, I'd either try to doze off for a few hours on the sofa or try to kill time before morning, usually cleaning her place until it was spotless. This was the first night that I had spent sleeping with her in her bed, and the first morning that I didn't have breakfast waiting for her when she woke up.

I made a pot of coffee and sat trying to clear my head. After drinking a couple of cups of it black, I called Tammy back. She had a nice voice. I pictured someone young and blonde, with green eyes and a cute button nose. When she asked when I could make it to New York, I suggested why not that afternoon, that if they could rent me a BMW convertible and put me up at the Plaza, I could be down there by four. She hesitated for a moment, then told me she'd have to clear it with Michael's schedule, but she'd call me right back. I was halfway through my next cup of coffee when she called to tell me that she was able to clear the time with her boss, but that they were thinking more along the lines of flying me down on the shuttle and putting me up in a Holiday Inn.

'Yeah, well, I'm thinking more along the lines of driving down in a BMW and staying at the Plaza. Tell your boss if he wants me in New York that's the way it's going to be.'

She hesitated again and told me she'd have to call me back. Ten minutes she called to tell me it was all set, she had booked me a room at the Plaza and had rented me a BMW Z4 convertible.

'We can only put you up in the Plaza for one night,' she told me.

I told her that was fine with me. While I didn't like that they were going to start nickel and diming me, especially after throwing six hundred grand in my face, I felt more of my old self – not letting anyone dictate terms to me. After I got off the phone with her, I took a shower, dressed casually in jeans and a T-shirt and loafers, slipped on the leather jacket that Nola had bought me as a gift, then took a cab to the clothing store where she worked. When I told her that we were going to spend a couple of days in New York at the Plaza, she let loose with a little squeal and just about flew into my arms with her arms wrapped tightly around my neck. Her manager had no objection to her taking a couple of days off. In fact, he seemed relieved by the idea of it. We took a cab back to her place and packed; me, an extra change of underwear and socks and another shirt, her with enough clothing to fill two suitcases. I called the number that Tammy had left me and within an hour a BMW was delivered.

The traffic was light through most of the drive to New York and I took my chances with the state troopers in Connecticut, sometimes keeping the BMW speeding along at 130 mph. We didn't hit any slowdowns until we reached the Hutchison River

Parkway and even then it wasn't that bad. Two hours and ten minutes after leaving Boston we were checking into the Plaza. It had been a warm late October day, at least warm enough to keep the top down, and Nola looked exhilarated from the ride, her hair windswept and her skin glowing a bright pink. Me, I had a lot of nervous energy built up. We had over an hour and fifty minutes before my meeting with Bennett, so Nola and I made use of the time. After we were done and I had put my clothes back on, I told Nola to order whatever she wanted.

'Champagne, food, massage, bikini wax, put whatever you want on the hotel bill. The publisher's picking up the tab, so let's give them something to get pissed off about.'

Nola curled up in bed, kind of like a cat, a satisfied smile showing.

'Don't worry,' she said. 'I'll find ways to spend their money.'

A woman after my own heart. I was beginning to feel a fondness for her, maybe even something a bit deeper. I kissed her on the tip of her nose and headed out. Harleston Books had a Fifth Avenue address, only a half dozen blocks from the Plaza. It was a nice day and the sun was still strong enough to feel good on my face, so I decided to walk it. While I made it down those half dozen blocks, I saw dozens of sleek and beautiful women all dressed to the hilt. It does the spirit good to see women like that. The energy on the street was intense, something you could feed off. I'd almost forgotten what New York could be like. My last trip there had been over ten years ago, and that was for some business for Red down in the Bronx. After the job was done I took a week off in Manhattan. Christ, it felt good to be back.

If Harleston Books was swimming in enough money to pay someone like me six hundred grand, I sure as hell wouldn't have been able to tell from their lobby. I was disappointed with what I saw. I don't know what I was expecting – maybe marble and granite and walnut trim with a chandelier bigger than the BMW

I drove hanging from their ceiling, and maybe marble busts of famous writers lining a back wall – but what was actually there could've been a lobby from any building. I'd been to Chinese restaurants on Route 1 in Saugus that had put more money in their décor than that lobby. I gave my name to the security guard working the front desk. Less than a minute later Tammy came down to get me. I wasn't disappointed in what I saw with her. I also couldn't have been more wrong about my earlier image of her – not that she wasn't young and cute and slender with a nice little button nose, but she was Asian with a last name of Chen and had dark eyes and long black hair that reached halfway down her back. She also had a dazzlingly beautiful smile and a firm handshake. As soon as I saw her and the way her dress clung to her body I regretted bringing Nola with me, but what's done is done. On the elevator ride up to Bennett's office we chitchatted about the BMW she rented me and my ride to New York. It was pleasant talking to her. If she held a grudge about me forcing the issue with the BMW and the Plaza she didn't show it. I liked her. I especially liked the spark in her eyes when she laughed at my jokes.

Bennett, the cocksucker, kept me waiting twenty minutes, supposedly on an important call to Hong Kong. Obviously a power thing to put me in my place, but since Tammy kept me company during that time I really didn't mind – at least not enough I couldn't keep myself in check. When he finally came out to meet me, it was like shaking hands with a damp sponge. The guy was taller than I would've thought from his picture, maybe six and a half feet, but Christ was he skinny. He couldn't have weighed more than a hundred and fifty pounds. Other than that, though, he looked like he did in his picture. The polished, well-crafted look of someone who's supposed to be smarter than everyone else around him. I wish he had been in the South End that day. I would love to have had Danny crack his skull with a brick so we could steal whatever we could off of him.

'I am so thrilled that you were able to come here on such short notice,' he said as he ushered me into his office, guiding me with one hand on my back. I didn't like being touched by him but for six hundred grand I kept my mouth shut. His office wasn't much. Instead of the leather and expensive woods I was expecting, it was more metal and plastic. The globe from the picture was next to his desk and there were a lot of bookcases stuffed with books, but other than what I could tell was a private bathroom off to one side and a picture window view of Fifth Avenue, not much to show that he was a big shot. I stopped in front of the window.

'If you turn more towards your left you can see Central Park,' he remarked.

He had taken a seat behind his desk, and was now sitting almost exactly the way I had pictured him during our phone call with his hands pressed together and his fingertips barely touching his pursed lips. I know it's crazy, the guy was offering me six hundred grand, and all I wanted to do was kick the shit out of him. I guess it was because he had the same sort of look as all the other cocksuckers who'd sneer down their noses at me thinking they were better than me. What the fuck? In an office like that? Because he went to some ivy league college and fell into this scam while I had to bust heads and take knives and bullets to the body to make my money? I took a deep breath to settle my rage, then pulled up a chair across from him.

'What the fuck am I doing here?' I asked him.

He broke into a gleeful laugh – I swear to God, that's the only way I could describe it. Noises like steam escaping from a vent came out of him. He held out his palm to me.

'I'm sorry, Kyle. Please don't think I'm laughing at you. It was just so priceless. Your directness was exactly what I was expecting. And hoping for.'

'I'll tell you what. Until we have a business arrangement, why don't you call me Mr Nevin. And why don't you tell me what type of book you want from me and quit wasting my fucking time.'

He nodded, still smiling, but not quite as much glee in his eyes.

'Fair enough,' he said. 'Mr Nevin, what I would like from you for your first novel is a fictionalized version of the kidnapping you were just acquitted of.'

'What the fuck? I had nothing to do with that.'

'If I thought you did, I wouldn't be making you this offer. But what I'd like you to do is put yourself in the mind of the actual kidnappers and write a fictional novel of how you might've committed this crime. I want this to be a tough, hard-hitting crime novel, something where there are no winners, only losers, and with the authenticity that you are more than capable of providing.'

I rubbed my jaw as I thought about what he said. My eyes shifted away from him.

'I don't know,' I said. 'The FBI might try using it as a confession and bring me up on more charges.'

'No they won't. I've already consulted with a top criminal defense attorney, and there's no risk of anything like that happening, but to ease your mind I can have you meet with the attorney tomorrow morning, all at our expense, of course.'

I squinted hard at him, still rubbing my jaw and wondering what type of lawyer he'd try to set me up with after already trying to bring me to New York on the cheap.

'Yeah, I think I'd better do that,' I said. 'I don't know. This wasn't the type of book I thought you'd want from me.'

'What were you expecting?'

'I don't know. Maybe one of those tell-all books that so many of my brethren are writing.'

He waved that idea away, his eyes deadening at the thought of it. 'There have been too many of those as it is. And to be honest, Mr Nevin, I find them unseemly on so many different levels.'

I made a face as I considered what he was proposing. 'You want me to write an actual novel. Shit. I've never tried writing anything other than that editorial in the *NY Times*. I don't know if I could do something like this.'

He smiled. 'That editorial was two thousand words. How long did it take you to write it?'

'I don't know. Maybe an hour, another hour to clean it up.'

'Two hours for two thousand words? Mr Nevin, the book is going to be eighty thousand words. You'll have no trouble.'

I half-heard myself tell him that I didn't even know where to begin with something like this.

His smile widened a bit and he lowered his pressed fingertips so that they rubbed through his beard.

'You won't have to. I'm going to have you work with a book packager. They'll help you formulate the plot and structure, as well as character development. All you'll have to do is connect the dots with the actual writing. It will mean sharing the copyright with the packager, as well as twenty-five percent of the advance and royalties for the first book, but there should be more than enough money for this book to go around.'

I calculated that out in my head. This would leave me a hundred and fifty grand less than what I was counting on, and I said as much to Bennett.

'Actually, it would only be seventy-five thousand less. The advance is for a two-book deal, with three hundred thousand for each book. If you learn enough working with the packager on the first book, we won't have to hire them for your second one. But Mr Nevin, if this book does as well as I'm expecting, it could easily bring in five million or more in royalties.'

I was mulling over everything he told me. I didn't have to be greedy about it. I could split five million. Two and a half million would be more than enough.

'Why not just have this packager write the book and put my

name on it?' I asked. 'You want to do that and pay me half the royalties, that's fine with me.'

His smile weakened. 'We can't do that,' he said. 'Nor would we want to even if we could. To be honest about this, with enough help anyone can write a book. And with enough money behind it I can put almost any book on the *NY Times* bestsellers list. What I can't do is make any book a blockbuster. Those are rare. For those you need the right package, and Mr Nevin, you're it. You've got the back story, the national attention, the rough good looks that appeal to both women and men, and you can actually write – trust me, there's absolutely no question about that. Your writing is raw, but it's also powerful, edgy, and exactly what this book needs. It's what I call "The Street". I'm convinced that this book will be a blockbuster and will sell into the millions. If I wasn't, you wouldn't be sitting here now.'

I must've looked like I was in a daze the way he smiled at me, like I was some little kid in short pants. He walked over to a bookcase, and after studying it thoughtfully, picked three books from it and dropped them off in front of me. *Red Harvest* by Dashiell Hammett, *The Killer Inside Me* by Jim Thompson, and *Dead City* by Shane Stevens.

'An eclectic collection of crime novels,' Bennett said. 'I strongly suggest studying these books. You can learn a tremendous amount from them. Not that I want you to ape their styles. You've got a unique style as it is, and that's what I want for this book, but it never hurts learning from the masters.'

He had put his hand on my shoulder in a paternal sort of way. I stared at him until he removed it.

'If this book is going to be worth millions, then what about upping the advance,' I said.

He moved back to his chair and sat down, leaning back with his hands clasped behind his head. He gave me an apologetic smile.

'I can't do that,' he said. 'This was what I was able to get approved by our board of directors. Besides, we need to give you an incentive to put in a diligent effort.'

I shrugged nonchalantly, said, 'If this book is such a potential blockbuster like you say it is, maybe I should shop the idea to other publishers. See if I can work out a better deal for myself.'

His smile tightened a bit.

'By all means,' he said. 'Of course, other editors may not be as visionary as I am. And of course, Harleston is one of the bigger and more respected publishers in the industry. Very few if any of our competitors have the resources to promote your book as intensively as we can. Before you even write your first line, I'll have articles appearing in major newspapers across the country talking about you being our latest and greatest literary find.'

He held his smile, his eyes steady on mine. I decided no sense in being greedy. Anyway, I liked the idea of having an excuse to run into Tammy again in the future. I nodded, and that brought enough of a slight cocksucker-type smile to his lips that I knew I could've squeezed him for more money.

'We'll talk more tomorrow after you have a chance to consult with the attorney,' he said.

'Yeah, sure.'

'Mind if I call you Kyle now?'

'Add another fifty grand to the advance, go right ahead.'

He laughed, told me he'd look into it.

Before we called it a night, he told me what was going to be expected of me if I wrote this book. The interviews, book tours, TV appearances. After that, I shook his damp sponge of a hand again, and as I was getting up he clapped me on the back and reminded me to take the books he had given me. I collected them, my head buzzing with the idea of writing a novel. On the way out I stopped by Tammy's desk and suggested that she help me spend a pile of her bosses' money by joining me someplace expensive for dinner and drinks. She hesitated, and I could see she almost accepted my invitation, but she begged off, claiming she had to work late. When I asked for a raincheck, she flashed me her dazzling smile and promised that she'd give me one. I really didn't expect her to drop everything and go out with me that night, but I was setting the foundation for later.

It was five-thirty when I left Harleston Books. The sidewalks were filled with even more sleek beautiful young women than before. The weather was still warm enough for them to be wearing tight skirts showing off their legs, and of course, high heels that accentuated their calves. Seeing them worked better than any blue pill I could've taken. A number of these women smiled at me as they walked past; a few of them, their smiles turned into something completely different as they realized why I looked familiar. It didn't matter. When I got back to the hotel room, Nola was waiting for me. She had put her clothes back on, and within seconds I was pulling them off, not that she objected. When we were done, she showed me a big satisfied smile and told me how I'd have to get book deals more often. The fucking truth.

We went out to dinner and dropped close to a half a grand on food and drinks, all of it charged to Harleston Books – I knew they wouldn't like it but they didn't think ahead enough to put a price limit on what I could spend. I was still thinking the whole thing was a joke, but I still spent a good part of the night reading the books Bennett gave me. My heart sank as I read them. I guess I had kidded myself that I could actually do what Bennett was saying, but reading those books I knew I could never write anything like them. This was a fucking game. A scam. Nothing more. I'd play my part in it, collect my six hundred grand, minus the book packager's cut, and expect nothing as far as royalties. If Bennett could turn the shit I gave him into a bestseller, all the more power to him. I'd have to respect someone like that. It would be a bigger crime than anything I could ever pull off. Jesus, what a world. Anyway, it would take hitting a lot of ATM machines to make the money I was going to make for this. But there was a price for this too. For six hundred grand I was going to become a fucking joke.

That was how it sized up.

Me, Kyle Nevin, a man who used to be someone.

Fuck it.

I sat stewing, thinking about the laughing stock I was going to become. If it was what I needed to do to find Red Mahoney, then that was what I was going to do.

Nola sensed my mood had darkened. Hell, a total eclipse wouldn't have been any darker. Worry lines creased her brow, but she knew enough not to say anything to me about it. Thank God for that. If she gave me any lip, fuck, I don't know. It was three in the morning then. I had to get moving, otherwise I'd tear the place apart with my bare hands. I left the room and headed to Central Park, hoping for any chance at all to let loose some of the pressure building up inside me. I needed to let it out before something inside popped, but I'll tell you, the only way it was going to be a fair fight would be if they had guns, and even then I wasn't sure. With the way I was feeling, it wouldn't have mattered to me what they had. As long as there was at least one motherfucka ready to get in my way, that was all I cared about. At least one. More would be better.

Chapter 13

I was back in my room by six and had calmed down quite a bit. I was given a chance to let out some of the pressure, but more important, I realized the joke was going to be on Harleston Books, not me. Everyone would know it was nothing but a scam – and that I was the one doing the scamming, taking the publisher for all that money for nothing but a pile of shit. If nothing else, it would increase my standing in the neighborhood. The street kid pulling one over on the fancy New York publisher. The idea of the book didn't bother me anymore.

Tammy called the hotel room early to let me know when and where I was supposed to meet the lawyer. It gave Nola and me just enough time to order up breakfast in bed, then I was heading off to a Park Avenue address. The lawyer was someone I'd heard of, Fred Magione, a big-personality type who had done mob work representing a number of the Italian family members out of New York and New Jersey, but also worked on Kevin Flannery's case. I had to give Bennett credit, he did his homework and found the right guy for me to talk to. He didn't cheap out there. First thing Magione did was give me an appraising look and ask about the cut over my right eye.

'That's nothing,' I said. I gave my bruised knuckles a quick look. 'You should see the three guys who tried jumping me.'

He got a kick out of that and we chatted for a while, first about Kevin Flannery and what a shame it was what his mom had to go through, then talking about who was in prison and who was still out on the streets. After his secretary brought us a couple of cappuccinos, we got down to business.

'A fictional novel is just that,' Magione said. 'Fiction. A story. It can't be considered a confession or an admission of guilt. As long as you don't libel real people, you're fine.'

Magione crossed his legs and took a sip of cappuccino. He had a toughness about him, and his five grand Savile Row suit did little to hide the fact that he worked out regularly. He looked like someone who could've gone either way, the mob or something legitimate, and somehow ended up in the middle as a lawyer.

'We're talking purely hypothetical here,' he went on. 'I'm not trying to imply that you had anything to do with that kidnapping business, but you have to expect that the FBI will be paying close attention to this book. If you put in anything that helps them find evidence connecting you to an actual crime, then you're fucked. But if you're that stupid you deserve to be fucked. Am I right?'

I sat thinking, scratching my chin. 'What about double jeopardy? I had a finding of not guilty. Even if they wanted to, they couldn't try me again, could they?'

'I only know what I read in the papers, but the charge against you was a federal kidnapping charge. No murder charges were filed, at least from what I read. If you were to write something that led the police to that kid's body, I'd expect murder charges to be filed, with a quick conviction and life sentence to follow. Now, we're only talking hypotheticals here because we both know you had nothing do with what happened to that boy.'

I nodded, asked Magione what he thought, if he saw any reason why I shouldn't write this book.

'None at all. Take their money, just like I'm going to. You

should see the bill I'm going to be sending them. In case anyone asks, you and me, we talked for three hours. And don't be an asshole either. Get yourself legal representation to look over any contract you sign. You want, I can give you some names.'

Without my asking, he wrote out for me a list of names and then escorted me through his office. At the door we shook hands. From his grip I asked him if he ever boxed. He smiled, told me he was a Golden Gloves winner three times.

'Me, ninety amateur bouts as a kid,' I said. 'Eighty-nine and one.'

'Got you one better. Seven pro fights. Five and two.' He paused, said, 'That was bullshit what Red Mahoney did to you nine years ago. Fucking rat bastard. He pulled the same crap on a couple of my clients here in New York. If you had hired me to represent you, I would've gotten the charges thrown out due to entrapment. I mean, fuck, at the time Mahoney was working as an agent of the FBI. If that's not entrapment, then what is? You ever run into him again, give him one of these for me.'

Magione punched a fist hard into an open palm; the sound of it made a loud crack that caused his receptionist to turn our way.

'I'm planning to give him a lot more than that,' I said. I leaned in close so his receptionist couldn't hear me, then asked if he could give me an introduction to one of the New York guys he represented, Joe Lombardo. He nodded, didn't bother to ask why I would want something like that, but his attitude towards me stiffened and became more cautious. I shook hands with him again and left. Thinking about Red had brought the ire up in me. It had been almost five months since I'd been sidelined in looking for the sonofabitch. Five months where he was able to live like a normal human being. Wherever the fuck he was hiding, that was five months longer than he should've had. While I walked back to the Plaza, I thought about how I could take advantage of this book business to flush Red out, and I settled on a plan of action.

After lunch I met with Bennett and a writer from Murder Books Incorporated, the book packager I was going to be working with. The writer looked a lot like the fucker from Scolley's who had been shooting bullets at me with his eyes – almost enough to where they could've been twins, except this guy had a much better disposition. He laughed at half the things I said, even comments that weren't meant as jokes. Still, it wasn't a bullshit laugh. Maybe he was stoned, maybe he was just nervous, I don't know. Anyway, I had no problem with the guy, and I told Bennett that after the writer left.

There were a couple of surprises when we went over the contract. Not many, but a couple. The first was that Bennett wanted the book finished within two months of signing the contract. As I had said before, I had decided the whole thing was a fucking joke, one that I wasn't going to take too seriously, but still it sounded odd to me, and I didn't like the idea of some ivy-league clown taking advantage of me.

'I thought it takes three years to write a book?' I asked.

Bennett smiled at that. 'Who told you that?'

'I was talking to a writer a couple of days ago.'

'I'm sure it could take some people three years. You've got anal retentive types who could spend three years putting together a grocery list. If you want I can give you names of very good writers who've written books in three days. It's all relative. For you, I doubt you're going to need more than a month to write this.'

'I don't even know what the fuck I'm writing.'

'Not an issue. Next Monday you'll come back to New York, and after a week of working with Scott you'll have it all figured out. Kyle, this is going to be nothing more than you connecting the dots, but with you doing it in your own inimitable style.'

'What if I need more time?'

He tapped his desk impatiently, his mouth shrinking to a small oval. 'That's not going to be an issue. If somehow it becomes one and you need more time, you can call me and we'll work something out. Okay?'

I didn't care for his attitude, but it didn't much matter to me how much time he gave me. If I had to write the book in a day, I'd do that. The only thing I wanted out of it was the money and the cover it was going to give me in flushing Red out of hiding. Anyway, there was no percentage in getting up and slapping the shit out of Bennett. If he kept pissing me off, maybe, but not for this. I went onto my second surprise. The payoff schedule for the advance. Bennett had been able to add an extra fifty grand to the advance, but according to the contract I'd only get twenty-five percent of my money on signing, fifty percent on acceptance of my first book and the final twenty-five percent on acceptance of my second book. To me it smelled like I was only being guaranteed twenty-five percent of the money that was being promised me, and I complained about it to Bennett.

'Sounds like a classic bait and switch to me,' I said.

'Not at all,' he insisted. 'The only way Harleston Books benefits is if you deliver both books. Kyle, my man, you need to develop some trust. I'm going to be putting my ass on the line for you. That's how much I believe in this book. Before the book's written I'll be spending close to a million dollars promoting it.'

He'd been slipping in that '*Kyle, my man*' shit all day and I didn't like it, but I kept my mouth shut about it. It took another hour to find one of the lawyers on Magione's list who was free to look over the contract. Tammy faxed it to him, and while we waited for comments to be faxed back, Bennett tried to engage me in small talk about my old days with Red Mahoney. I fed him a few stories, nothing that could ever get back to me. I joked around a bit, told him my second book could be something true-life, with the title *The Hunt for Red Mahoney*. He actually gave the matter some thought, asking how much money I'd need to track Mahoney down. I changed the subject quickly, then kept my mouth shut until we had the contract worked out. After I signed it, Bennett wrote me out a check for the first part of my advance. It was a lot less money that I had originally been expecting, but still, it was enough to get me started. My lawyer tried to add to the contract for Harleston Books to put me up in the Plaza for any trips I needed to make to New York as well as providing me a laptop computer. Bennett wouldn't budge as far as the Plaza went, but he did agree to get me a laptop. I decided with the money I was being given I'd pay my own way for the Plaza. I slid the check into my wallet, then Bennett and I shook hands, with his being even damper than it was the other day. He promised me that Tammy would have the laptop waiting for me when I showed up Monday.

On the way out Tammy congratulated me on my deal, giving me a quick hug and a kiss on the cheek. The dress she was wearing was even tighter than the one she had on the other day and it showed more leg. Her smile was just as dazzling, maybe with a touch of vulnerability to it. I could tell she was waiting for me to use my rain check, but my head was buzzing with things I needed to do, and besides, I had Nola waiting for me. Her smile weakened a bit as she realized I was leaving without suggesting a celebratory dinner. That would have to wait, not that I didn't want to fuck the shit out of her right then and there.

I had a lot of things I needed to do before Monday, but I figured Nola deserved a day out on the town, especially since she didn't say a word about me coming back to the room that morning bloodied and bruised. The two of us took a walk around Central Park. The bodies of the doped-up muggers I had left by one of the jogging trails were gone. Whether they were carried away or had been able to crawl off on their own I had no idea, nor did it much matter to me. When I left I couldn't care less whether they were dead or not, and I didn't bother checking. After Central Park we headed to Times Square. The place had been cleaned up since I'd been there last. It was now like fucking Disney World. We had dinner at a steak house, then took in a show. After that we headed back to Boston. I drove at a leisurely pace, knowing the troopers would be out in force. We didn't get back to her condo until three in the morning. Nola was near dead on her feet. Me, I was too wired to even think about sleeping. After dropping Nola off, I took a drive up to New Hampshire.

That weekend I bought a used Honda Civic. It wasn't much different than the one Danny had owned. Nola was disappointed by my choice, but I wanted something nondescript.

'You promised me you'd be driving a BMW before the end of the year,' she pouted.

I should've known better than to take her car shopping with me. I sighed, not really up to any of her bullshit.

'The year's not over,' I said. 'When I get my next advance check, I'll buy a BMW. This will be fine for now.'

After I dropped her back at her condo, I made a trip to Logan airport to collect license plates.

Later that night we went back to Scolley's. My book contract had already made the news, and I returned there the conquering hero. People were buying the two of us drinks all night. I don't think I ever saw Joe look prouder.

Nola didn't like that I was going back to New York by myself, but I explained to her that I was going to be working hard all week with the book packager, and I couldn't be distracted by that beautiful ass of hers. That mollified her enough, and as she traced a finger along several of the cuts on my face, I thought about what I was going to be doing that week and it got me to the point where I was able to leave her more than satisfied. Hidden under the spare tire was a hunting knife and an automatic with a silencer that I had taken from the arsenal at Red's cabin, along with ammunition and several license plates that I had borrowed from Logan's long-term parking. It was ten past nine by the time I was parking the Honda in a garage down in the Village. Earlier I had called a rental agency and had arranged for the same model BMW I had driven the week before to be waiting for me. I drove the BMW convertible to the Plaza and had the valet take it. Anyone checking in later with the Plaza would see that I had left my car there all week, not that I expected that to happen, but better safe than sorry. I had dinner at a place near Union Square that was serving twenty-dollar martinis. I tried a few but didn't really notice much of a difference between those and the six-dollar variety. I felt calmer than I would've thought, none of the nervous energy I was expecting. It was midnight when I got back to my room and, as I had promised, I gave Nola a quick call. Surprisingly, when I tried I fell right to sleep. Even a bigger surprise, I didn't wake up until seven the next morning. Christ, I could hardly believe it. As close to a full night's sleep as I'd had in over nine years.

The next morning I met Tammy to collect my laptop. My jaw dropped seeing how she looked. She had put on extra makeup, some green eye shadow and a hot pink lipstick, and that along with the way she fixed up her hair and the ultra-short green dress she had squeezed into made her all the more beautiful. She blushed a bit seeing the effect she was having on me, which made me all the more nuts. We joked around for a while before I left. I think she was expecting me to ask her out for later, but I had other plans for that night.

Murder Books Incorporated had their offices on West 32nd Street, and I took a cab there to meet the writer, Scott Powell, that I was going to be working with. I wasn't much in the mood for it – I would rather have been back at Harleston Books flirting with Tammy, or better yet, getting her back to my suite – but I wanted the second advance check so I played by the rules and did what I was supposed to. After a while, though, it wasn't that bad. For most of the day we mostly batted around ideas. In a way it reminded me of how it used to be with Red when we were planning out a job. Scott was a pleasant enough guy, easy to talk to, and I liked some of the stuff he was coming up with. The main character for the book was going to be a thinly veiled version of me – an Irish badass who has been working for a Red Mahoney-type mob boss until he's set up the same as I was. Bennett wanted the book to be *tragic*, something where my character is violent but deep down has a heart of gold and is struggling to reform himself. The problem is he can't help the path he takes. The thought of that was laughable, and even to an amateur like me clichéd as all hell, but that's what Bennett wanted. Scott came up with the idea of having the character driven by an obsession for revenge on the Red Mahoney character. Jesus, I loved that idea.

'He gets his revenge,' I said.

Scott was chewing on an end of a pencil, giving me a puzzled look.

I explained. 'He finds this rat bastard and he gets his revenge.'

Scott was mulling the idea over, nodding. 'That's really good. He'll get his revenge but it doesn't help him any, he's still as fucked up as ever afterwards. I like that. I think we could do something very cool with that.'

He jotted some ideas in his notebook. I didn't much care about that part of it, but I liked the idea of adding a Red Mahoney-like bastard getting his in the book. No matter where Red was hiding, I knew he'd get himself a copy of my book when it came out, and I could imagine him seething while reading that part of it. And maybe sweating a bit afterwards, knowing that everything that happened to his character was going to happen to him in real life once I found him.

Around five Bennett dropped in to see what we had done. Scott went over his notes with him, and I could see Bennett getting excited by the way things were taking shape. He had a few comments of his own, and I have to admit they weren't bad. He gave me a thin smile and told me that Tuesday morning I was going to be meeting with a reporter from *People* magazine.

'It will be a soft interview about your journey from the mean streets of South Boston to budding literary prodigy,' he said with a sly wink. 'The reporter's name is Sammi Johnson and she'll be contacting you at your room at nine. If she asks, the first draft of your novel has already been written. Don't go into any more details other than what we've already talked about.'

I nodded, told him it wouldn't be a problem. We worked out the rest of my story, then, as Bennett got up to leave, he stopped to ask us both if we wanted to join him for dinner at a new hot spot, some trendy Italian and Japanese fusion restaurant. I begged off, telling him I was wiped out from the day and wanted to hit the sack early. Bennett gave me a funny smile and told me we'd have to do it another night that week. Scott looked a bit deflated. I guess as a mostly struggling writer he wanted any free meal he could get. After Bennett left, I slipped him a couple of hundreds, told him to make a night of it. He started to protest but I wouldn't take no for an answer, not that he tried all that hard to change my mind. The two of us packed it in for the night then, and I went back to my room to change clothes. After that I had a quick dinner before heading to the Village to get my Honda. I still had a three and a half hour drive back to Massachusetts to make that night.

Before leaving I swapped license plates with one of the ones I had borrowed. I didn't want to take any chances of a toll booth or an overpass having video surveillance. During the drive I kept my speed at twelve miles over the limit. When I entered Connecticut I lowered it to five miles over. I didn't want to be stopped by a state trooper. If I was I'd have to do this all over again another day.

Tommy Mahoney had always been a diehard Bruins fan. I remembered that about him. He had season tickets by center ice and never missed a game if he could help it. I was gambling that he was still the same. Yeah, it was a gamble but I thought it was a good one since he was still using ex-Bruins players in his TV ads. Me, I used to also be a diehard Bruins fan until the 1978–79 season. The two years before that the Bruins and the Canadiens were the two best teams in hockey, but the Bruins just couldn't get over the hump and beat them. That 78–79 season was their year. *Terry O' Reilly, Gerry Cheevers, Rick Middleton, Brad Park.* Shit, they had the Canadiens beat on their own ice except for a bullshit *'too many men on the ice'* penalty with a minute to go that stole it away from them. I lost interest in hockey after that. Over the years I still went to games with Tommy, but my heart was just never in it.

When I entered Massachusetts I found the game on the radio. The Bruins ended up losing. In the old days, Tommy's routine would be to have pizza in the North End after a game. If they won, he'd hang around drinking until two in the morning. If they lost, he'd have his pie and head home. I had about an hour's drive to get to his house, which timed things out pretty well.

Tommy these days was living out in the suburbs. Weeks earlier I checked out the layout and found a place within quarter of a mile from him where I could park inconspicuously. The area was poorly lit and the neighbors lived a good distance from one another. Before leaving I had dressed in a black T-shirt and black jeans. I had a change of clothes with me in case things got bloody. As far as I could tell no one saw me as I cut through several backyards and made my way to the side of his house. Then I waited. The temperature had been dropping of late, but it didn't bother me. The thought of what I was going to be doing kept me warm.

He never saw me as he drove up his driveway and into his three-car garage, nor when I slipped in after him. I don't think he had a clue I was there until I shoved a dirty rag into his mouth and banged his head off the cement floor. He didn't lose consciousness, but he was woozy enough that he didn't put up any fight while I tied his wrists together behind his back. I flipped him over and waited until the clouding in his eyes cleared up. I wanted him to be fully aware of what was happening. When his eyes focused on me and he recognized who I was, the sonofabitch tried screaming for help. The rag mostly muffled his screams, but the heartless sonofabitch tried screaming anyways. He had to know that if any of his family heard him and came into the garage I'd have to massacre all of them, but it didn't stop him. I let him go on, half hoping that that would happen. When it didn't, and he started gagging from his efforts with his face beet red, I took the hunting knife from my waistband and went to work. The last thing I wanted was him checking out by means of a heart attack. I wanted him to know everything that was going to be happening to him.

I cut his shirt off, then took my time carving the words 'RAT BROTHER' on his chest. It took time, especially with the way he was squirming, but that was fine as far as I was concerned. I think at that point he would've told me anything I wanted to know about Red if I'd let him, but I didn't care to hear it from him. Besides, I doubted that he had much to tell. Red was too cagey to stay in one place too long, and any contact between the two of them would be one-sided. It didn't matter. The only person Red cared about in this world was Tommy. He loved his brother and what I was doing to him would hurt him deeply. And from everything I was going to do to him Red would know without a doubt who was behind it.

After I was through with my carving, I started to cut off pieces – the same pieces that Red had cut off when he demonstrated on a rat years earlier to Kevin Flannery and me and a few others. I attached the silencer to the automatic I had brought, and by the time I flipped Tommy over and lowered his pants, he was mostly gone, but I stuck the gun barrel into the same place Red had, and emptied a full magazine into Tommy's body. Nobody heard a thing, at least no one bothered checking out the garage. I pulled off my latex gloves, wiped off the little blood I had gotten on me, then packed up and left the garage. Within ten minutes I was heading back to New York. For the first hour of the trip I was hyped up by the violence and the thought of how it was going to affect Red, but after a few hours of listening to rock tunes I had mostly mellowed out. I was feeling good, more relaxed than I'd felt in years. Before reaching Manhattan, I dropped several packages weighted with bricks into different waterways. It was after four in the morning when I brought the Honda back to the garage in the Village where I was keeping it, and fifteen minutes after that before I was back in my room. The way I was feeling I could've slept for twenty-four hours. I had no doubt about that. Unfortunately I had a wake-up call for a quarter to nine. As soon as I closed my eyes I was out like a light.

Chapter 14

I almost slept through my wake-up call. Over the last nine years the thought of five hours of sleep would've been a wet dream, but that morning I could've slept enough to make up for all the bad nights I'd had. Reluctantly, I pushed myself awake. I was groggy but more alive than I'd been in years. I stared at the clock next to me until I could focus and see that I only had five minutes before I was supposed to meet the reporter from *People* magazine. I made my way to the bathroom, slicked my hair back with a wet comb, gargled with mouthwash and slipped on a polo shirt, jeans and a pair of loafers. Tommy's murder had already made national news. I had just enough time to catch a story on CNN about it before the reporter called me from the lobby. According to CNN, a police spokesman described the murder as the most brutal he'd ever seen and that it was obviously done by a depraved individual. While they had their suspicions, they weren't sure yet whether it was related to Tommy's older brother, the fugitive John 'Red' Mahoney, but based on the condition of the body they thought it was a strong likelihood. Christ, go out on a limb, why don't they? One of the background shots showed Tommy's wife and two oldest daughters red-eyed and weeping. Seeing all that got a buzz of energy running through me. Somewhere Red was also watching all that and I knew it had to be killing him. My feet barely touched the carpet when I went to the lobby to meet Sammi Johnson from *People* magazine.

The reporter was like a lot of the sleek beautiful women I'd seen walking around Manhattan. Blonde, slender, blue eyes, in her early thirties and dressed to kill. Her nose was a little longer than it should've been and she had a weak mouth, and maybe not enough on top, but she was still nice to look at. She had a photographer with her, and I took them both back to my room where I ordered all of us breakfast. She offered to put it on her expense tab, but I told her not to worry about it, that Harleston Books would be covering it.

The interview went well. I was in rare form, had both of them grinning at my jokes. The story I gave was that after my editorial appeared in the *NY Times*, Bennett contacted me, suggesting that I try writing this book, and after writing a first draft in a month the rest was history. I talked about growing up as a kid in Southie, my amateur boxing career, and how Red Mahoney recruited me because of how fearsome I was in the ring. At one point she asked me if I knew Thomas Mahoney.

'Yeah, I knew him.'

I could see the excitement in her eyes as she asked if I thought what happened to him was related to his brother. I gave the impression of thinking it over and told her from what I saw on the news that it was a possibility, but that you never know with these things – that it could just as well be someone with a vendetta against Tommy trying to throw the police off track. I suggested that if I were the police I'd check for any life insurance policies he might've had. I knew that answer would infuriate Red if he saw my interview. After that I got things back on track.

The interview lasted an hour. The photographer took a few more shots, then they both left. I knew I nearly charmed the pants off both of them, and that part was confirmed, at least on Sammi's part, when ten minutes later she knocked on my door alone with a sheepish grin on her face, telling me she had a few follow-up questions. It was an hour later when she put her clothes back on and left with a pink blush on her cheeks. Any talking we did during that hour wasn't going to be repeated in a family magazine. Jesus, she wore me out.

> To Ed.: Full disclosure, that blonde reporter didn't come back to my room, but the way she was looking at me, Christ, I'm sure if I had suggested it she would've. Anyway, your call whether you leave this in, but the photographer kept mentioning how he had to run across town for another shoot, so it will be her word against mine. —K. N.

Not much else of interest happened the rest of that week. Later that same day I stopped off to chat with Tammy, but got mostly a cold shoulder from her. I guess she was pissed that I didn't appear to pick up on all the signals she had sent my way the day before. Anyway, when I saw her she was dressed like she didn't give a shit. I decided she could wait until my next trip to the city. That afternoon I received a call from Joe Lombardo on my cell, telling me that he had heard that I wanted an introduction. Joe's son-in-law was sent to Leavenworth when I was already there and I had taken care of him, first giving him a bunch of supplies from the commissary when he arrived; stuff like canned tuna fish, toothbrush, soap, mouthwash, all the little things that make a stay in a place like Leavenworth bearable, and also making sure the animals there knew they'd better leave him alone. The son-in-law had a slight build, and he looked like he needed someone looking out for him; besides, Italian or Irish, he was in the same circle as me. Joe knew about all this and thanked me for what I did. I told him what I wanted, that I needed contacts in Europe who could do some work for me. I explained the work I needed, and he told me he'd get back to me with some names. Before hanging up he told me it was a shame what happened to Red Mahoney's little brother. I agreed in the same tone of voice he had used. Which was that neither of us really thought it was much of a shame.

After that the week was mostly quiet. I spent my days batting around ideas with Scott, and my nights catching up on years of lost sleep. I'm sure if I was back in Boston everyone at Scolley's would be talking about Tommy, and I'm sure everyone would be asking my thoughts on it. But being in New York I was mostly isolated from it. The stories about it mostly faded from CNN. It sounded as if the police had nothing. I ended up going out to dinner with Bennett and Scott one night, and Bennett did comment on the murder. I could see suspicions tightening his face as he remembered me begging off from going out to dinner the night it happened, but I guess he decided it was too far-fetched to think of me driving back and forth from New York in one night to do it. Watching me a little more carefully than he should've, he made a comment how while he didn't necessarily like benefiting from someone else's tragedy this was going to help our book. That anything bringing attention to Red Mahoney would help.

My last day in New York, Friday, Scott had a thirty-page outline for me and as we went through it it played through my head like a movie.

'Jesus, Scott,' I told him, 'this is good. Why the fuck aren't you writing your own books?'

For a moment I could almost see the answer on his lips, '*Because I haven't kidnapped any ten-year-old boys.*' Fortunately he caught himself. I liked the guy and would've hated to lose respect for him giving me a crybaby answer like that. He gave me his *I-don't-give-a-shit-about-anything* grin and told me he just might someday.

'You never know, maybe I'll even pass you on the *NY Times* bestsellers list. Kyle, just do a good job promoting this puppy. It may be small, but I've still got a piece of the action on it.'

'I better do a good job writing it then.'

His eyes and his smile both dulled a bit. 'Yeah, that too,' he said.

Before leaving the city I stopped off to see Tammy to tell her the next time I was in town we'd hook up. She seemed a bit taken aback by that, but nodded. I worked on her a bit more and even coaxed a small smile out of her.

Out around Westchester County I traded in my Honda for a used BMW 330i sports coupe. Nola was happy to see it when I got back to Boston. That night we went to Scolley's and all the talk was about Tommy. Most, if not all, showed little crooked smiles at the edges of their mouths as they talked about what a shame it was. When we returned to Nola's condo, I had no trouble keeping things going for hours. It was as if I were a teenager again. Tommy and his rat bastard brother were at least good for something.

I decided to take the weekend off and wait until Monday before starting on the book. While I still thought the idea of it was mostly a joke, I have to admit to getting a little excited about the book. Maybe it was because the outline Scott gave me was so damn good, maybe it was the *People* magazine interview and some of the other articles Bennett was able to get written about me, or maybe it was the good mood I had drifted into knowing how much Red had to be suffering, but I actually started thinking I could pull this off. Over the weekend I reread the books Bennett gave me and on Monday morning I was up at the crack of dawn with the laptop open and ready to start typing away. The problem was all I could do was stare at the blank screen. When Nola got up I started typing some garbage so she'd think I was working, but as soon as she left I went back to staring at nothing. After a few hours of that I tried some shadow boxing and then going for a run, but afterwards it was the same. I started to feel a cold sweat realizing that I just couldn't do it. I was willing to write anything to fill up the two hundred and fifty pages I owed Bennett but I just couldn't figure out how to start. By the time Nola came back I still hadn't written a single word. She asked if she could read what I had written so far. I told her I'd rather wait until I had the whole book done. When she suggested Scolley's, I begged off, telling her I was wiped out from my day. The last thing I wanted to do was go to Scolley's and feel like a fraud.

The next three days were more of the same. I tried, fuck did I try, but I just couldn't get that first sentence written. Thursday afternoon I went to Scolley's. I had to go somewhere. The place was mostly empty but sitting at a table trying hard not to notice me was the same writer from before – the one who had bitched and moaned to me because I was able to get a book deal while he couldn't sell his masterpiece. I kept staring at him until he gave me a slight nod. I got up and brought my pint to his table to join him.

'How's it going,' he said, shifting uncomfortably and trying hard not to pay any attention to me.

'I signed my book deal,' I said.

'Yeah, I read about you in the *Globe*. Quite a deal for a first-time author. Most writers are lucky to get ten thousand for a first book.'

We sat in silence after that. For a few minutes I gave him a hard stare while he kept shifting uncomfortably. Finally I broke the silence.

'How'd you like to make ten grand?' I asked him.

He shifted a dubious eye towards me. 'What do I have to do?'

'Write my book for me. That's all. You don't tell a fucking soul, though. If you've read about me you know what will happen to you if you do.'

I explained further, told him about the thirty-page outline and how I needed it done in two months. He made a face like he had just swallowed spoiled milk.

'I can't write a book in two months,' he said.

'Why not? The outline lays it all out. It doesn't have to be fucking perfect. It won't have your name on it.'

He rubbed his chin as he thought about it, finally nodded.

'What the hell,' he said. 'Sure, I'll do it. At least I'll be published. Even if nobody knows about it.'

He finished his beer, then the two of us left. I told him I was already missing my deadline for the first chapter, and he'd have to work on it over the weekend and have it for me by Monday morning. He agreed. When we got to Nola's condo, I put a copy of the outline on a disk and gave it to him. I also wrote him a check for a grand, told him I'd pay him more after he got more of the book done. I drove him back to his apartment. During the ride he seemed to get more excited about the idea. He promised he'd email me the first chapter by midnight Sunday. I warned him again what would happen if he breathed a word of this to anybody.

'That's okay. At least I'll know they published one of my books,' he said.

After I let him off I drove back to Scolley's. At five, Bennett called on my cell, asking where the first chapter was that I was supposed to have delivered.

'I'm having some trouble with it,' I said.

'Kyle, my man, just write the damn thing.'

'It's not that easy.'

He paused for a moment, then somewhat strained, 'We have a contract. Kyle, you don't want to default on it. Just apply yourself. Okay?'

'I'll work more this weekend. I'll have it for you by Monday.'

He didn't like it but he accepted it.

We hung up. I joined Joe at the bar and shot the breeze with him until around seven. Nola must've figured I was there 'cause she came in around then. I bought her a few drinks and later we left to the North End to my favorite restaurant. We had cause to celebrate. I had my first goddamn book written. At least it was on the way.

That writer was a man of his word. At eleven o'clock Sunday night I received an email from him with the first chapter. I sent it right off to Bennett. Twenty minutes later I got a call from him.

'You didn't write that, Kyle,' he said.

'What the fuck are you talking about?'

'Kyle, I can tell MFA writing when I see it. That writing screamed MFA. I know you didn't write it. What you sent me is unacceptable.'

I sat trying to think, a queasiness working its way into my stomach. To bide time until I could think properly I asked him what MFA stood for.

'Masters in Fine Arts. Usually in creative writing. Kyle, if I wanted this type of writing I would have found an MFA to write this book. What I want is your unique voice. I want the same raw energy that I saw in your *NY Times* editorial. You can write, there's no doubt in my mind about that. Just apply yourself and send me the first chapter by tomorrow at five. No more of this fucking bullshit. Both of our asses are on the line here.'

He hung up then. Nola gave me a puzzled look, asked me what was wrong. I didn't answer her. I sent that asshole writer an email back telling him he was fired, then I sat for a long time staring into space, trying like hell to ignore all of Nola's questions. Finally she left for the bedroom. Once I was alone I took the books Bennett had given me and gave them one more try. I stayed up reading them. When I was done I sat in front of the laptop until I forced myself to write the first sentence. I didn't stop until I had a chapter written. Then I sent it to Bennett and told him if he didn't like it he could suck my cock. Nola had already left for work by then. I paced the apartment like a caged animal until I received a response back from Bennett. He told me he didn't like it, he loved it. It was a struggle, but I kept writing then.

That Friday I had the first sixty pages done. For the most part I followed the outline, but I added a few characters and made a couple of small detours. It was like I could see the whole thing in my mind. My stomach was a wreck as I watched Nola read the pages I had written. Damn, she was inscrutable – with the way her brow was furrowed up I had no idea what she was thinking. Finally she finished. She looked up at me, and a look of awe slowly spread over her face,

'It's absolutely terrific,' she said.

'You really think so?'

'Yes, definitely.'

She came over to me and gave me a hug, her mouth searching out mine. I kept it short so I could send the pages to Bennett. I started pacing then. Nola gave me her bare trace of a smile, asked if I wanted to wait in the bedroom for Bennett's response, maybe work off some of my nervous energy there. I shook my head, told her I couldn't. It was an hour later that Bennett called to tell me the same as Nola. That he thought what I had sent him was gold. After I got off the phone with him I took Nola into the bedroom.

Chapter 15

It was weeks after Tommy's murder that a couple of police detectives tracked me down to Nola's apartment. They knew that I had interrupted Tommy's lunch at a Beacon Hill restaurant six months earlier, and they wanted to know what we talked about and where I was the night of the murder.

'What we talked about, that's personal,' I told the two officers. 'As far as where I was, the Plaza Hotel in Manhattan. I remember turning on CNN the next morning and seeing the story about it. It saddened me, Detective. Even though his brother fucked me over royally, I always thought of Tommy as a friend.'

The heavier of the two officers – his skin the color of boiled ham – stared at me blankly, the other smirked.

'A friend, huh?' the one who was smirking said. 'A lot of people like you for this, Nevin. That's what we keep hearing.'

I frowned like any injured man would. 'If the murder was related to Red Mahoney, he fucked a lot of us over. I was just one of many. As far as what you might be hearing, there are people out there with vendettas against me. What can I say?'

'You want to know what you can say? How about telling us about the talk you had with Thomas Mahoney. That would be a nice start.'

'It wouldn't help you any. It was personal and I'm not saying a word about it, at least not without a trade. You want to tell me who's pointing fingers at me, then we'll see.'

'We're not telling you that, Nevin.'

'Then I'm not telling you about a private conversation I had over six months ago. Now if you'll excuse me—'

The heavier detective, the one who had been staring blankly at me, took a small step towards me, his face reddening under his military-style buzz cut. I could smell the sourness of his breath as he moved closer. I guess he expected me to back up, but I stood my ground.

'Thomas Mahoney told associates of his you threatened him,' he said.

'I don't know why he'd say that, but I have to disagree. Anything else?'

By then they were both staring at me blankly.

'We'll check out where you said you were that night,' the heavier red-faced detective said. 'You'll be hearing from us.'

He wasn't being truthful about that, because that was the last I heard from either of them.

As far as my book went, Bennett ended up being right on target about it. Once I got over the hump, I had the book written in a month. It was no longer a joke to me. It wasn't a joke to Nola and the few others that I let read it. They were all amazed by it. When Joe Whalley read it he kept shaking his head, muttering how brilliant it was. Afterwards he damn near cried. Bennett confided in me that it was a hell of a lot better than he was expecting. We finished all the rounds of editing in less than two weeks. Then we waited for responses to the galleys. The night the book was sent to the printers, Bennett flew up to Boston to take me out to dinner. Once I found out that Tammy wasn't joining us, I brought Nola along.

'I've changed the first run from three hundred thousand to a million five copies,' he told me over drinks, his face flushed from the alcohol. He was a bit of a lightweight. At that point we only had martinis and two bottles of wine. 'The reason I fast-tracked this, the same reason I pushed you so hard to get the book written as fast as you did, was we wanted to strike while the iron's hot, and Kyle, my man, the iron is fucking burning up right now. I've got you on *Letterman* next week, *Oprah* the week afterwards.'

'You're kidding?'

'Nope.' He gave me a thin smile. 'I've got TV producers and magazine editors lining up for you. We're going to keep you busy right up until the book's released, and then we've got the book tours. But I have a surprise. Some early reviews and quotes from the galleys.'

He fumbled with his briefcase and took out a small stack of papers. While I read through them, Nola stood behind me so she could read them over my shoulder. Bennett, the more he drank, the more he kept eyeballing her. I guess he thought I was too absorbed in what he had given me to notice, but he was trying his hardest to take off the little she had on with his stare – almost as if he could melt her clothes away. I couldn't blame him, I don't think she ever looked better than she did that night. Anyway, I didn't let it bother me as I read through what he gave me. I recognized most of the names of the authors providing quotes. Over the last two months I started taking this writing business more seriously and was spending more time at bookstores noticing who the bestsellers were. The names attached to the quotes were writers I recognized as bestselling authors, and they were all saying the same thing: how powerful and authentic the book was and how it was one of the best debut novels they'd ever seen.

'Wow,' Nola murmured. 'These are amazing.' She rubbed the back of my neck. 'You should be so proud of yourself, Kyle, honey.'

I turned so I could reach behind me and take hold of her hand and brush it against my lips. Then I turned back to face Bennett.

'Do you think any of them actually read my book?' I asked.

His smile turned a bit wooden.

'Maybe one or two of them,' he admitted.

It didn't matter. As long as those quotes were on the front and back covers that's all I cared about. I next read the early reviews and damn near blushed.

'Fuck me,' I said.

'Those reviewers certainly read it,' he said. 'And they're mostly honest reviews. Of course, a few of them might have been swayed by the quotes. But my own opinion, I agree with them. I think they're right on target.'

Nola sat back down. I gave her the reviews to read. Her skin flushed with pride as she went through them. She reached over for my hand to squeeze it.

Bennett, a bit tipsy, raised a glass of wine, some of it sloshing out of the glass. Nola and I did the same without spilling any of our wine.

'Here's to a blockbuster of major proportions,' he said. 'By the way, my last surprise for the night. Movie deal's being negotiated as we speak. It's going to be seven figures, Kyle, my man.'

I was speechless.

Needless to say it was the best dinner of my life. And later, when Nola and I were alone, it wasn't too shabby either. It was as if I hadn't touched a drop of alcohol all night. As if I had taken a dozen blue pills. And Jesus, she was on fire.

The next six weeks while we waited for the book to be released were more of the same. Things couldn't have been better between Nola and me. I was sleeping sounder and more peacefully than I had in years, most nights sleeping straight through to morning. The few times thoughts of Red would seep in it hardly even bothered me. As far as those blue pills went, I flushed them down the toilet knowing full well I wasn't going to be needing them anymore. Of everything that was happening, what affected me the most was the respect I was now getting when people recognized me. In the past, it would be out of fear. Now it was something different, more genuine, and in its own way it was better.

As far my TV appearances went, they all went smoothly except for one malicious bitch. This one was for a syndicated show, and she was laying in wait for me. Her handshake was as damp and cold as a pile of slush. The first thing she asked was how I felt the family of the kidnapped boy would react on reading my book.

'My book is only a work of fiction,' I started to say. 'I hope they would view it as that and realize it has nothing to do with their own tragedy.'

She snorted while I answered her. I swear to God.

'So this book isn't being written to exploit their pain?'

'Of course not. It's fiction. It's not based on any particular crime.'

She made a show then of consulting her notes. 'The central character is based on yourself, isn't he?'

'No. He's a composite of people I knew growing up in South Boston.' Bennett had given me that answer during one of our sessions. *A composite.* A beautiful answer to shut people like her up, but she wasn't about to be shut up.

'You say he's not you, but doesn't the book start with this character, Kevin Shannon, being released after nine years in prison because he had been betrayed by a mob boss reminiscent of John "Red" Mahoney?'

'I said the character is a composite. There are certain aspects that might be related to me, but he's not me. Besides, I only served eight years after being screwed over by Mahoney.'

I was grinning then, trying to lighten the mood, but she was having none of it. She kept digging, her claws fully out.

'So this is a joke to you. A family is in pain, not knowing what happened to their ten-year-old son, and this is a joke to you.'

Somehow I stayed calm. I didn't let her act get to me. I just gave her a cold steel eye and repeated how the book was simply a fictional work and had nothing to do with that family. Again, she shuffled through her notes, then looked up contemptuously.

'Your character in this book kidnaps a young boy as soon as he's released from prison to finance hunting down his old mob boss who is now a fugitive. And you sincerely expect us to believe this isn't you simply laughing your head off at all of us suckers?'

She was trying to rile me up. Make me look like some psychotic. I didn't bite. Still keeping my voice calm I cited how the DNA evidence proved I had nothing to do with the kidnapping.

Again with her notes, then, 'I consulted with one of the FBI investigators on the case, and he explained that the DNA evidence found most likely came from a close family member of yours.'

Now I was getting a little hot, but I think any other reaction would've looked funny. 'The only other family member I had living at the time was my brother, Danny. He's dead now. Are you accusing my dead brother of committing this crime? Or maybe it was my dad. He left home when I was thirteen and I haven't heard from him since. I guess it could've been him. Or maybe some half-brother or sister that I don't know anything about. Or maybe none of them. You see, you fucking bitch, the operative words are *most likely*, not *with a certainty*. But you see, none of this even matters. Under oath they were claiming it was my blood when they knew damn well it wasn't, so how the fuck can you believe anything they're telling you now?'

She signaled to stop the video recording. I think she could also sense she was losing her studio audience, that they were starting to side with me.

'Mr Nevin,' she said, indignant, 'there is no point in using profanity. This is not live, we have ample opportunity to edit out those words.'

'That's nice,' I said. 'Do you have the balls right now in front of this audience to accuse me of being involved in that boy's kidnapping, or are you going to keep taking your cheap shots?'

She blanched. She wanted to accuse me, but that would be slander, and she'd be transferring everything she owned to me.

'I haven't accused you of anything. I'm doing my job and asking you questions that need to be answered.'

'I believe I answered them. Several times. And fuck you. I came here to talk about my book, not to listen to this bullshit.'

I ripped the microphone from my shirt and stormed off the set. The audience gave me a standing ovation.

Later, when I told Bennett about it, he got a chuckle over the whole thing, especially my grandstanding at the end.

'That conniving little bitch,' he said. 'You're the last author of mine I let go on her show, and I'll make sure she knows that.'

Other than that one incident, things went well. The story I had worked out with Bennett played well with my other interviews, and they were more than happy to go along with it. Yeah, I might've been a tough badass bank robber, but I only got caught once. Of course – I'd tell them with a sly wink – that might've been the only bank I ever tried robbing. And yeah, I might've hung out with a tough crowd when I was younger, but I never hurt anyone seriously, at least when I wasn't in the ring fighting as an amateur boxer. That was the story I told them and other than that one interviewer, no one had a problem with it. As far as why I chose the topic I did, I told them it came out of a conversation I had with my publisher, but that it was also therapeutic – that after being falsely accused and almost framed for the kidnapping, it was all I could think about. I would explain how I wanted to write something sympathetic to the victims of such crimes, something that would show the perpetrators as not necessarily evil but flawed human beings who were unable to envision all of the ruined lives that would be left in their wake – that what I was trying to write went beyond being simply a crime novel, but something that touched on the very nature of crime and victimization. That more than anything I was hoping this novel could also be therapeutic to the family of that ten-year-old boy. That was the story Bennett and I worked on. Yeah, when we first came up with it I thought it was nothing but a crock, but over time as I worked on the book I started to see Bennett's vision, and maybe even believed it to some degree. At least at an intellectual level, if not at a gut level. Anyway, I had no problem selling it, but then again, I can be awfully fucking convincing when I want to be. The times I was interviewed in front of an audience, I'd find a way to work Danny's death into it, about how my carelessness caused the fire that killed him, and how I wanted to atone for that by doing something positive with my life. By the end of the interview there wouldn't be a dry eye in the house.

The *Boston Globe* columnist who always had a hard-on for me kept writing his bullshit columns, asking people to remember Sue Connor, Mary Martinelli, Jennifer Coughlin and Wendy Grotowski, the four girls found dead in Flannery's mom's basement, also Jimmie Clark who had been killed in the bank robbery with me, and all the other people killed in bank robberies that he suspected I was involved in. He also had the balls to suggest I was behind the killing of Tommy Mahoney, a murder he called the most depraved in Massachusett's history. He had no proof of my involvement with any of it: Tommy, those four girls or any of the other robberies, but he couched his language to make his accusations only strong implications, nothing libelous that I could sue his ass over – at least according to the lawyers I consulted. It didn't matter. He could've been pissing in the ocean for all the good it did him. It didn't stop me from getting a ten-million-dollar movie deal (of which Harleston Books took twenty-five percent), or all the A-list celebrities attending my book launch party, or the big Hollywood stars buddying up to me to try to get the inside track on playing the lead in the movie, or the rave reviews my book received, or the book selling out its first print run in two weeks – something Bennett told me was unprecedented. After all that it was time for the book tours. What I had worked into the contract was for me to tour Europe first. Thanks to Joe Lombardo, I had people watching Red's bank accounts over there, and I knew there was activity in an account of his in Edinburgh. I had that city added to the tour. I knew Red would be searching me out to pay me back for Tommy.

The funny thing was that after all those years of dreaming and obsessing about it, paying Red back no longer seemed to matter, at least not as much as it once had. But I had already put the ball in play.

Chapter 16

Nola came with me to Europe. I left her in London while I went off to Edinburgh for two days. Now I was hiding behind a dumpster at the hotel I had checked into. Hours earlier Red had snuck in the back entrance. At first I didn't recognize him. He had gotten so much frailer and thinner since I'd seen him last, his hair no longer the shocking bright orange he used to dye it but now its natural white. It was shorter too, done in a bristle cut and looking like the end of a shaving brush. It made his overall appearance both shabbier and grayer. I only saw him for a few seconds as he moved quickly through the alleyway leading to the back door, but I was now sure it was him. As I had expected, he had read my newspaper interviews in London and knew where I was staying, although even without that he would've found out. He was always as resourceful as he was cagey. He must've bribed someone at the front desk to find out what room I had checked into, which was also something I had expected. As far as anyone at the front desk was concerned I was still in the room. Red must've been told that. I would have to imagine that he'd be both surprised and disappointed to find the room empty. Knowing Red, he was right now seething over the front desk clerk's incompetence, not knowing I had slipped out of the room and down the back staircase.

At this point Red might've suspected I was setting him up, but how could it be anything more than a nagging suspicion? For it to be more than that he'd have to know that I knew he was in Edinburgh, and how was I supposed to know that? He probably thought I had slipped out to pick up some hookers without wanting to be seen. That would be like Red, never giving me any benefit of the doubt. I was deciding whether to call the front desk and ask for some fresh towels to be brought to my room as a way to flush Red out, but he beat me to the punch and left by the back door before I had a chance to make the call.

He was less than five feet away when he walked past me. There was no masking the rage burning in that wasted face of his. Jesus, he had lost a lot of weight. I could see the bones shining through the paper-thin skin wrapping his face. As thin as he'd become there was no question that that was Red. I could've taken care of him right there in the alleyway, but that could bring up uncomfortable questions if his body were found that close to the hotel. I followed him instead, and he was stewing too much in his own juices to notice.

A mile away I was still mostly hiding in the shadows when he darted into an alleyway. I followed him into it, then stood confused, still hidden by the darkness, wondering what the hell happened. It looked as if that slippery sonofabitch rat bastard had disappeared. I turned at that moment and made kind of a matador move stepping to one side. If I hadn't I would've been stuck in the kidneys with a six-inch blade. It wasn't because I saw or heard anything. It was more that I sensed he was there, as if I could feel it on the short hairs on the back of my neck. The moonlight glinted off his switchblade and reflected bone white on his face. His eyes were nothing but cold ice chunks as he moved in on me. Red was well-skilled with a blade, and as thin and wiry as he was, he was pure fierceness. But I was also close to thirty years younger than him and had fifty pounds more muscle. I also had quick hands, and knew more than just how to box. His first attack was his best shot, and after that he really didn't have much of a chance. He made quick, short slashes, his face showing nothing but savagery. I sidestepped each of them until I could move in, blocking both his knife hand and hitting the side of his skull at the same time. The blow dazed him enough that I could grab his knife arm and break it. I forced him to his knees. While I did this he tried switching the knife to his other hand, but it dropped and clattered harmlessly away.

'You will burn in hell for what you did to Tommy,' he forced out, his breathing ragged.

'Save me a spot. We can burn together.'

I kept twisting his broken arm until I forced him to lay prone on the ground. Here was the person I used to look up to. The person I wanted most to be. For years he had been a god to me, now he was nothing but an old man, his body crumpled and broken as it lay among the garbage and filth littering the alleyway.

'I read your book,' he spat out, his mouth bloody, his face dirty and torn from being pushed into the cobblestones with bits of broken glass all around. 'I thought it was pure *shite*.'

'Everyone's a critic,' I said.

Originally I was going to spend hours with Red. Now all I wanted to do was get it over with. I kicked him over and pushed down with my foot against his throat until he was dead. Jesus, I was shaking as I left that alleyway. All those years of wanting this, and now wanting nothing to do with it. I went back to my hotel room, cleaned up, and then went out to the nearest pub to tie one on and to get that image of Red's glassy dead eyes out of my head. By the time I rejoined Nola in London I was mostly fine.

The European book tour lasted two weeks. It went well, but it was tiring and I was glad to be home. I never read anything about Red's body being found in an alleyway in Edinburgh. They obviously never identified his corpse as John 'Red' Mahoney. If they had it would've been an international story. They must have just assumed he was an old man, victim of street violence (in which one of the punk kids must've left his switchblade behind). His body would've been taken to the morgue to wait for someone to claim it. Left unclaimed, Red would end up in a pauper's grave. It was a quiet death. One that wouldn't cause much more of a stir than a whisper. I decided to put it out of my mind. I wasn't going to shed any more tears over him.

When I got back to Boston, Bennett had an eighteen-city tour lined up for me, but I convinced him to push it out a week, that I was too bone-tired as it was. To appease him, I agreed to go on one of the network morning shows that was begging for me. It would be live, so he warned me to be on my best behavior.

The Monday night we were back, I took Nola to Scolley's. It had been the first time we'd been there in over a month. I brought Joe a few bottles of rare single malt whiskies that I bought during my time in Scotland, and he examined them proudly. Before too long phone calls were being made and Scolley's was stuffed to the rafters with people wanting to welcome me home. It was a loud, raucous night, one which I was glad for. By the end of it I'd just about gotten the look of Red's dead face out of my mind.

Tuesday night I took off to New York. I had my appearance scheduled for the live show the next day, and I had to be in the studio by eight in the morning with my interview set for eight-forty. I brought Nola along. I decided I really had no interest in hooking up with Tammy, and further, wanted to make things permanent with Nola. I was comfortable with her, and beginning to care deeply about her. Besides, I was still feeling too antsy about the whole Red business to want to be alone.

I didn't sleep well that night and was up well before my wake-up call. I just had this uneasiness in my gut. I knew something was wrong but couldn't quite figure out what it was. When I saw the face of the morning show's producer, I knew they had some sort of trap set for me. All these wild thoughts went through my head. The one that kept me frozen in my seat was that someone in Edinburgh had witnessed me killing Red in that alleyway. I could barely stand it as I waited, wondering what the fuck they had on me.

When the time for my interview finally came, the morning show's host gave me a curt nod and didn't even bother to shake hands with me. She addressed the audience, telling them that they had discovered disturbing news about me. I sat there expecting the absolute worst, thinking that a videotape of me crushing the life out of Red Mahoney must've surfaced. When I saw what she actually had I nearly broke out laughing. On a screen they showed the following paragraph I had written for my book:

My destination was a gray colonial. When I rang the bell the door was opened by a thin man with a tired face that had no color in it except a pinkish spot the size of a half-dollar on each cheek. This, I thought, is the asthmatic sonofabitch Charlie Winslow.

What the fuck was that supposed to mean? I just stared at her as if she were nuts.

'Did you write that?' she asked.

'Yeah. So?'

What was displayed shifted, and alongside my paragraph they fitted another one, almost word for word identical. Instead of '*Colonial*' it was '*frame cottage*', instead of '*pinkish*' it was '*red*', and instead of '*asthmatic sonofabitch Charlie Winslow*' it was '*lunger Dan Rolff*'.

'Mr Nevin, the paragraph next to yours is taken from Dashiell Hammett's classic crime novel, *Red Harvest*, written in 1929.'

'What do you know,' I said, half under my breath.

'Excuse me?' she asked.

'Yeah, they're similar, but they're not the same,' I said. 'You can see some of the words are different.'

She was staring at me as if I were lowest form of garbage she'd ever encountered. I didn't want to look at the audience, but I could sense they were doing the same. Jesus, it had gotten quiet.

'Do you realize how serious plagiarism is?' she asked, her tone about as warm as ice.

Yeah, I used some of Hammett's book to help me get mine written. I mean, fuck, I had less than two months to write it, and never had written anything before. What the fuck did anyone expect? Anyway, I had just used the book as an aide, something to help me move along when I was stuck. But I didn't say any of that. I just sat there feeling my stomach twisting into a knot, knowing that this was worse than it seemed.

'Yeah, I read *Red Harvest*,' I said to break a long silence. 'It's a great book. I must've internalized that paragraph.'

She proceeded to bring up on the screen other paragraphs, all almost word for word identical to the ones next to them.

'We counted twenty-three paragraphs identical to *Red Harvest*. They're all on our website now. What do you have to say for yourself?'

All I could do was mutter that I must've internalized all of them. As soon as the commercial break came I nearly stumbled off the sound set. The host didn't bother looking up at me. A minute later Bennett called on my cell demanding to know what the fuck I did. I hung up on him. He called back again seconds later.

'You better be polite,' I said.

His voice strained to the point where he could barely talk, he said, 'This is a big problem, Kyle. You can't steal another writer's work and call it your own.'

'Every one of those paragraphs I changed at least one word.'

'Are you stupid or something? You can't do that—'

'I warned you already about being polite. And what the fuck are we talking about? Twenty-three paragraphs? Five pages out of two hundred and fifty? Fuck, I only used *Red Harvest* to help me when I was stuck. If you had given me more than two months to write my first book, I wouldn't have had to do that.'

I could tell he was struggling to keep himself under control.

'I want you to go home now, Kyle. I don't want you to say a word to anyone. I'll manage this but keep a low profile until I do. Understood?'

'Yeah, sure, whatever.'

'Is there anything else I need to know?'

'What do you mean?'

'Is there anything more than those twenty-three paragraphs that I need to worry about?'

'Those should be about it.'

He hung up then without saying another word to me. I stared at my cell phone wanting to smash it. It started ringing. According to the Caller ID it was one of the reporters I had given an interview to weeks earlier. I turned the phone off. Then I went back to the Plaza to pick up Nola. She must've watched me on the morning show. She looked absolutely crestfallen, but she didn't say anything about the show. During the ride back to Boston neither of us spoke a word to each other. Later, after we were home for several hours still not talking to each other, Nola came up to me and told me she Googled me and came up with over ten thousand hits, most of them talking about what a joke I was. I went to the computer and read a few of them. I also found a press release that Bennett had put out stating that he was supporting me fully, that he believed me about internalizing those passages, and that I was working on a new version with those offending passages removed. I turned my cell phone back on to see if he had bothered trying to call me to give me that news, but there were too many messages to try to go through. As soon as the phone started ringing again I turned it off. I got up to go to Scolley's. Nola, in a frigid voice, asked me where I was going. I answered her by punching a hole in the wall.

At Scolley's, Joe Whalley and the others there commiserated with me.

'What's the big fuss about this?' Joe asked. 'So a few words here and there are similar. Jesus, they're acting like you committed some major felony.'

'Like kidnapping and killing a boy,' some asshole said, but he was heading for the door before I could react. Joe threw an ashtray at him and nailed him on the back of his head before he could make it out the door. I got up to follow him outside but Joe stopped me.

'It's not worth it, Kyle. He won't be welcome here anymore. And about this other business, I wouldn't worry about it. None of it sounds as if it's deserving of this big hue and cry. It will pass.'

I nodded, told him how my publisher was managing it.

'There you go,' Joe said.

I stayed out at Scolley's until three in the morning. When I got back to Nola's condo, I found a terse email from Bennett. He had taken it upon himself to compare my book with the other two books he had given me and found other passages that he claimed I had stolen. He told me that if those were discovered, he would pull the plug on the book. He warned me not to spend any of the money I had, that if my contract were cancelled I'd be giving it all back.

The next four days things only got worse. More passages were found from *Red Harvest* bringing the total up to thirty-seven. Some of those were total bullshit, where they stretched the supposed similarities to a point of being ridiculous, but what the fuck could I do? The papers had a field day with me, but the bloggers were the worst. Jesus were they unmerciful. During those four days I couldn't sleep and spent my nights reading all the shit written about me on those blogs. The fourth day was when some asshole found the paragraphs I had used from *Killer Inside Me*. He listed nineteen on his website, and the news of it spread like wildfire. By this time Nola was barely even looking at me. When I'd go out on the streets, people were either averting their eyes from me or looking through me. It was like I had become a ghost, just like Kevin Flannery and Red. The holy trinity of Southie, the three most feared men, and now all three of us were nothing but ghosts, Red literally, Kevin Flannery and me figuratively. When I went to Scolley's that night, no one bothered to say a word to me, not even Joe. I sat in a corner and drank, never feeling more alone in my life. There were more than a few whispers in the place that I was no longer welcome.

I found a motel to stay in that weekend. I didn't want to see Nola, didn't think I could stand seeing all that disappointment and disgust in her face. Monday Bennett released a statement to the media canceling my book contract and offering to buy back all copies of my book that had been sold. According to his statement, the film studio that had bought the movie rights were also canceling their contract. Furthermore Harleston Books and the studio would be seeking all monies that were paid me.

I tried calling Bennett, but he wouldn't pick up his cell. I called Tammy and asked if she'd put me through to Bennett.

'I'm sorry, Kyle, but he's not going to talk to you.'

I was choking up then and could barely talk.

'You realize how insane this is?' I asked her. All at once I broke down sobbing. Jesus, it was the first time I'd cried since I was five and my dad smacked in me the face for getting in the way of the TV. I could barely breathe I was sobbing so hard. I tried not to let Tammy hear it. When I could I told her, 'You add up everything I'm accused of stealing, and it's not more than nine pages. Nine pages out of two hundred and fifty. And none of it even matters as far as the book goes.'

'I'm so sorry, Kyle.' And she hung up on me.

I sat in that motel room and sobbed like a baby. It wasn't the money or the loss of prestige or even being made into a joke. What I realized then was how important the book was to me. It was my legacy, something to make up for all the crap I'd done in my life. Something to give my life meaning. I couldn't let it end, not like this. When I could, I cleaned up, got a grip on myself, and headed off to Nola's. She was gone, but there was a note for me telling me she wanted me to pack up and move out of her condo, that she couldn't stomach the idea of seeing me again. Fine. I didn't come back there for her. I took my laptop and left, spending the next two hours averaging over a hundred and twenty miles an hour as I drove to New York. If any cops had stopped me, mine would've been the last car they ever stopped. Fortunately for their families none did.

When I got to Harleston Books, the security guard at the front desk tried to get in my way. I sent him head first into the side of his desk and walked over him and then took the elevator up. Tammy looked surprised to see me. Before she could say a word I was inside Bennett's office, locking the door behind me. He looked like hell, maybe even worse than I did. His face haggard, like he hadn't slept in days, the flesh from his jowls sagging, and his eyes buried under circles so dark that it looked like soot had been smudged around them. He blinked at me, staring like he couldn't believe I was standing there. Slowly he came to life.

'Get out of here now or I'll call security,' he said, his voice cracking with emotion.

'You can't just pull the plug like this,' I said. 'All this stuff can be fixed. It can still be a great book.'

He started laughing then. It was an insane laugh, something

that you'd expect to hear from a hyena. He got up from his desk and moved towards me.

'You don't get it? It didn't matter how good the book was. You could've given me any piece of shit you wanted and I would've spun it as gold. But you had to do the one thing I couldn't fix. You had to cheat. But I guess it's in your blood. I should've known better than to bet my career on a cheap fucking thug like yourself.'

'Why can't we just fix this?'

'Why? Because it's over for both of us. You took me down with you, Kyle, my man. Right now I'm waiting for the board to fire my ass. I'm ruined, just like you are. Now get the fuck out of my office!'

He reached to grab me. I started to push him away but he did some kung-fu-like move, and next thing I knew I was sitting on the floor tasting blood. Bennett positioned himself in a kung fu-like stance.

'I'm giving you fair warning that I'm a black belt in Tien Shan Pai. Now get out of my office before I throw you out!'

I wiped a hand across my mouth and saw a streak of blood across it. I got to my feet slowly, breathing hard. Next thing I knew I had grabbed an office chair and rushed him with it. He had no idea what to do. I guess that was never covered in his Tien Shan Pai training. He ended up on the floor, wedged between his desk and the chair I rammed into him, while I pounded away at his face. Five minutes later there was nothing left but pulp. The office door behind me opened. Tammy must've gotten security. Bennett was dead, there was no question about that. Me, I was splattered with his blood, gore dripping from my arm. When I stood up and Tammy's eyes met mine, the only thing in them was horror. Any pity or sadness that was there before was long gone.

'I'm going to have to tie you two up,' I told them calmly. 'Otherwise I'll have to kill you.'

Neither of them put up any fight. This went well beyond anything the security guard was ever expecting to deal with. I used the cord from the phone to secure the two of them together. Then I cleaned up the best I could in Bennett's private bathroom. By the time I left I only had some blood smudges on my shirt, but nothing too obvious.

As I drove out of Manhattan, I knew exactly what I had to do. There was only one thing that made any sense. I had a baseball cap pulled low over my head and sunglasses hiding my eyes, but I really didn't have to worry about being recognized. I knew I had time. I figured it would be hours before my face would be broadcast nonstop over the news. As far as my car went, I never bothered registering my BMW in Massachusetts, besides I still had some borrowed license plates, so there was no reason for any State Police to be pulling me over. The first grocery store I came across I stopped at and bought several weeks' worth of food. Then keeping close to the speed limit I headed towards New Hampshire.

On the way to Red's cabin, I made a detour to Janet's house. It had bothered me for a long time that she never offered any condolences about Danny or any congratulations about my good fortune with my book deal. What really stuck in my craw, though, and what I had been trying to overlook for all this time, was her not telling me about my daughter. I decided to wipe the slate clean. I had filled up a milk bottle with gasoline and when I got in front of her house I doused a rag with the gasoline, stuck it in the bottle, lit it and tossed it. The bottle hit the house like a fireball and exploded. I watched as the fire spread and the house became engulfed in flames. I could hear a young girl screaming from inside. After a minute or so I drove off. Maybe next time Janet will fucking tell me when we have a kid together. I would have liked to have made more detours, especially to Nola and that asshole writer who tried to get his fifteen minutes of fame by telling the *Boston Globe* I tried hiring him to write my book for me – the asshole even had the balls to say he turned me down because he found the whole thing so contemptible – but I decided I didn't have time for any of that, not if I wanted to make it up to Red's cabin in one piece.

When I arrived, the cabin stood empty feeling every bit the abomination it was, but somehow it seemed right that I'd end up there. I brought my groceries inside. The generator started right up and I went back to my car for the laptop. Then I went to work, writing nonstop, taking breaks only to make fresh pots of coffee or to eat cold beef stew from a can or to light a fresh cig – yeah, I had started smoking again, nonstop, like a fucking chimney. This time around I decided to write creative non-fiction (I bought books on writing months ago – I knew all the terminology). The book was going to be everything that happened from the day I stepped out of Cedar Junction. Not so much an explanation but an exploration of the criminal psyche. I mean, what the fuck, it was the one thing I truly understood. It was going to be as honest as I could make it, showing all my warts, all my flaws, and hopefully be something that could be held up as a great book that would be read for years to come – if by no one else, at least by criminal psychologists trying to understand fucks like me. I had a gut feeling that this was my only chance to write something real. That when I was done there'd be no time left to do anything else.

I worked nonstop on it, typing away like crazy, just letting the words fly out of me. A buzz ran through me from almost the first minute. Even if I wanted to I wouldn't have been able to sleep. But I didn't want to – all I wanted to do was get this book written. It was like something stuck in me that I had to get out. Maybe it would make up for my first one. At least this one I'd be able to swear on my mother's grave had nothing borrowed.

I worked seven days nonstop on it, no sleep, no breaks lasting more than a few minutes. At times I was jittery as hell but I never felt tired. Over ninety thousand words in one week. Jesus, the books I could've written. I guess I could've given myself up and had all the time in the world to keep writing in prison, but that wasn't the way I was going to go out. Anyone reading this will understand that, just as they'll have a good idea of the only way I could go. Scolley's will be in flames by the time I'm done, as will Nola's condo and all the other cocksuckers who had forgotten that they needed to fear me.

Outside of clearing up one loose end, all that's left now to finish this is one final edit and adding a few notes to whoever ends up having the balls to publish it. Maybe whoever takes over for Bennett will change their mind about canceling my two-book deal. If they don't, let it go to the highest bidder. As far as the money goes, I'm sure there'll be plenty of victims' families lining up to sue my estate.

Now for the loose end. Yeah, Red and I killed those four girls and buried them in Flannery's mom's basement. Connor was right about that, as was that cocksucker columnist at the *Boston Globe*. Red had been sleeping with them and claimed it needed to be done – that they overheard conversations of his that could put us all away for life and were starting to spread what they heard. It was a lie. I didn't find out until it was too late that Red had me kill them as some sort of sexual perversion of his, that me killing those girls while he watched turned him on. Once it dawned on me that that was what was happening, I told him I'd cut his fucking heart out if he ever tried a stunt like that again. Why he wanted them buried where he did, I don't know. Maybe he'd had a beef with Flannery and was trying to stick it to him, or maybe it turned him on knowing they were right there in the neighborhood. Whichever it was, he never told me. May the sonofabitch rot in hell.

To Ed.: Change of plans. It was a good thing I had this book written in a week. As I was finishing up the editing and my notes, I heard noises outside and saw what must've been at least fifty cops setting up. The only way they could have found out about the location of the cabin was through Flannery. I guess he turned out to be a rat like all the rest. Sign of the times. They probably don't know about the tunnel that leads from under one of the floorboards to about twenty yards behind from where they're setting up. They also probably don't know the extent of Red's arsenal, which includes dozens of hand grenades. As soon as I finish this last note, I'm arming myself to the teeth and taking those grenades with me through the tunnel, see if I can go out in a bang. I'm sure they'll get me, but with some luck I can take half of them out before that happens. In any case, it's going to be a massacre. Fuck it, if nothing else it should help sell books. —K. N.

Small Crimes

A sampler from Dave Zeltserman's earlier
novel, published by Serpent's Tail

Chapter 1

This was going to be our last game of checkers. Usually we played in my cell; this last game, though, we were playing in Morris's office. Over the last seven years we had played tens of thousands of games. Every fourth or fifth game I'd win, the rest I'd let him beat me.

Morris Smith ran the county jail here in Bradley. He was a large round man in his early sixties, with soft rubbery features and small wisps of hair framing his mostly bald head. I liked Morris – at least as much as I liked anyone. He could have made my life difficult the past seven years; instead he treated me about as well as he could've.

I spent a few seconds studying the board and saw that I could force a checker advantage and a sure win, but I could also set myself up to be triple-jumped. I pretended to be deep in thought for a couple of minutes and then made the move to let him force the triple jump.

Morris sat silently, his small eyes darting over all the possible moves. I saw a momentary glint in his eyes when he recognized the combination leading to the triple jump, and watched with some amusement as he tried to suppress a smile. He pushed his checker in place with a large, thick hand that shook.

'I think you made a mistake there, young fellow,' he said, his voice coming out in a low croak.

I sat there for a long moment and then cursed to show that I realized how I had screwed up. Letting loose one last profanity, I made the move I was forced to make and watched as Morris pounced on the board, making his triple jump and picking up my checkers.

'That should be about it,' he said.

We played out the rest of the moves. I knew Morris took great satisfaction in removing the last checker from the board. When the game was over, he gave a slight smile and offered me his hand in a conciliatory shake.

'You gave me a good game,' he said, 'except for that one mistake.'

'What can I say? You've been kicking my ass for seven years now. I just got to admit I've met my match.'

Morris chuckled, obviously pleased with himself. He glanced at his watch. 'Your paperwork is all done. You're a free man. But if you'd like, I could order us some lunch and we could play one more game.'

'I'd like to, but it's been a long seven years. I've been craving a cheeseburger and a few beers for some time now.'

'I could have that brought here.'

'Well, yeah,' I said, hesitating, 'but you could get in trouble doing that, Morris. And, besides, it wouldn't taste the same in here. No offense.'

He nodded, some disappointment showing on his round face. 'Joe, I've grown to like you over the last few years. I didn't think

I would after what you did to get yourself in here. Can I give you some friendly advice?'

'Sure.'

'Why don't you start fresh someplace else? Maybe Florida? Myself, soon as I retire in three years, I'm moving to Sarasota. You can keep these lousy New England winters.'

'That's not bad advice, but one of the conditions of my parole is to stay in Bradley—'

'You could petition for a change of address.'

'Well, yeah, I guess I could, but my parents are getting up there in age, and I'd like to make up for lost time.'

He shrugged. 'I hope you at least think about it. I don't think Bradley's a good place for you anymore.'

'I appreciate the advice. But I don't have much choice in the matter. At least not right now.'

We stood up and shook hands. I turned away to pick up my duffel bag and Morris asked whether I wanted to call my parents for a ride. I told him I'd get a cab. I made a quick phone call, signed whatever paperwork I had to, and was led out of the building by Morris. A cab was waiting for me, but there was a man bent over, talking to the driver. The cab pulled away, and as the man stood up I recognized him instantly. I'd have to with the way his face was carved up and the thick piece of flesh that was missing from his nose. At one time, he had been a good-looking man, but that was before he had been stabbed thirteen times in the face.

Morris looked a bit uncomfortable. 'Well, uh,' he said, 'it was a pleasure having you as my guest, young fellow. If you ever want to stop by for a lesson on the theory of checkers, feel free.' Then, seriously, 'Try to stay out of trouble.'

He gave me a pat on the back and waved to the other man before disappearing back into the building. The other man stood grinning, but it didn't extend to his eyes. Looking at him was like staring at an open-mouthed rattlesnake.

I nodded to him. 'I don't want any trouble, Phil,' I said.

Phil Coakley just stood grinning with eyes that were hard glass. Phil was the district attorney in our county. I knew he'd been stabbed thirteen times in the face because that's how many times they told me I'd stabbed him. That was a good part of the reason I'd spent the last seven years in county jail.

'I'm sorry for what happened,' I said, keeping my distance.

Phil waved me over, his grin intact, but still nothing in his eyes. 'I don't want any trouble either, Joe,' he said. 'As far as I'm concerned you've paid your debt to society, and what's done is done. I just want to clear the air, make sure there are no hard feelings. Come on over here. Let's talk for a minute.'

I didn't like it, but I didn't feel as if I had any choice. When I moved closer to him, I could see the scarring along his face more plainly, and it was all I could do to keep from looking away. The damage was far worse up close. He looked almost as if someone had played tic-tac-toe on his face. As if he were some grotesque caricature from a Dick Tracy comic strip. Parts of his face were uneven with other parts, and that chunk of flesh missing from his nose, Jesus Christ. As tough as doing so was, I kept my eyes straight on him.

'I hope you don't mind, Joe,' he said, 'but I asked your taxi to come back so we could talk for a few minutes.'

'Sure, that's fine.'

'I've been waiting out here almost an hour. Your parole was supposed to be completed by noon.'

'You know how Morris is. He takes his time with things.'

Phil gave a slow nod. 'Look at you,' he said, 'Joe, I think jail agrees with you. Your beer gut's gone. Damn, you look better now than you've looked in years. But I guess you can't say the same about me.'

'If there was any way I could go back and change what I did—'

'Yeah, I know, don't worry about it. What's done is done.' He paused for a moment, his grin hardening again. 'I often wondered how you were able to serve out your time in a county jail. Arson, attempted murder, maiming a district attorney, and you end up in a county jail. I've been trying for the last seven years to have you moved to a maximum security prison, but I guess you were born under a lucky star. Even drawing Craig Simpson as your parole officer.'

I didn't say anything. He gave a careless shrug, still grinning. 'But that's all in the past,' he said. 'You paid your debt, even though seven years doesn't quite seem long enough. What was your original sentence? Twenty-four years?'

'Sixteen to twenty-four,' I said.

'Sixteen to twenty-four years.' Phil let out a short whistle. 'It seems to me like a hell of a short sentence for what you did. And you only had to serve out seven years of it in county jail, all the time being waited on hand and foot by old Morris Smith.'

'It hasn't been all that easy. My wife divorced me—'

'Yeah, I know. My wife divorced me, too.' He paused. 'I guess she had a difficult time looking me straight in the face.'

He had lost his grin. I just stared at him, stared at the mass of scar tissue that I was responsible for. After a while, I asked him what he wanted.

'I just wanted to clear the air,' he said. 'Make sure there are no hard feelings between the two of us. Also, I want to talk a little police business with you. After all, you were a police officer in this town for twelve years. You hear that Manny Vassey's dying of cancer?'

'I heard something about it.'

Phil forced his grin back and shook his head slightly. 'The man's only fifty-six and he's dying of stomach cancer. Manny always was a tough bird. Normally I wouldn't have a chance of cracking him, but, when a man's dying, sometimes he needs to unburden himself. You know, at one point I think every drug, gambling, and prostitution dollar that flowed through Vermont went into his hands. You remember Billy Ferguson? I think you investigated his murder.'

'I remember.'

'I guess you would,' he said. 'It's not as if we have a lot of murders here, and I don't think we ever had one as brutal as that one. How many years ago was that?'

'I don't know. Maybe ten.'

Phil thought about it and shook his head. 'I think it was less than eight and a half years ago. Only a few months before you maimed me. I'll tell you, Joe, that was one hell of a brutal murder. I don't think I ever saw anyone beaten as badly as Ferguson was.'

He waited for me to say something, but I just stood there and stared back at him. After a while he gave up and continued.

'Billy Ferguson was in way over his head with gambling debts,' he said. 'As far as I could tell, he owed Manny thirty thousand dollars. I suspect Manny sent one of his thugs over to collect and the situation got out of hand. Do you remember anything from your investigation?'

'That was a long time ago. But as I remember, we hit a brick wall. No fingerprints, no witnesses, nothing.'

'Well, I'm not giving up on it. I'm making it a point to visit Manny religiously.' Phil laughed, but his grin was long gone. 'I'm spending time each day reading him the Bible. I think he's beginning to see the light. With a little bit of luck I'll get a confession any day now and clear up Ferguson's murder along with a few other crimes that have always bugged me.'

I didn't bother saying anything. He was wasting his time, but he'd find that out for himself. Manny Vassey was joined at the hip with the Devil, and there wasn't a chance in hell he'd ever find God or confess to anything. My cab pulled back up to us. Before I could say a word, Phil grabbed my duffel bag from me and swung it into the cab's trunk. 'Be seeing you around, Joe,' he said as he walked off.